Cobalt!

Books by the same author

The Final Shah Mat
published via Amazon   2014

The disconnect between people and politicians. A plot by former Soviet generals to revenge the collapse of the Soviet Union by encouraging California to leave the United States of America.

The Acionna Projects
published by Austin Macauley   2016

Water – the globally abused resource without which we cannot survive. A plot involving strategic sites in China, Europe and America.

The Hwanung Solution
published by Matador   2017

Climate change – the melting of the permafrost and iced rivers and its impact on peoples' lives, escaping viruses, a hunt for treasure and a love story.

www.davidmiddleton-author.com/bookshop

Cobalt!

David Middleton

Matador
9 Priory Business Park,
Wistow Road, Kibworth Beauchamp,
Leicestershire. LE8 0RX
Tel: 0116 279 2299
Email: books@troubador.co.uk
Web: www.troubador.co.uk/matador
Twitter: @matadorbooks

ISBN 978 1838593 551

British Library Cataloguing in Publication Data.
A catalogue record for this book is available from the British Library.

Printed and bound in the UK by TJ International, Padstow, Cornwall
Typeset in 11pt Aldine401 BT by Troubador Publishing Ltd, Leicester, UK

Matador is an imprint of Troubador Publishing Ltd

This book is dedicated to my Mom who elected to adopt me when medical advice was telling her not to. She gave me a chance in life that is an unpayable debt. Also to recently deceased cousins who were giants in my life, Tony and Frank Wainwright. Both heroes in my mind. I was distraught when Tony got hold of my first book. In huge anxiety and trepidation I asked him what he thought of it. I shall never forget his answer. "Why didn't you do this years ago?"

I remain indebted to numerous people but especially my long suffering wife Jennie, grown up and discerning offsprings Caroline (responsible for redrawing the map of Africa for me) and Anthony, Peter Gibbs who is back in my life after 30 years away and advising now on publishing and promotion, mentor Debbie Dorman, hawk-eyed error spotter Mike Dodman and long-time friends Kevin Walsh and Merle Gibbs. They all gave me great encouragement and guidance. Thanks also to Steve Wallace who first suggested I should look at cobalt as the subject for a book and to the invaluable help of Professor Peter Slater of the University of Birmingham.

Cobalt! My fourth novel is a standalone story though many of the main characters are re-established from the previous books. It is another adventure that provides a cocktail of fact and fiction (see Fact & Fiction Appendix). The focus this time is on the element cobalt without which we cannot have our sophisticated electronic lives. Yet much of it is scraped from the ground by children, many less than ten years old. It is a diabolical example of our greed and the gap between the haves and have nots.

About Me

Always a keen writer, I was given a chance at the age of 20 to become a news reporter on the weekly local newspaper, the Walsall Observer. I spent a few years in local newspapers and radio before becoming a motor sport photo journalist. Via time in commercial PR, I moved into the world of exhibitions and conferences which took me across Europe, Japan and the USA. In 1988 I had my "green epiphany" standing on a bridge in Pittsburgh. In 1991 I helped launch the MEBC, a business group dedicated to the subject of sustainable development. I became its CEO. I was also Secretary General of TURF – The Urban Renewal Foundation. I later added the role of CEO of the UK branch of the World Business Council for Sustainable

Development to my activities. I retired from these responsibilities in 2013. Since then I have become involved in various projects.

See www.davidmiddletoncommunications.uk

I have now taken to writing fast moving adventure stories with the central themes based on various elements of sustainable development in the hope this may be an effective vehicle by which to carry important messages to as wide an audience as possible.

See www.davidmiddleton-author.com

Preface

I have spent more than 20 years promoting sustainable development, a set of values which seeks to ensure my generation passes this planet on to the next generation in some sound order. Against that objective we will sadly fail. But many of us who believe in the principles of sustainable development in which financial, social and environmental values are equal feel we have failed to get our message to the general public. Even President Barack Obama says this in the documentary epic by Leonardo DiCaprio "Before the Flood".

My novels try and help by weaving truth and fiction into stories of espionage and political intrigue that seek to entertain but also promote sustainable development values. They will not only satisfy my personal ambitions to become a novelist but will, I hope, carry the sustainable development story to a wider audience than I have reached to date.

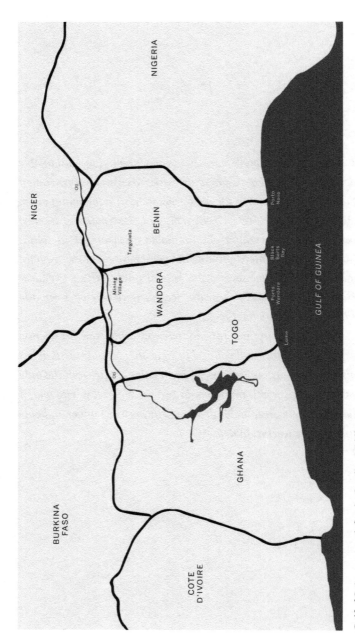

Gulf of Guinea map redefined – Caroline Middleton

"There can be no keener revelation of a society's soul than the way in which it treats its children."

Chapter 1

The tension is palpable but the voice cuts straight through it. "OK guys and gals. We're right on the money. Still counting. Still running – straight and true. Big bang and fireworks in four minutes."

A quarter of a mile ahead, somewhere in the murky depths of the Gulf of Guinea, if Marcel Bartoll could see what was approaching from behind at around 45 knots he would recognise it instantly. If the scientific team monitoring his every move was not so focussed on their forward cameras, maybe one of them might see it emerge from the gloom. But by then it would be only seconds from impact. Even if they had seen it, even if they had wanted to warn Marcel, what do you say when it is far too late? What do you say to someone you know is about to die? What do you say when there is nothing you can do – but watch?

A sceptical onlooker might have thought the stubble faced man with unkempt hair probably watched far too many American WW2 movies. Ever since the launch a few seconds ago he continues to stare at his stopwatch and listen intently to what can be heard through his headphones. His words, spoken in English, have a pseudo-American sounding drawl. But he is very obviously not American. Eastern European perhaps? Maybe Russian?

In their dimly lit claustrophobic metallic environment, every inch crammed with banks of gauges, switches, dials, buttons, pipes and cables, and which has a unique smell of hot electrics and stale male bodies, his colleagues, concentrating on their respective responsibilities, hear him. They say nothing. Just a few glance in his direction. His words are hardly understandable thanks to the well-worn, very dead and severely frayed stub of a fat Cuban Corona stuck in the corner of his mouth. It looks as if during its lifetime it may have been more chewed than smoked. It has certainly not been lit since they came aboard.

"Three minutes and counting."

The target, Marcel Bartoll and Karl, have no sense of impending disaster. For Marcel, nothing could destroy this exquisite moment. He is in his element – in the place of his passion and which, like a drug, he cannot get enough of. He adores the serenity, solitude and sheer beauty of deep sea exploration, especially in such a small submersible he and pilot Karl are in. Marcel loves probing places no human has ventured into before, the adrenalin pumping sense of adventure and risk, the excitement of descending into the unknown, the magnificence of the deep.

"Two minutes." The man with the pseudo-American voice continues the countdown.

"Current 11 knots." Unlike the other, this is a voice Marcel and Karl can hear. Electronically distorted, it comes from one of the team monitoring their every move from the expedition ship high above them. It cuts through the near silence to give a routine status update.

In the background the electric engines propelling the submersible hum quietly. Now and then there is a gentle hiss as more gas is released from the ballast tanks. Otherwise it is a silent world.

"Cliff top wall on camera two." This second voice, identifiably female, is also tinny in its electronic distortion. Marcel, sitting in the glass-like dome of his craft, sees it too on one of his monitors and now strains to catch sight of what the enhanced vision of the camera has already seen but what the human eye yet cannot.

The forward lights of his vessel struggle to penetrate the murky gloom of the Gulf of Guinea to illuminate what he is searching for – the top of the cliff face of the recently discovered oceanic trench in this part of the Atlantic Ocean off West Africa. In this underwater fog, everything looks bland and colourless – sea and seabed alike.

"It's like trying to look into a very muddy pond," Marcel told anyone who was listening. Karl nods in agreement. But then into sight comes something different, just discernible parallel lines. He can see them cut into the seabed even though it is still impossible to discern the ocean bottom. He saw these incisions before when the remote vehicle first found the trench. He jabs his finger at them to ensure Karl too sees them. His heartbeat quickens. He knows he is near. Karl inches the craft closer and follows the cuts until at last there it is, the edge of the cliff face at the top of the trench.

Karl manoeuvres their craft forward. They are travelling quite fast now because of the current and it takes an effort to swing the craft rapidly through 180 degrees so they are now looking towards the face of the cliff. A laser beam from the submersible hits the top of the trench wall and dances and shimmers on the rock face. It gives a measure and sense of scale to what is being seen. Marcel's venture into what has become unofficially known as the Guinea Trench is about to start. His sense of excited anticipation is raised several notches.

Apart from the thrill of being where no human has been before, this is a pretty uninspiring place with little sign of any forms of life. That is what he expected. Oceanic experts know the variety of marine flora and fauna here is extremely limited when compared to that of the nearby western tropical Atlantic. What is known as biological poverty results from a lack of coral reef ecosystems because of low salinity and the high turbidity of the water. It is also known that crustal disturbances in the Miocene Epoch millions of years ago created a climate here less receptive to life forms than in neighbouring seas. That made the discovery of a previously unknown sea anemone even more surprising.

How deep the trench is has yet to be determined. The SNEL expedition that originally found it used a deep sea robotic submarine to collect tiny samples of unknown life forms found at a depth of around 1,000 feet. Nothing has yet been to the bottom of the trench and nobody has any idea how deep it is. The minute samples of life forms were recovered from an area of cliff face at the top of the trench where, much to everyone's amazement, the robot sub found the orange coloured sea anemones with white tentacles waving in the current. Scientists were not only puzzled as to why these plant-like, water-dwelling predatory animals were where they were but also how they survived with such low levels of life forms around them. How did they sustain life?

The venom within the tentacles of the sea anemone proved to be completely new to the scientific world. A great deal of excitement followed when it was suggested that the Guinea Trench Anemone, as it quickly became known, might provide medical breakthroughs in a variety of areas, not the least being its potential as a treatment for some forms of cancer.

Exploration of the seabed off the coast of Africa in the Gulf of Guinea was sparked in the aftermath of a tsunami. How much damage had occurred to the seabed and marine life was a matter of intense interest to oceanic experts already concerned about rising levels of pollution and the decline in the life-sustaining capabilities of our seas. In a moment of unforgettable excitement, the remote deep sea probe from Marcel's company discovered the Guinea Trench, explored its upper area and captured small specimens from the sea anemone.

Marine scientists aboard the exploration vessel knew that in recent times organisms such as echinoderms, sea anemones, tunicates, and mollusks have demonstrated biomedical potential. Some of these animals produce a mixture of toxins, commonly known as venom, to protect themselves from predators and to catch prey. Some have stinging cells on their tentacles that inject venom into the animals they touch. It is the venom that excites the biomedical fraternity because often the compounds it contains have the potential to be developed into new drugs.

Experiments on one microscopic amount of venom from the Guinea Trench plant-like cousin of the jellyfish caused great speculation as to its potential value. What was needed were more specimens and some assessment of the quantity of anemone in the trench. That was Marcel's brief. And with the cliff wall now in view Karl carefully and very slowly guides the craft down into the trench then along the cliff face just a few feet from its top, peering all the time for any signs of the orange coloured plant-like animal. Marcel can already confirm that the few hundred yards of parallel fissures marked into the seabed eventually curve gently downwards to the lip of the trench and that the cliff wall is sheer and vertical and plunges deep and out of sight.

The cliff face itself is marked with upward stripes suggesting some historic volcanic action. In this dark and virtually colourless world, even though he was expecting it, Marcel is shocked when the sub encounters what appears to be a plant stuck in the rocky cliff face. It has an orange centre and white tentacles long enough to wave in the currents.

Now the task falls to Marcel. This is what he is here to do. Despite the strong and fluctuating currents, Karl has to maintain the submarine in one position while Marcel extends its telescopic arm to grab the sea anemone. It does not help that the target is waving almost majestically from its position on the cliff face to which it soon becomes apparent it is very significantly attached.

"Thirty seconds." The eyes of the man with the tattered cigar remain locked onto his stop watch.

The grab hand of the sub closes in on the strange plant-like animal at a position close to the cliff face and the telescopic arm starts to pull. Marcel's heart pounds with concentration and excitement.

The explosion when it happens violently rocks the substantial 45 metre long multi-purpose sub-sea expedition support vessel commissioned by SNEL for this expedition. Those least experienced on board thought it would flip. Crew members and the scientific crew from SNEL monitoring Marcel's activities far below are thrown around, some sustaining bad gashes and bruising. The explosion sounds like a dull but very distinct thud. Seconds later the sea near the expedition craft erupts in a ball of furious water and air. The violent bubble is accompanied by plumes of sea that fountain into the air, some crashing down onto the research vessel and flooding its decks. Research team and crew members hang onto their chairs or grab anything for support. Others are sent flying, some crashing painfully into solid objects. The comms team, including Lotty who had been the main contact with Marcel, are all screaming in pain as their eardrums are attacked by the noise of the explosion through their headphones.

"What the fuck?" cries SNEL Project Leader Maria Cummings as she staggers back onto her feet in the wheelhouse. Lotty, lying on the floor amongst a chaos of stuff that has been thrown there, is hanging onto consciousness. Petrified at the thought of what has happened to the man she loves, she is nearly hysterical, crying out Marcel's name.

In the chaos Bill Hutton has only one concern. He grabs the microphone from one of the fallen communications operators.

"Marcel. Are you there? Marcel. Karl. Come in Marcel. Marcel. Karl. Answer me."

But there is no response from the deep.

"Marcel. For God's sake. Answer me!" Hutton cries in anguish, looking forlornly at Maria. Lotty sobs. There is no response from the deep. Silence.

Nearby and unseen, the 30 year old ex-Soviet navy diesel engined submarine swings sharply to starboard and heads away from the scene of carnage. Job done.

Chapter 2

The sea surge had taken Wandora's coastal population by surprise. It was not high but it was extremely powerful. The idyllic paradise of silver beaches curving around the deeply forested coast with turquoise shallow waters and palm trees was transformed in an instant into hell itself. Offshore fishermen, holiday swimmers, sunbathers, those in the beach bars were the first to be hit. They had no chance. The few who saw the rushing waters before they smashed ashore tried to run but no human can outrun such an incoming force. People, bars, beach huts, boats of varying sizes – all were swept away as the torrent hit. Only a few escaped – mostly those in recently built, modern, multi-storey holiday apartments fronting onto the beach. Even here, people on ground floors were overwhelmed by water that swept all before it, smashing windows, crashing through doors and gushing through the lower levels of buildings. Those on the balconies above could only watch in horror as events below quickly unfolded. They prayed for the structural integrity of the buildings in which they stood. For those who survived, the screams of those who perished that day would live with them forever.

Progressing rapidly inland the sea, together with a growing accompaniment of debris and bodies, swept up

Porto Wandora's normally dusty high street. Cars, trucks, carts, goats, cows, cyclists, pedestrians – the normal jumble of the capital's traffic, was instantly overwhelmed and engulfed by water. Individuals clung to anything they could grab. Many structures disintegrated, disappearing under the swirling waters taking with them anyone who clung to them in forlorn hope.

Most buildings collapsed but then most were pretty flimsy. Porto Wandora's architecture is – or was – a miscellany of shanty huts, wooden homes, shops and workplaces, and colonial-style brick and concrete buildings occupied by those who could afford them. Many but not all of the latter survived, battered and scarred but still intact, standing in desolate isolation with their surroundings flattened.

It was a day of death, of miracles, of human tragedy, of extraordinary heroic deeds and unselfishness, of unbelievable devastation. Unlike other marine seismic disturbances which create mountainous cliffs of surging water, this sea upwelling sneaked in so as to give no warning to the innocent. Less dramatic in its arrival, it was, nevertheless, cataclysmic in its destructive power.

It is thought the catastrophic and unheralded disaster originated from a subterranean volcano somewhere near the Cape Verde archipelago, some 350 miles off the main African coast. More than 7,000 years ago this area, notorious for its volcanic activity, is believed to have created perhaps the largest tsunami in history when the eastern flank of the island of Cape Verde blew off. This latest event was minute in comparison but disastrous for

10

the thousands who became its victims all along the coast of that western part of Africa.

It shattered the small African state of Wandora (population just over four million) which extends in a narrow belt of territory some 500 miles inland from the coast of the Gulf of Guinea. A former Portuguese then French colony, it only recently celebrated 50 years of independence. It started as a poor nation, remained poor through its colonial years, and is still poor now despite its independent status. Given freedom to manage itself, Wandora split into various factions, teetered on the brink of a multi-faceted civil war and fell into its current state of nervous stability. The tsunami further deepened Wandora's sad situation.

Disaster sometimes brings out the best in people. So it was with Kevin Forsythe. For most of his working life Kevin had been what some might describe as a pink gin career civil servant. He was the epitome of a Noel Coward Englishman. Now in his late 50s, if asked what he thought of his working life he would probably tell you "Dear boy. It's been mostly a load of old balls, old bollocks and Old Raj" – the last being reference to his much-loved Scottish gin with its connotations to what he considered the glory days of the British Empire.

Kevin Forsythe has lived in Wandora for six years. He moved here from another African state when the British government decided to close its Consulate there as part of a global 'realignment of resources'. For the first time in his career Forsythe, who fully expected to conclude his life in a long and happy, gin-fortified retirement courtesy of a generous pension from HM Government, looked at a future that offered nothing. He was delighted and relieved when opportunity came along to switch to the private sector and manage the Wandora office of a French water company.

Sadly for Kevin that came to an abrupt end. The company had been called in to solve a water crisis. Its solution to water shortages in villages created by the excessive use of water in Wandora's burgeoning mining industry, was to develop new wells and use the water from them to supply the villages. But the solution went, in the words of Forsythe, "tits up big time." It was eventually realised the water company was drawing water from aquifers that originally supplied the country's villages. Rather than cure the problem the actions were making it substantially worse. The company was sacked. Kevin lent heavily on friendships developed in the Wandoran government and eventually secured the task of managing the country's roads and buildings, quickly gaining the confidence of the President and being rapidly promoted to Minister.

But when the tsunami hit, smaller though it might have been compared to more recent devastating examples around the world, Kevin Forsythe, in his capacity as Minister of Buildings and Infrastructure, suddenly demonstrated a side of him not seen before. The tsunami wiped out Porto Wandora. Fishing boats were thrown inland. Roads disappeared. Many homes, stores and offices just collapsed under the pressure of water. The final death toll remains uncounted. In its aftermath the country's major town is smashed and in chaos. It is taking a huge effort by local people, the army and volunteers to regain any semblance of order. The French, UN, USA and various NGOs have all sent help. The arrival of helicopters is a godsend. It was probably his army training that saw Kevin become a central figure in turning disarray into something resembling functioning order. He has become the liaison between all the helping agencies and a co-ordinator of the clean-up. It has given him a new lease of life.

Quite a few government buildings survived the watery onslaught and Kevin's was one of them. Never the most orderly of places, three days after the tsunami it is in turmoil. Boxes, crates, the occasional oil drum, three ancient bicycles, tools, spades, brooms, piles of assorted and unfiled paperwork and even a tethered goat litter the spacious area Kevin calls his office. Now a constant stream of people come and go, jostling for attention from the small team of Kevin's staff as he tries to orchestrate some semblance of order out of madness. There is much shouting. Frustration is rife as people try to rebuild their lives. Arguments and scuffles constantly break out amongst locals who have called into the office seeking help. In the midst of the chaos he has almost ignored the approach by Pete Turner. A young English geological graduate who has become caught up in Wandora's disaster, Pete was supposed to be travelling the world on a gap year but somehow got stranded in Wandora almost 15 months ago. A combination of depleted funds, the blissful nature of the place and enough odd jobs to scrape enough money to buy food, drink, shelter and the occasional small treat, meant his global trek was suspended for the foreseeable future.

He and Kevin had developed a friendship well before the disaster. Pete often capitalised on Kevin's generous friendship when they spent time together talking about worldly things or playing chess and drinking gin cocktails or palm beer on the sandy terrace of La Cabane du Pecleur on Porto Wandora's main beach. Like all the beach bars, this was annihilated by the flood which simply picked up such structures and destroyed them.

Yesterday Kevin had been deeply relieved to find Pete amongst the survivors.

"You got a minute?" asked Pete, walking into the disorder and general bedlam of Kevin's office without the usual knock on the door. Such a courtesy was no longer possible. The door had gone – swept away in the flood.

"Dear boy. For you, anytime. To sleep – perchance to dream. Not much time to sleep at the moment, old son, and I dream of beach time drinks again. But some hope! And I can't even shut the fucking door! So it's open house. Do come in." Pete noted the normally immaculate Kevin looked far from his dapper self. The former civil servant fastidiously wore a tie and a hat. Nobody else wore a tie in Porto Wandora. Today it was loosely knotted and hung limply across a dishevelled shirt. His light canvas field jacket was crumpled and dirty. The usual pristine white Panama hat looked slightly stained and battered. Normally clean shaven thanks to a daily routine starting with his trusty cut-throat, utterly out of character Kevin now had stubble.

The rotund, bald headed Englishman swept his hand in a theatrical gesture to indicate the state of his office, the state of the building and the state of the general pandemonium everywhere.

"So what brings you to my emporium of chaos?"

"It's this. It's a bit odd," Pete said, holding out a lump of rock about the size of his hand.

Kevin peered at what Pete held, then looked back at the youngster with a quizzical look. "If I am not mistaken dear boy that's a bit of rock," he responded, stating the blindingly obvious and with a reasonable quantity of sarcasm.

"But look at the colour."

Kevin hesitated, again scrutinising the lump in Pete's hand. "I don't want to get too technical but it's a sort of greyish lump with hints of blue. Yes, I would even extend my limited descriptive abilities by calling it a bit of blueish grey rock! Yes, it is without doubt, a lump of coloured rock." His tone remained sarcastic.

"Ah yes!" responded the persistent youngster excitedly. "Exactly! When did you last see a stone this colour and this size in Wandora? Between an extremely sandy coastline and an inland desert not that far away, I've never seen a stone anything like this in all the time I've been here."

"So what, dear boy?" Whilst the young geological student was clearly animated by his find, Kevin was far from being so.

"I'm wondering what it is? I'm guessing it was thrown up by the tsunami. If so, what is it and where did it come from?"

There was a pause as Kevin Forsythe extended an arm around his young friend.

"Now, my dear boy, it may just have escaped your notice but I am the focal point in trying to engender some semblance of order from chaos. I have dead people floating past my front door. People homeless. People lost. People without food, drink or shelter. A country shattered by an extreme act of nature. I have the army, NGOs and even the United Nations knocking on my door – if I still had one – looking for guidance. And in the midst of all this you stand before me and seek my attention – to a bit of rock!" He swatted his hat at a long feathered bird that dared to enter his building in search of food, missed and turned his attention to the next demand.

Summarily dismissed by his friend, Pete Turner pondered what to do. There was something about the chunk of rock that fascinated his geological mind. Its grey/blue colour made it very conspicuous and so out of character with anything else he had seen in Wandora. His bet was it came from the sea. Thrown up by the tsunami perhaps? What was it? Could it be of value?

Inland, up towards the northern extremity of the country and heading towards an area of rapid desertification, Wandora's fledgling mining industry was giving new hope to the nation's dire economy. It was a predominantly Chinese led activity but Pete was aware of the number of geologists involved. Perhaps one of them could tell him what his discovery was? But something held him back. If he showed it to them would they simply take over whatever it was he held? The solution when it came to him was, he thought, quite inspirational. There was a man in England he had worked with for a while. An environmentalist. And if he did not know what this bit of rock was, he probably would know someone who did.

With some difficulty he chipped a piece off the rock, stuck it in an envelope with a scribbled accompanying note, and headed to the airport which had established limited operations since being damaged in the floods. Amidst the bedlam there he found an old contact from an airline that flew to the UK. He asked a favour. Could the envelope be posted in the UK please?

And so a chunk of Pete's rock ended up in the UK postal system with the name and address of the recipient clearly written – Gene Bond and an address near Birmingham, England. The note with it asked three questions about the enclosed sample of rock found in Wandora. What was it? Was it of value? Could it have come from the sea?

Chapter 3

The discovery of the oceanic trench generated a lot of publicity and put SNEL into the spotlight. But, for commercial confidentiality reasons, after the initial burst of media attention the sea anemone story faded into the past and those involved did nothing to provoke any further external interest. Marcel kept close contact with the laboratories that were inspecting the tiny sample of the previously unknown plant-like marine animal.

SNEL first became involved with the Gulf of Guinea in the aftermath of the disastrous tsunami in Wandora. The English sub-nautical specialist company slashed its prices to win the contract against fierce competition to explore the seabed of the Gulf of Guinea and to identify the extent of the damage the tsunami had caused. The discovery of the trench had been a significant moment in the history of the company and was widely and enthusiastically celebrated. It was just the sort of oceanic research work Marcel hoped the company would do. To discover the trench was amazing and would do wonders for the company's reputation.

When Marcel formed SNEL it could have been argued his thinking was a typical demonstration of youthful naivety fuelled by his passion for deep sea diving and a burning ambition to have his own business. It had little or nothing to do with good business reasoning. Born in the port of Cherbourg to a family in which small boats were an integral part of life, the passion for diving developed in his early teens. Then, just as Marcel started to take more than a passing interest in the opposite sex, Erika arrived. Dazzling and effervescent, the young English girl from Devon was also obsessed with diving. Stunningly attractive, tall, shapely, with bright red hair and a short temper, Erika encouraged Marcel to move to England where they lived and dived together for several blissful years. It all ended abruptly and without warning. The impetuous Erika suddenly became infatuated with a fast talking, deep pocketed, smart youngster who worked in the City of London and kept a high powered boat at Cowes. Marcel was mortified by his loss. But by then he was already scraping a living from diving. The departure of his girlfriend saw him dedicate all his efforts into developing his young business based on the English south coast. He thought of returning to France but all his business contacts were in England, as by now were most of his friends. So he stayed.

His passion for his subject fuelled his energy and determination. Now aged 28, this was, he believed, his one and only chance to create and build a sustainable business. To anyone willing to listen he argued the time had never been more opportune to develop a specialist diving company based on ocean research – to earn income from data gathering about the state of life in the oceans.

"Two thirds of ocean life remains undiscovered," he told anyone showing a spark of interest. "There may be as many as a million species of life down there that we don't know about. There may be 5,000 new varieties of fish yet to be found. We currently discover about 150 new species of fish every year! I think that's extraordinary. And when you think how many medical treatments are derived from marine life who knows what might be down there that could help us?"

"There are times when I think we know more about Mars and Neptune than we do about our own planet! How crazy is that?"

"Insensé!" he would shout when over excited, thumping his fist and reverting to his native tongue.

"People are planning how to mine asteroids! Would you believe! Yet we still don't know what minerals are at the bottom of the seas. We've landed 12 men on the moon – roughly 230,000 miles away. Guess how many men have visited the deepest point below our seas? One! Yet that's a journey of only seven miles."

"Incroyable! There's so much we don't know about our own planet. I think as a species we've lost the plot!"

The new company picked up contracts, mostly from the academic and research sectors though nothing ever of any great substance to delight the bank manager. A turning point came when Gary Marchant joined the company. Younger than Marcel and with a reputation for being highly commercial and successful, the two men had known each other for a few years, having met at diving events. When Marcel became aware of a tender issued by a minerals extraction company for commercial seabed exploration, rather than ignore it as he might have done in the past, he approached Marchant who he knew to be discontented in his current job. Marchant agreed to a deal whereby he would compile and submit a response to the bid for SNEL and join the company if it was successful.

It was. Marchant was appointed a director of SNEL and nobody could argue he had not added greatly to the value of the business. Slowly, almost imperceptibly, SNEL drifted into two halves divided by different objectives, cultures and philosophies. Business captured by Marcel was driven by his eco-passion. The commercially ambitious Marchant chased business wherever he saw it. The relationship between the two men moved from being friendly to becoming tetchy and distanced.

Marchant, preoccupied by the demands of his fast moving commercial contracts, was as joyous as anyone within SNEL about the positive publicity gained from the discovery of the trench. However he could not see any real immediate or direct commercial advantage. He did not become involved in any follow up activity. Nor did the discovery of a plant-like animal excite him. In his mind it would take ages – possibly years – for the laboratories to properly evaluate the potential of the sea anemone. If that was something for SNEL to continue to explore that was up to Marcel. He, Gary Marchant, had other things to do.

Chapter 4

Gene Bond Esq.
Environmental Consultant

Wythall
Near Birmingham

Professor Pete Slater
The Centre for Strategic
Elements and Critical
Materials
University of Birmingham
Edgbaston
Birmingham

Dear Mr Bond

I am grateful for you making contact and sending the sample piece of rock for analysis.

I can advise you that the rock is rich in cobalt, from the German word meaning goblin. It is a hard, stable metal unaffected by air or water and only slowly affected by acid. Cobalt is one of the three ferromagnetic metals, so it is often used in alloys for magnets. The rock is mainly composed of minerals. The niobium-dominant mineral is columbite (after niobium's original American name, columbium), and the tantalum-dominant mineral is tantalite. Tantalum is used to manufacture tantalum capacitors used in electronic products such as iPhones, iPads, laptops and the like. What is particularly interesting is the presence of large amounts of cobalt as usually we would expect to see a more abundant metal such as iron instead. With the move away from fossil fuelled vehicles to ones powered by electricity, the demand for cobalt has grown rapidly since it is a key component in Lithium ion batteries. It recently doubled in value.

Given the unusually high levels of cobalt we would be keen to know more about the origins of this rock. We would like to extend an invitation to you to visit the University to learn about our new Centre for Strategic Elements and Critical Materials and to exchange information.

Best regards

Pete Slater, Professor of Materials Chemistry

Chapter 5

The sun peered over the horizon, its beams striving to break through the slight haze of sand kicked up by a sharp breeze. Where they succeeded, a golden shimmer spread across the scrubland. Thin dust clouds hung in the air, inhibiting vision, deadening sound and stinging Nakki's eyes. She was close by the outskirts of her village now, following a path impacted by thousands of similar, barefooted footsteps over generations. Her back was bent from the weight of the water buckets, the journey from the well almost done. This part of her daily life had become routine for the 12 year old and though it was physically demanding she relished momentarily being away from her family and the people of the village so as to enjoy on her own the silent beauty of her surroundings. She plodded barefooted along the well-trodden pathway, her mind in a state of peaceful limbo, empty just now of the challenges of daily life. She would deliver the water to her parents' hut then be off to work in the mine for hours before snatching some time to study what little she had in educational books. Life was tough. This usually was the best part of her day.

Screeching into the air, the serenity of the morning was shattered as a flock of birds took flight with much flapping and excited squawking. It startled Nakki. Her heart fluttered. Instinctively she wondered what had disturbed them. Was it a predator? A lion? Would she be threatened? She had an instinctive fear of lions when they were in their mating season. Male lions would attack anything. The questions did not remain unanswered for long. The silence and tranquillity of this most northern tip of Wandora was shattered by the ear-splitting ratatatat sound of a heavy machine gun as a hail of bullets raked the thatched buildings of the native inhabitants and the prefabricated concrete buildings of the Chinese workers and officials. Nakki's village was being shredded by gun fire and bombed by grenades.

Her scream was unheard in the cacophony of noise from the village. She dropped to the ground at the sound of the first rounds being fired, crawling to a small thicket of bushes and squeezing her body in as far as she could. Prickly spikes scratched and clawed at her. It hurt and she could feel blood trickling down her arms. But she dared not make the slightest noise despite the racket coming from the direction of the village a mere 100 yards away. The insurgents had crossed the nearby tributary of the River Oti, the country's most northerly border. Undetected they had virtually surrounded the small community before opening fire. The result was carnage. Uncompromising death and destruction. Concrete chunks and splintered wood flew through the air mixed with body parts when grenades landed close to villagers. Fire quickly took hold in some buildings, smoke billowing upwards to mix with the sand haze.

The few security personnel there to provide protection to the Chinese workers and officials did their best. But their response was pitiful. They were simply mown down, outnumbered and outgunned. There was no discrimination. Villagers old and young, male and female, and Chinese miners, officials and guards all suffered the same fate. They were annihilated. Some tried to flee. Others tried to hide. The few rounds fired by the Chinese guards in response to the attack were puny against the small army with their Russian Kalashnikov assault rifles and grenade launchers.

Petrified and trembling in uncontrollable fear, Nakki initially watched the extermination of her village as a group of some 30 men emerged from the surrounding scrubland. Through the clouds of smoke and sand she could see their vague shapes as they moved amongst the smouldering remains. Occasional bursts of gunfire marked where survivors were summarily executed. It was unconditional slaughter. She could not bear to look any longer and buried her head in her hands and sobbed. Eventually, as the death toll rose until no villager, miner or guard still lived, the noise of the battle slowly subsided.

Nakki silently sobbed herself to sleep.

News of the massacre eventually reached Porto Wandora where the President called an emergency meeting of his inner sanctum. They met in his main offices in the renovated and modernised part of the ancient fort of São João Baptista de Wandora. Now the official residence of the President, the imposing building with its original battlements, arrow slits and ancient canons, overlooks the entrance to Porto Wandora. Built originally by the Portuguese and developed during the years of the slave trade, there was a certain irony in the rumour that the pirate 'Black Bart', – the Welshman Bartholomew Roberts – sailed from here. Wandora was also thought to have been home port for a while to the notorious pirate ships The Royal Rover and The Royal James of pirate, Howell Davis, also a Welshman. History was repeating itself with modern day pirate activity rife across the Gulf of Guinea.

Why the attack? Why in Wandora? And by whom? These were the dominating questions. Now only a few hours after the event, the ramifications were hitting the President from every direction. The Chinese government had sent a message of protest, demanding a meeting with their high ranking officials who were already on their way from Beijing. The Chinese minerals extraction company was demanding news and an explanation, its operation in shreds. The Americans, UN and various aid organisations helping in the aftermath of the tsunami, were demanding action by Wandora and reassurances their people were not in danger. If the insurrection spread they would, they said, withdraw.

But so far there were no answers. Moussa Ehouzou, responsible for national security, said the identity of the attackers remained a mystery. News from the north was of a group of men who had attacked the village and were now heading south, killing and slaying as they went. Rumours were rife with social media rightly or wrongly identifying the culprits as being a breakaway from the notorious Al-Shabaab. The story being promoted was that since this brutal terrorist group had lost ground in the Yemen and Horn of Africa, fragments had headed west. Some had reached Nigeria where rumours suggested they now linked to the Boko Haram group.

27

But why Wandora had been attacked was, so far, a question nobody could answer.

While the President was Commander-in-Chief of Wandora's near 3,000 strong army, it was upon the shoulders of Minister of Defence, Frederic Gnanligo that operational responsibilities fell. The attack in the north could not have been worse timed as far as he was concerned. His army was currently dispersed across the nation helping the rescue and rebuild activity in the aftermath of the tsunami. He had neither the resources nor, if truth be known, much faith in the idea of sending troops to combat the incursion.

Kevin Forsythe was mostly a spectator at the meeting. He had nothing to offer of material value. But as he sat in the meeting listening, he could not help but speculate that someone, somewhere was taking advantage of the nation's chaos and hitting it when it was especially weak. Who and why he had no idea. But looking around the group of trusted friends of the President, he reckoned he could place a bet with some certainty that at least one around the table knew the answers.

Five hundred miles north, lying huddled up as close to the centre of the prickly desert bush as she could get, Nakki woke from her nap – a fitful sleep – a reaction to the horror she had witnessed. White, brown and thick black smoke now billowed in the morning breeze from the buildings of the village. The smell of burning timber, rubber, oil and human flesh filled the air. Through the haze Nakki could see the perpetrators of the carnage celebrating their work in some sort of spontaneous dance accompanied by occasional bursts of gunfire into the air.

Now a new noise came to her. Vehicle engines. Into the village swept a line of four Toyota Land Cruisers. The instant they stopped heavily armed uniformed soldiers exited the second, third and fourth vehicles in a well practiced routine. The celebrating insurgents stopped their dancing. Their guns fell silent. There was instant deference to the new arrivals. The first Toyota had hardly stopped moving before three tall, suited men emerged from the rear doors and another from the driver's seat. All wore identical pin-striped suits, dark glasses and carried assault rifles. They formed a circle around the man who emerged from the front passenger seat. Nakki could see he was a very large, bearded man who wore loose, colourful clothing that waved and ballooned in the breeze.

The big man looked slowly around him at the burning village and the fighters who now stood silently before him. He knelt, scooped up a handful of soil which he took to his mouth as if to taste it before letting it slip through his clasped hand to fall to the ground. This, the man said silently to himself, was the first time in his extraordinary career that he had stood in a country he would soon own. It might be battered and near bankrupted but he knew it possessed huge potential thanks to its deep sea harbour – gateway to his expanding African markets. He was soon to find it had even more to offer – a secret wealth beyond imagination somewhere off its coast. It was more than the entrepreneurial chaos creator from South Korea could hope for.

Chapter 6

Gene Bond turned the collar of his coat up and bent into the cold wind and the fine rain as he walked from the railway station across the canal bridge and into the campus of the University of Birmingham. Ahead of him and up the slight hill, Big Joe, the affectionately nicknamed clock, struck the hour. Now more than 100 years old, the more correctly named Joseph Chamberlain Memorial Clock, in memory of the Birmingham manufacturer, mayor and politician, is thought to be the tallest freestanding clock tower in the world at 100 metres high. It is sometimes mistaken for being Big Brum, Birmingham's answer to Westminster's Big Ben. Big Brum stands adjacent the Council House in the city centre some three miles away.

Gene Bond's world seemed to work in phases. He knew it was only coincidence but it did seem odd that for a while his work would be dominated by matters to do with energy, then pollution, then waste, and so on. Currently it seemed concern for the oceans was on everyone's minds, more specifically the growing problems of pollution and especially plastic related pollution. The recent David Attenborough television series about the devastation of the oceans had caught the public's attention. For someone based in Birmingham, more distanced from the sea than any other city in the UK, this upsurge of marine-related business was ironic. But Bond found locating himself in the city at the centre of the country to be convenient for someone with clients and projects scattered across the nation albeit a long way from the sea.

Self-employed, he calls himself a sustainability consultant but this covers a multitude of interests. There was no simple definition of his job and it was a challenge to him when anyone asked him what he did for a living. It was not easy to answer. He had become passionately interested in how, since industrialisation, the modern global community continues to cause havoc to the planet and its hugely complex and often fragile eco-systems. His work involves helping organisations – companies or cities and towns – function differently so as to stop destructive activity, such as pollution and waste generation, and to adopt new technologies such as renewable energy, hybrid vehicles and locally generated power.

In recent times his name has caused him great consternation and dismay. Through a series of what he considered to be severe misfortunes, he became involved in exploits normally associated with the world of espionage and terrorism. The press instantly locked onto Bond's name and took much joy in exploiting the story of a British man named Bond being involved in such activity. Gene Bond considered himself the antithesis of anything to do with the image of Bond, Ian Fleming's creation, and cursed the author for selecting Gene's family name for his fictional spy. He cursed his dad for being a Johnny Cash fan and emulating the famous song 'A Boy Named Sue' by giving him such an effeminate sounding first name.

He equally cursed Georgi Patarava. Much of the blame for this espionage and terrorism nonsense into which he had been dragged away from his usual, normal, sedate and sane world, was linked to his close friend. He first met Georgi, a Georgian, many years ago when Georgi worked at the Kensington based London Embassy of the then Soviet Union. Bond was interested in how the Soviet Union was dismantling its war machine and moving it into other manufacturing activity. The term 'tanks to ploughs' had been widespread for a while. Bond was exploring prospects for UK businesses. The two spent a little time talking business, much time talking politics, the environment, sport, and women, and even greater time consuming copious amounts of Caucasus brandy. The drink, according to the label on the bottle, "attracts by its history, its grandeur, hospitality, beauty of women and nature, braveness of men, love of feasts, respect of guests, polyphony songs and hot dances." It was, they agreed, a drink totally in harmony with their own interests and values.

Georgi was now running the London communications centre of the Brussels based European Secret Service, an organisation that does not officially exist. Indeed, most members of the European Parliament do not know it exists. It was not, Georgi contested, an anomaly that Bond had been sucked into his world. "The more vital resources become depleted and under greater demand, the more people will try and exploit them –

legally or otherwise," he said to his friend. "The criminal world will become increasingly interested in anything that has growing value – and today that includes energy, water, rare minerals and the like, or new technological solutions."

And so it had proved to be with Gene Bond becoming very reluctantly involved with three major adventures with Georgi, all to his considerable consternation and very much against his better judgement.

Bond was bemused about the content of a small parcel when it arrived from Africa until he read the accompanying note from Pete Turner. He immediately recalled the young geological student who had spent a week with him tracking his business activity as part of the work experience of his academic course. The youngster was quick minded, quick witted and a generally bright and likeable young man. Bond remembered Pete planning a global tour so was not surprised to see the package came from Wandora in Africa though he had never heard of the place before. He struggled to find it on his National Geographic desktop globe. But yes, there it was, a strip of a nation in a line of countries bordering the Gulf of Guinea.

As for the content of the package, it was a ragged piece of grey/blue rock appreciably smaller than a golf ball. Bond accepted Pete's accompanying thoughts that such a coloured rock is rare, if not totally unknown, in the sandy environment of Wandora. Pete's note said the original lump of rock was about the size of an open hand. He had found it on the edge of a beach and the geologist had pondered if it might have originated out at sea and been thrown in by the recent tsunami. The tsunami rang a bell in Bond's memory. He recalled reading about a small African state being decimated by such a disaster. Researching via the Web, he found numerous accounts of the catastrophe. The whole Gulf of Guinea coastline had become a disaster area.

There were two issues to be investigated. What was the rock? Could it have come from the sea? Bond had two contacts he felt might be able to help. He had read with passing interest that the University of Birmingham, located some eight miles from his home, had not long ago launched a new research centre to do with rare materials. The Centre for Strategic Elements and Critical Materials had, according to the article, already established a global reputation. And in considering the marine element of Pete Turner's question, in searching the Web for information about the tsunami in Wandora, the name of a British company based in Southampton came up. SNEL – Sub Nautical Exploration Limited – had apparently undertaken a survey conducted with remote deep sea vehicles to see what damage the tsunami had done to the seas off the West African coast. On checking what news items he could find, Bond noted the expedition had apparently found a previously unknown sea anemone which, according to newspaper reports, might have medical benefits. That the story had subsequently disappeared suggested either the prognosis was wrong or that it was right and was now being supressed for commercial sensitivity reasons.

Bond had risked sending the rock sample on to the university and was delighted to receive the short report back telling him what the rock was and inviting him to visit the Centre. It was too good an opportunity and he organised to meet. Bond had read about cobalt as being a material essential to our modern information technology driven world. He recalled seeing articles about children mining the stuff but he knew nothing in detail about it. He was intrigued about its role especially in electric cars. He again turned to the Web to find out more. What he discovered horrified him.

Newspaper reports, reports from NGOs and government organisations, television news reports – all told him how cobalt is mined mostly in the Congo to provide an essential element for the modern day communications tools used globally. But by far the worst aspect of what he read was how young children, some as young as just four, are exploited in the mining process. One extensive report with accompanying photographs painted a shocking image of a moon-like landscape, predominantly mud with no visible greenery at all, and youngsters digging for minerals with their bare hands or acting as labourers carrying full sacks of earth to points of disposal then taking the empty sacks back to the mines to be refilled. A day's work could be as long as 12 hours and if no minerals were found no money was earned so no food was bought.

Bond was horrified. This was as extreme an example of the 'haves and have nots' of the modern world he had ever seen. How could it be in this day and age that sophisticated communications, now a part of daily life especially in the developed world, were reliant upon four year old children scraping a living in the most hideous of circumstances? He was close to tears as he watched a Sky News video report from the Congo which tracked the fortune of two youngsters. Their story was frightful and quite unbelievable.

The more he researched the more it became apparent that the world's use of such materials is on the increase as demand for more and more electrically based technology expands, not least for electric cars. At the same time, the value of these mined minerals was feeding more and more criminal activity and, across Central Africa in particular, terrorist groups.

Bond was thoroughly damp and chilled by the time he walked across the centre of the campus to their designated meeting point, the café in the new Alan Walters Building, a large, imposing, concrete and glass structure, one of many within the continually expanding university. Lectures could be seen in many big windowed rooms and students were scattered around the place in groups or individually, some in casual conversation, others in earnest study. Professor Slater turned out to be a young, tall man in jeans, jumper and hooded coat who deposited his case on the floor before shaking Bond's hand and apologising for meeting in such an open area. "The Centre for Strategic Elements and Critical Materials is a virtual centre with no physical home of its own," he explained. "It covers numerous faculties across the university – chemistry, economics, law, physics, social sciences and others in a programme that's exploring critical materials and their reuse."

Over two large coffees, the professor told him that with the global population set to increase from around

7.2 billion to 9.7 by 2050, and with vast numbers of people in developing countries such as India and China emerging into the high consumer middle class, pressures on critical resources are only going to grow. That pressure also builds as society moves its energy provision away from being based on fossil fuel to renewable energy.

"Cobalt is," said the professor, "used in batteries and batteries are becoming increasingly important in a global chase to find effective ways of storing electric power. The more we generate power locally the more we need to find ways of storing it for when we want to use it."

The University's teams were also deeply involved in seeking an alternative to 'wet' batteries. "The problem we have with batteries for powering cars," said the professor, "is they have liquid content. That makes them potentially dangerous so they're housed in a heavy protective casing. That causes added weight and big headaches when it comes to recycling them. They're very difficult to break down so as to recover and reuse their component parts – like cobalt. We can take pressure off the rare material supply chain if we can find cost effective ways of recycling batteries which we are working on as part of our ReLiB project. Until then, the demand for such minerals will continue to rise."

"Could cobalt be found in the seabed?" Bond asked.

"There have been some reports of low concentrations on the deep ocean floor but not at the levels in the rock you sent. Ultimately, we know so little about what's on the seabed anything is possible," said the professor.

To further explore the question as to whether Pete Taylor's lump of rock could have been thrown inland during the tsunami, Bond turned to SNEL, the company he recalled as being involved in the discovery of a sea anemone off-shore the African coast. Bond thought if anyone should know the answer to his question, SNEL should. He wrote to their Managing Director in the strictest of confidence, telling him about the lump of grey/blue rock and how the people at the University of Birmingham had identified it as containing cobalt. In their opinion, could it have been thrown inland by the tsunami?

That the letter was intercepted by someone else within SNEL was to cause turmoil in a number of directions.

Chapter 7

Gary Marchant had not been in the office for several days and wondered what sort of reception he was going to get. Tensions were running high. The relationship between himself and Marcel was deteriorating and all the SNEL team knew it. Not that he was that bothered but he did notice with some small sense of relief that Marcel's car was not in sight as he swung his BMW into the small car park and into the bay at the head of which hung a sign with his name on it. SNEL's base in Southampton is actually in Marchwood on the opposite side of the River Test to the city, located down a lane that could do with some serious filling of potholes. Onwards past the entrance to SNEL, the single vehicle track ultimately leads to the water's edge. A good number of trees still stand close to the offices but nowadays they tend to look forlorn, listless and grey as if succumbing to the steady corrosion of nature by the relentless march of industrialisation. The locals refer to the area as being "snaggy" – run down. At the end of the lane is a wide expanse of river with shipyard cranes prominent on the Southampton side opposite.

Marchant was accompanied by his leggy assistant, Vanessa. Had her dress been any shorter it might have been cause for an arrest for indecency. The neckline was similarly daring. It plunged deeply revealing a significant amount of cleavage when she stood and a clear view of her ample bosom – unfettered by a bra – when she sat or bent forward. They were returning from a long weekend break culminating in an extended lunch at the thatched Pilgrim Inn a mile or so away from the office. They had eaten well and drunk even better and spent the time planning their forthcoming holiday during which Gary intended to ravish the delectable 'Van' as much as possible. Their relationship was now known to pretty well everyone in the company and the initial novelty and gossip had died down. Generally considered Gary's mistress and called a "tart" when the other girls in SNEL gossiped about her, the founder, Marcel, considered Vanessa's presence distasteful and inappropriate, her professional abilities questionable and her pay excessive.

"What the hell about her business competencies and skills when she's got the sort of assets she's got!" Gary had retorted dismissively in one of their heated discussions about her. It simply fuelled the rift between the two men. Marcel despaired about the growing arrogance of his business partner and his general attitude. It had changed significantly since he first joined SNEL. Initially Marchant shared Marcel's passion for diving and concerns about sea quality degradation and marine life pollution and environmental issues in general. Then he started to make money and he changed. Marcel had once liked the man. Not now.

Entering the office, Gary grabbed a handful of envelopes from his correspondence pigeonhole located in the reception area. As was his normal custom born out of curiosity and a keen sense of wanting at all times to know what was going on within SNEL, even if that was contrary to his apparent disinterest in corporate matters, when nobody was in reception he would take a quick look at what was in other pigeonholes. It was not his customary practice to open the correspondence of fellow directors but this one letter sparked his curiosity. It stated on the front to be from sustainability consultant Gene Bond. It was a name Gary recalled from the past. He remembered a previous letter from the same person expressing interest in the discovery of the sea anemone. He wondered why Bond would be writing to Marcel again. So he opened the envelope. If later questioned why he had done so he would simply claim it had been in the wrong tray. He would say he only realised it was for Marcel after opening it.

The letter asked for a meeting or telephone conference with Marcel about a piece of rock that had been discovered in Wandora on the African coast of the Gulf of Guinea. Bond had had the rock analysed and it transpired it was a mineral called cobalt. Bond recalled the deep sea exploration undertaken by SNEL in the aftermath of the tsunami and wondered if any of their findings or data from their exploration might help identify if the cobalt sample could possibly have come from the seabed off the Wandora coast.

Gary scribbled "Sorry – opened in error. Was in my pile of letters" on the envelope and replaced it with other envelopes waiting for Marcel.

Gary knew nothing about cobalt. It was only later in the day he decided to Google the mineral. He read the results with growing interest.

"Cobalt is a naturally occurring metallic ore. Tantalum is extracted from it. That is used for capacitors in electronic circuits as its high capacitance property allows the storage and instantaneous release of electric charge with minor power loss."

"Tantalum is strategically important and valuable. Sectors in which it is extensively used include defence industries, aviation and medical technology. The characteristics which make it valuable are its resistance to extreme heat and chemical corrosion, hardness and ductility."

His interest stimulated by what he read, he opened other entries on the Web. Another told him: "Cobalt is found in major quantities in the Congo which possesses 80 percent of the world's supply. When cobalt is refined it becomes a heat resistant powder that can hold a high electric charge. The properties of refined cobalt are a vital element in creating devices that store energy or capacitors used in a vast array of small electronic devices, especially in mobile phones, laptop computers, pagers, and other electronic devices."

And: "Rwanda, Uganda, Burundi and their proxy militias are the primary exploiters of cobalt in the Congo. In an 18 month period Rwanda made $250 million as a result of exploitation of cobalt in the Congo. Although Rwanda and Uganda possess little or no cobalt, during the period of the war in the Congo, their exports escalated exponentially. For example, Rwanda's cobalt export went from less than 50 tons in 1995 to almost 250 tons in 1998."

He found a United Nations note reporting on the "Illegal Exploitation of Natural Resources in the Congo." It said: "The consequences of illegal exploitation have been twofold: (a) massive availability of financial resources for the Rwandan Patriotic Army, and the individual enrichment of top Ugandan military commanders and civilians; (b) the emergence of illegal networks headed by either top military officers or businessmen."

He read a Daily Mail report from the Luwow Mine in the Democratic Republic of Congo. The accompanying pictures were appalling. It read; "Scraping through shovels-full of silt for the precious mineral with their bare hands, miners use these primitive methods to harvest cobalt – the magical conductor that powers your iPhone, Samsung Galaxy or other smartphones. Covered head-to-foot in the ore-laden mud, hundreds of workers toil for 12 hours a day – in scenes reminiscent of the 19th century gold-rush."

"Wielding picks and shovels, legions of strong men delve deep into the mountainside to retrieve the precious natural deposit which enables our high-tech mobile world of emails, social media and the internet."

But it was the value and heavy demand for the stuff that really got Gary excited. Research showed a variety of prices for cobalt, as high as $600 a kilogram in one report but Reuters saying; *The financial markets have an unlikely new hero. In recent months, the best way to make a serious amount of money in a short amount of time has been to buy cobalt. The price per ton of the metal has soared by almost 70% already this year, driven by a near-insatiable demand for rechargeable batteries and the growing popularity of electric cars."*

If what Pete Turner sent Bond was an indication of some source of cobalt out in the Gulf of Guinea that had been disturbed by the tsunami, the value could be astronomic. His mind raced with excitement. Rwanda had made $250 million in 18 months! The big questions were – was the one rock evidence of a sizeable source of the stuff? If so, how much was out there? And where?

Casually so as not to raise anyone's concerns as to why he was interested, he asked around SNEL about activity being undertaken in the aftermath of the deep sea surveying work they had undertaken. It transpired that Marcel had had a number of meetings with various organisations all interested in the potential of the sea anemone they had found. There was, as far as he could determine, nothing from the exploration that referred to any minerals, cobalt or otherwise.

With a growing interest in another expedition, this time manned, the objectives of which would be to gather more samples of the sea anemone and to try and gain some sort of measure as to how much there was of it, Marcel's team had been making contact with a variety of organisations. Vanessa found they had established contact with The Gulf of Guinea Interregional Network, a body set up by several African countries primarily to combat the growing problem of piracy at sea. Some 20 countries located down the west coast of Africa were involved. The call from Marcel had been received with some considerable interest. Heavy support came from the European Union through its Critical Maritime Routes Programme. Marcel spoke to officials there who confirmed their interest in the sea anemone as part of their remit concerning sea quality. Yes, they told him, they might be interested if further research was undertaken.

Marchant found people in Marcel's team had even spoken to high ranking officials in the Wandora government, in particular to an official who spoke English, one Kevin Forsythe, even though the subject was way off his normal agenda. When he asked questions about this in the office, he was told the Wandora civil servant had sounded very officious, pompously full of his own self-importance, but had been very helpful.

Clearly there was much interest in the sea anemone. Now Marchant turned his attention to the cobalt rock. If there was a seam of it off the Wandora coast, could it be mined? What were the likely costs? What were the potential gains?

His research into deep sea mining was disturbing. The more he delved into the subject the clearer it became that the harvesting of the sea anemone – if that is what it came to – might be compromised by deep sea mining – if that prospect came to fruition. At a time when concern was growing around the world about the increased pollution of the planet's oceans, the prospect of mining minerals from the seabed was sparking much concern.

He set Vanessa to research what she could on the subject and one report he found especially interesting. It was from a Bromley Murton, a marine scientist specialising in minerals to be found on the sea floor. The article introduced him to something he had never heard of before – Marine E-tech. During his work Murton had apparently found on the seabed the material tellurium at concentrations 50,000 times higher than in deposits on land. The article said; "Tellurium is a key component in thin-film high-efficiency photovoltaic cells. If we want to move towards a low-carbon future, then we need raw materials like tellurium. We calculate that based on the average concentration of tellurium and thickness of the ferromanganese crusts at tropic seamount, if all the tellurium was used to make solar PV panels, they could provide up to 60% of the UK's electrical energy generation capacity."

Gary was disturbed to read about the potential consequences to marine life of deep sea mining. He read; "For biology that is directly impacted by deep-sea mining, there is total destruction. However, it's a matter of assessing the importance of that impact – at a species level, are we going to lose species or just individuals? When we cut down pine trees for timber, it may be bad news for the tree, but has little impact on the species of pine. Of course, if it's a major isolated tree that hosts lots of other life whose felling would cause a great loss of biological diversity, then you have to think twice. Another way to look at this is on the seafloor – the seamount we studied is only 40km in diameter. As such, if it were mined, it would impact only 10,000th of 1% of the Earth's surface. In contrast, farming impacts 40% of all land and cities 3%. On a practical level, if deep-sea mining happens, then we must devise methods to minimise impacts."

"Human life needs raw materials to survive. Population continues to grow and societies to develop.

As land-based grades diminish, and the resource gap grows, despite recycling and the circular economy, new sources of materials have to be found. The question is whether deep-sea resources can provide a safer and less harmful supply compared with land-based mining."

To Gary the research was showing one thing. If offshore Wandora there was a seam of cobalt on the seabed, and if there was enough sea anemone to harvest to be viable for use by the pharmaceutical industry, recovering both was highly unlikely. So, given the choice, where should the research, funds and effort go? To Gary there was only one answer – but it would be at odds with Marcel's ambitions.

Chapter 8

The big man in the flowing, colourful gown stood opposite the small African man who wore an immaculate, expensively tailored grey suit and white shoes that could have been cleaner. He considered him with contempt. Nobody should ever, he thought, become so cornered in the way he had cornered this man. It was pitiful.

"It's simple," the South Korean told the Minister from Wandora in a gentle, matter of fact voice. "You cooperate and you will be a rich man. You fail me and first you will see your family die one by one before you too will be sent to your maker. Is that quite clear?"

Sum Taeyoung's interest in Wandora had developed fast but that was characteristic of the founder of the Seoul based Sustainable Development Brokers International. He was, amongst many other things, an opportunist.

SDBI is a globally operating consultancy. It uses experience gained by people in the developed countries to help those emerging from poverty and despair in poor nations. It especially covers issues such as water provision, air pollution and local energy production from renewable sources like solar panels and wind turbines. It is a highly successful, well considered business.

But it also acts as a cover. Sum Taeyoung, an Anglicised South Korean educated at Oxford, the LSE and Harvard, grew to despise the western free world. It was, he came to believe, born out of aggressive imperial empire building by England, Portugal and Spain and more latterly America. These nations, he believed, had abused people, violated their lands and asset stripped nations around the globe. It was his avowed intent to revenge the plight of people who had been its victims. And to that end, behind the authentic activity of SDBI, he built a clandestine organisation the objectives of which were chaos creation in the free world and trafficking in armaments and drugs. Whilst born out of altruistic values, this shadowy world of Sum Taeyoung was also by far the most financially rewarding. And it was this activity that caused him to look towards Africa, now considered to be the fastest growing and biggest market for illicit drug trafficking.

Africa, a continent in turmoil caused by conflict, weak governments, corruption and natural catastrophes, also offers huge prospects for armaments sales, especially to the vast numbers of illegal armies, gangs and even wars rife across the world's second largest continent both in land and population size.

His supply chains for both arms and drugs had been secure for years leaving Taeyoung's main concern for some time being the establishment of a viable and secure entry point into the continent. He first heard of Wandora when he read about it in the aftermath of the tsunami. In many respects it was ideal. Its bankruptcy meant its officials would be easy pickings. Its deep sea port held great potential not only for ships carrying illicit cargo but also for exporting the minerals for which the Chinese had acquired the extraction rights.

The attack on the northern village was immediately followed by a message to Taeyoung's Chinese contacts, of whom he had many, some in positions of high power in Beijing, advising them that his own team had successfully wiped out a Boko Haram force that had taken over the minerals mine in northern Wandora. The Chinese could now be assured of their safety and resume mining activity. Taeyoung would take responsibility for their ongoing safety and to that end he was leaving his own significant, well armed presence in the mining area.

The message to Beijing remained unanswered as Taeyoung took the next step in his plot. He chose to meet the Minister responsible for security around the mines. They met in the Palm Trees Hotel, one of the tallest and more modern buildings in Porto Wandora and one that had largely escaped the consequences of the tsunami. It claims to be five star but by any regulated standards would be categorised as barely three. However it is the best the capital has to offer. Taeyoung had taken a long-term reservation on what was claimed to be the 'Presidential Suite' – a group of interconnecting rooms on its eighth and highest floor. Taeyoung established base here – until a more permanent arrangement could be organised.

The men met in the suite's lounge. Taeyoung had ordered two very large stemmed bowl glasses of well iced imported South African artisan gin in a cocktail the recipe for which he had handed personally to the hotel's head barman. The South Korean had enthused about the age-old spirit's newly enlivened local African interpretation in which juniper gives way to infused shrub leaves from the floral region of South Africa.

Sum Taeyoung sipped his as he wandered around near the open windows leading to the balcony beyond which could be seen palm trees, a golden stretch of beach and the sea. His Ministerial guest sat tense and anxious. A sweat patch had appeared on the front of his shirt. His drink remained untouched.

"I am pleased to inform you China Minerals Inc. has agreed to recommence its mining activity in Wandora," Taeyoung told Moussa Ehouzou. "But it's conditional."

"Conditional on what?"

"On the Wandora Government signing a contract with SDBI for that company to provide security for the mining area." There was no truth in that. Beijing had still not responded. But the Minister responsible for security was not to know.

Taeyoung saw the man in front of him squirm.

"That might be difficult."

It was as if he had not spoken. The South Korean stared straight into the Minister's eyes, as if he could read his mind.

"And because the Chinese are concerned about logistics and especially the export of extracted material, they also need to ensure the port is secure. So the contract regarding the mining area will extend to Porto Wandora."

"But that's our capital." The Minister moved edgily in his chair. "To hand over security to an outside contractor – it is unheard of."

"But it will be now," Taeyoung assured him. "You will see to it. And it inherently means SDBI forces will control the route between the mine and the port."

51

The Minister was shocked. These demands were preposterous.

"And you will be able to tell the President that you – you alone – have secured the return of the Chinese to the mines. You will be the hero of the hour – the saviour of the economy of Wandora!"

The Minister shook his head. It was impossible.

"And when you succeed your work will be acknowledged by a substantial deposit in a secure Swiss bank account to which only you have access." The Korean paused. "But if you fail, your family will be eliminated. You will live to witness that – before you too die. I was going to add that the choice is yours but, as you fully realise, you have no choice. Do you?"

The Minister paused but eventually resigned himself to the inevitable.

"No," he agreed.

Sum Taeyoung rose and stretched his hand out across his desk. The handshake from Minister Moussa Ehouzou was damp from fear induced sweat and limp from lack of conviction.

Taeyoung's connections with the Chinese Government's Ministry of Commerce had developed over several years. He had nurtured a number of particularly useful individual contacts with high ranking officers and it was to one of them the South Korean followed up the meeting with Moussa Ehouzou. He again expressed how mortified he had been to learn how China's workers had been massacred. He understood the importance of mineral extraction both to China and to Wandora. He explained in guarded and limited terms how his growing business interests in Africa meant he had developed his own security force. As a demonstration of its capabilities, his team now controlled the mining area of Wandora. He was pleased to report he now held a long term contract for security matters from the Wandora Government. With that in place SDBI was now able to provide guaranteed safety for Chinese workers in the mines. He would welcome the Chinese Government encouraging China Minerals Inc. to contract with SDBI over the matter, and with some urgency. It was in the interests of both the minerals company and SDBI that such an arrangement was made quickly.

The Chinese official agreed. The contract from China Minerals was swiftly secured. Taeyoung now held contracts from the Wandora government and the mining company. Security in both the northern part of Wandora and its port was now in the hands of SDBI. To underpin his position, Taeyoung pointed out to his Ministerial friend that if any element of the Wandora Government had difficulties with these arrangements they should raise them with him. For them to do so direct to Beijing might be to totally prejudice the prospect of mining being resumed.

In the President's main office in the São João Baptista de Wandora the latest emergency meeting called by the President discussed how to respond to the proclamation received from the South Korean.

"Has anyone met this man?" asked the President. He leant forward on his studded red leather chair and glared at his Ministers assembled before him. Now in his 61st year and second term of office, he trusted nobody. He had taken over the management of a country that was virtually bankrupt and riddled with corruption. It was a huge frustration to him that just as he seemed to be making some tangible progress and significant improvements could be found throughout Wandora, it had been massively undermined by the tsunami. His economic lifeline, the Chinese interest in minerals in the north of the country, was threatened by the massacre there and now this South Korean had appeared with a set of proposals that appeared preposterous but could not to be ignored.

The President sat at his imposing desk, the national flag draped across the wall behind him. To his left the whitewashed wall was dominated by a large, opulently framed picture of himself whilst on the opposite side hung a large abstract oil painting that nobody understood but which the President declared he had produced himself. While painting was known to be one of his hobbies, nobody believed he was the creator of the strange monstrosity of which he was so proud.

The eleven Ministers sat at a long table that was at a right angle to the President's. Heads shook in negative response to his question including that of Moussa Ehouzou, Minister for National Security.

"He seems to have manoeuvred himself into a very powerful position," the President continued. "It appears the Chinese will only resume mining exploration if we agree to the terms of SDBI. But the reality of that is we are handing over a significant element of the security of our nation to an outside, commercial organisation. That sounds fraught with dangers to me. But if we don't, we lose the revenue from the mining contract. And as we all know, that is currently propping up our economy. What do you think?"

He glared at his Ministers, challenging them to respond. Most had their heads down, apparently reading the copy of the SDBI declaration in front of them. Conspicuously – because he was the only one looking straight back at the President and because he was the only white man in the room, Kevin Forsythe found himself under the glare of the President and felt obliged to say something. Nobody else did.

"I was wondering, Mr President, if we ever found out who was responsible for the attack on the mining village?" As he spoke, the Englishman turned to look at Ehouzou who seemed ever more interested in what was on his table before him.

"Moussa!" the President barked in the absence of any response from the Security Minister.

"Yes President?" he said meekly, at last looking up.

"Mr Forsythe asked a question. Who attacked the village? Do you know?"

Moussa Ehouzou, a small, square bodied man with a receding hairline but plaited locks falling from the back of his head, had his hand to his mouth as if biting the back of it. He mumbled a response.

"What? Speak up man," the President snapped.

"We don't know, Mr President. We think it may be a gang made up of ex Al-Shabaab and Boko Haram fighters."

"And why did they attack?"

"We don't know Mr President." Moussa Ehouzou knew perfectly well the who and why. The who was

55

a motley array of mercenaries paid to do so by Sum Taeyoung. The why was they had been set up by the same man. No sooner had the gang created carnage in the village than an SDBI force had taken over the mining area and the original insurgents had gone on a killing and looting rampage further south into Wandora.

"It's not good enough!" The President banged his fist on the desk before him in emphasis.

"Our forces are so depleted in the aftermath of the disaster," pleaded the Security Minister in defence, then added in a mumbling voice that could hardly be heard, "And thank God for the South Korean who at least has got the Chinese back into the mines."

The President pondered the matter for some time before declaring "I will sign nothing before I meet this man Taeyoung. Moussa – you will make the arrangements."

Kevin Forsythe tidied up the documents on the table before him and stood to depart. It had never been like this in Whitehall, he reflected. He was, he thought, sitting in a den of iniquity. He wondered what on earth could happen next?

Chapter 9

Tension within SNEL was at boiling point. Marcel circulated a plan to his fellow directors to secure funds for a more extensive exploration out to the Gulf of Guinea Trench to bring back more samples of the sea anemone and to try and gain some measure as to how much there was of it. He advocated a manned submersible.

To anyone who knew the full story it might have seemed funny that neither Marcel nor Gary mentioned the subject of cobalt. But while Marcel suspected Gary had read the letter from Bond, he did not mention it to his co-director. Conversely, Gary remained silent on the subject too. Gary, keen to research whether it would be possible to mine cobalt from the sea if there was a seam there, did not want that prospect jeopardised by any progress Marcel might make in gaining support for an expedition to find the sea anemone.

The company was clearly dividing into two camps. On one side Marcel, the company founder and supported by two other directors, Steve Oldbury who looked after finance and Charlotte McDonnell, better known as Lotty, who now headed up admin. Both had been with Marcel from the early days of SNEL and certainly longer than Gary who represented the other camp. Though Marcel had the strength in numbers of directors on his side of the argument, the commercial division led by Gary had been successful enough to build a team of staff that outnumbered that of Marcel's by some 4:1.

There had been developments in both camps. Marcel was assembling a growing portfolio of pharmaceutical companies, research institutes, international agencies and NGOs potentially interested in further exploration to do with the sea anemone. The prospect of funding a manned submersible exploration of the Trench was becoming potentially more likely.

In the other camp, Gary accumulated more and more evidence of the growing demand for cobalt. There was no doubt that as the world moved away from its reliance upon fossil fuels – the UK, for instance, announcing it would ban the sale of fossil fuel powered vehicles from 2040 and was even considering making that 2030 – so the demand for batteries to store power was growing. And the more it grew, so did the demand for cobalt. During his research he found an article by Professor and conservation biologist, Richard (Rick) Steiner of Oasis Earth based in Anchorage, Alaska. He is a specialist in finding solutions in energy and climate change, marine conservation, offshore oil and environment, habitat protection, endangered species protection, and sustainable development.

But it was Steiner's concerns about deep sea mining and its potential impact on life in the oceans – and therefore the Gulf of Guinea Sea Anemone, that especially interested and worried Gary. He read; "There's a problem. The deep ocean, where mining is proposed, constitutes the largest and least understood biological habitat on earth. It is an Alice-in-Wonderland world of extremes, extraordinary adaptations, bizarre organisms, beauty and mystery. It is characterized by darkness (infused with sparkling bioluminescence), extreme pressure, cold temperatures, high biodiversity (perhaps millions of species, most yet to be identified), slow growth and reproductive rates, and high sensitivity to disturbance (low resilience). Given our poor understanding of deep sea ecosystems, growing industrial interest, rudimentary management, and insufficient protected areas, the risk of irreversible environmental damage here is real."

"Environmental risks and impacts of deep sea mining would be enormous and unavoidable, including seabed habitat degradation over vast ocean areas, species extinctions, reduced habitat complexity, slow and uncertain recovery, suspended sediment plumes, toxic plumes from surface ore dewatering, pelagic ecosystem impacts, undersea noise, ore and oil spills in transport, and more."

"Full-scale nodule mining would affect thousands of square miles of ocean floor, kill attached invertebrate communities, and create huge subsea sediment plumes that would flow and settle over thousands of square miles of seafloor. Such sedimentation would smother seabed habitat, reduce habitat complexity and biodiversity over vast areas, and post-mining recovery would be extremely slow. Mining of cobalt crusts on seamounts would cause enormous, possibly irreversible impacts to unique, productive seamount ecosystems."

"Clearly, we need to avoid such ecological damage. Before any deep sea mining moves ahead, we would need much more extensive scientific research – species identification, community ecology, distribution, genetics, life histories, resettlement patterns, resilience to disturbance, and at least a 10-year continuous time series of observations to understand dynamics of proposed mining sites over time. In addition, we need more robust management regimes at the International Seabed Authority and in coastal nations, royalty-sharing and liability agreements, stakeholder engagement, and significant advancements in subsea technology. Until this is achieved, the only wise policy is a global moratorium on all deep sea mining."

"Industry and governments recognize the huge challenges in mining the deep ocean but are resolved to move forward anyway. As justification, they invoke the "peak minerals" argument, depletion of land-based minerals, and a projected increase in mineral demand in the world economy. But mining proponents habitually avoid discussing the opportunity to reduce mineral demand by increasing the efficiency of metal use in the global economy, cradle-to-cradle design, recycling, and landfill mining. To build a sustainable economy, we will have to break the "economy of waste" – mining raw minerals, using them once or twice, discarding them, and continuing the demand for mining raw minerals. Surely at some point, with smart renewable metal use, we will have enough minerals already up into the global economy and won't need to keep digging holes for more. The sooner we get there, the better."

"This emerging industry would result in serious impacts to our oceans, so it is critical for civil society to engage now, in the early stages of exploration and development. It would be truly unfortunate if we allow the same industrial paradigm that destroyed much of the terrestrial ecosystems of our home planet to do the same in the deep sea. It is time to change this model."

The worry to Gary was the impact this sort of argument would have in support of Marcel's proposition. It again sharpened the view that it was either farm the sea anemone or mine the cobalt, assuming both existed off the African coast in viable quantities. It was one or the other – not both. But if Marcel got his funding and his new exploration found the sea anemone in sufficient quantity for the pharmaceutical industry, then deep sea mining in the area would become impossible.

Eventually the tension burst into an explosive confrontation between the two former friends meeting in Marcel's office in Southampton. The door was shut but passing staff could not help hear the raised voices.

"You can't keep blocking my attempts to get a new expedition together," complained Marcel.

"I can when it's not in the interests of the company," Gary told him.

"How the hell can't it be in the interests of SNEL?" Marcel countered. "It's exactly the sort of work SNEL was set up to do."

"But the effort in trying to secure funding is diverting people away from work that's fee earning," Gary argued. "Look how many hours – probably days – have been spent researching places of potential funding then making applications. Then there's no guarantee we'll get the work. We'll be competing against far bigger companies than ours."

"But we won the first contract," Marcel reminded him.

"Only by slashing our prices and just covering our costs. It made no contribution to our coffers," Gary pointed out. "What you're doing now is exciting the market to undertake more exploration then watching as bigger companies than ours get contracted to do it."

"But the value to us if the sea anemone can produce medical benefits would be massive."

"Bollocks! You don't know that," Gary disputed.

"It's bound to!"

"No it's not! SNEL might get paid for the exploration – and it's a bloody big "might" – but that'll be it. You'll not get any royalties on products that might arise from the sea anemone." It was an argument that could be turned against his own interests, thought Gary. But that was his problem and not one Marcel knew anything about. Yet. He had already researched the issue of ownership of any mining undertaken offshore Wandora. As far as he could tell, it was a matter for the Wandora Government. As with most if not all countries, its territorial waters should extend out 12 nautical miles in line with the 1982 United Nations Convention on the Law of the Sea. Surely anything thrown ashore by the tsunami could not have been more than 12 miles from the coast? It seemed unlikely.

As far as mining was concerned, Gary found the International Seabed Authority decreed that "Top of Form the international seabed area beyond national jurisdiction has been declared the Common Heritage of Mankind. The mineral resources of the Common

Heritage are administered by the International Seabed Authority. Recognizing the economic and technological imbalance between developed and developing countries, the United Nations Convention on the Law of the Sea places emphasis on the equitable sharing of benefits derived from the minerals of the area. To give effect to the concept of the Common Heritage of Mankind, the Convention especially aims at ensuring equitable participation by developing countries." That clearly did not apply within the 12 miles rule.

"You can't dictate what this company does or doesn't do," Marcel told Gary in no uncertain terms.

"And you can't stop me exploring opportunities I can see," Gary retorted, his voice now loud.

"We'll take this to the Board and decide there," Marcel declared.

"Do what you bloody well like," Gary shouted back in a departing gesture. "It'll make no difference to me." The one statistic that stuck in his mind and dominated his thinking and his ambition was the $250 million made in 18 months from cobalt mined by Rwanda. He slammed the door as he left Marcel's office.

Steve Oldbury waited what seemed like an appropriate amount of time before entering Marcel's office.

"It's getting very difficult," Marcel said in a voice that clearly indicated he had been shaken by the confrontation with Gary. "I've said we'll take the matter to a Board meeting. We need to do that sooner than later. I hope I can rely on the support of you and Lotty."

"Of course," Steve tried to reassure him. "You shouldn't feel you need to ask. But I have some news for you that's going to blacken your day even more."

Marcel put a hand to his forehead. "What now?"

"You'll never guess what I've found Gary has done!"

Chapter 10

Pete Taylor was amazed at the report from Gene Bond. The "bit of rock" so described by Kevin Forsythe was, it transpired, cobalt. From his geology course he knew about cobalt, about minerals critical to the information technology of the developed world, how children are used in the mining process and how valuable it is – and growingly so. The million dollar question now was – where did this bit of rock come from and is there a quantity of it there? But what to do next? The young geologist simply did not know the answer. He also worried about what he was starting – maybe a wild goose chase all on the basis of one bit of rock. He had searched around the area where he had found the solitary sample but found no more. In the end he decided he had to confide in his friend.

"Cobalt? Means nothing to me dear boy," Kevin Forsythe admitted. "Seem to recall a Chevy car by that name …but no. Sounds like a soap product!"

Clearly a mere lump of rock still did not spark interest in the former civil servant, now a politician. Whilst holding this polite conversation with Pete his mind was very obviously largely on some of the more challenging matters that had shattered his plans for tranquillity in the twilight of his career years.

They were meeting in Kevin's apartment, a well-appointed, third floor set of reasonably sized rooms located in a modern building near the renovated castle and surrounded by its own security fence and a keypad operated gate. A picture window dominates one end of the lounge and opens onto a balcony overlooking the bay with the castle in the foreground to the left. Adjacent apartments are occupied by other civil servants, a few government ministers and an equal number of people from the business community. A CD of classical music plays from an expensive sound system that wirelessly relays to other rooms.

Kevin and his young friend sit at a glass-topped table on which is Pete's rock specimen – on some sheets of kitchen roll to protect the glass – and two silver coasters on which rest elegant, large bowled gin glasses containing copious helpings of Old Raj.

Pete felt uncomfortable in these surroundings. It was all too neat and regulated. He much preferred it when they met at a beach bar. But the bars were still being rebuilt after the tsunami. So, nervously, he did his best to explain in layman's words what Gene Bond's note told him about his bit of rock. "When it's refined it becomes a heat resistant powder that can hold a high electrical charge. It's a vital element in the creation of capacitors that control the current flow inside miniature circuit boards. These capacitors are used in things like cell phones, laptops and other IT the modern world takes for granted."

Still little response.

"Without it the modern world would not be able to function," he adds in the hope of saying anything that will capture his friend's interest.

"That sounds a little fanciful. Are you not, my boy, over-egging the story?"

Pete agrees. "The last thing I want to do is start a wild-goose chase over nothing," he tells his friend.

"Romeo and Juliet!" Kevin responds in triumph.

"What?" There are times, sometimes many, when the young geologist has little idea what his significantly older political friend is talking about.

"Romeo and Juliet," Kevin explains. "Romeo says 'Switch and spurs, switch and spurs; or I'll cry a match' to which Mercutio responds 'Nay, if thy wits run the wild-goose chase, I have done, for thou hast more of the wild-goose in one of thy wits than, I am sure, I have in my whole five.' It's where the phrase wild-goose chase comes from. And I do wonder, my young friend, if thou hast not launched another wild-goose chase."

Pete felt increasingly exasperated. "I just worry that my one bit of rock is opening up such a big story. But it's all true about cobalt. The modern world is dependent upon it and increasingly so. Demand for cobalt is rocketing. And much of it is dug and scraped out of the ground by kids in the Congo. Without it none of the sort of IT you and I take for granted can work."

"Goodness," Kevin muttered thoughtfully. Pete wondered if at last he'd caught his friend's attention.

"I know you found this lump somewhere nearby. You say it's normally found in the Congo?"

"The biggest source is there," Pete confirmed.

"Oh gosh. The Congo." There was some obvious anxiety in the response. "And does it have much value?"

"According to the research I've done, because of the technology boom, cobalt once reached about $400 a kilogram. But recently it doubled in a month."

Kevin remained lost in his thoughts. "Goodness," he finally repeated.

At last Pete thought his friend was showing some real interest. "And is the price likely to remain that high?"

"I'm no expert on the value of minerals," the young geologist admitted. "But everything I read tells me it's bound to go skyward."

Kevin Forsythe was now solicitous. "Why?"

"Because the demand for cobalt is heavy now but with the world's auto industry turning to electric powered cars – which are fundamentally dependent upon the stuff – it can only go one way. I've seen a report by Hermes which forecasts a 30-fold increase in demand for cobalt by 2030."

"Hermes?" Kevin picked the bit of rock off the table, turned it in his hand whilst looking at it intently.

"One of the largest institutional asset managers in the UK."

"They should know," Kevin agreed quietly.

"Guess so," said Pete.

"So what do you plan to do now?"

"I've no idea," Pete confessed. "That's why I'm here."

Kevin continued to examine the bit of rock. There was a long pause before he said "Well, my boy, as the Bard would say – as good luck would have it – we, or more accurately, you, have a chunk of the stuff. 'The devil's children have the devil's luck' someone once said. Can't remember who. Is this the devil's luck?"

Pete was beginning to lose track again of what his friend was saying. Not an unusual situation. He could not think of a response.

"If there's a lot of this stuff here in Wandora – or at least on our seabed, it would, unquestionably, be a breakthrough for our economy. As important as the northern mines. Maybe more so. But how the hell do we progress in this corrupt Godforsaken place?"

Pete remained silent. The question was not aimed at him. It was rhetorical. Kevin was talking to himself. Thinking out loud. There was more silence. The piece of rock rotated in Kevin's hand. A couple of minutes passed before he looked at Pete.

"We need some advice and guidance. But where from?"

The question was asked without expectation of an answer.

Kevin thought further.

"How about this chappie Bond? Could he help? What I need is enough solid information to develop into a well considered business plan of integrity that I can take straight to the President. What do you think?"

Pete's heart had jumped. It was a cracking good idea. Gene Bond was highly regarded as an independent agent. Clearly he had done some homework before responding to Pete's call for help.

"Good idea," he enthused. "What do we do next?"

Kevin pondered the bit of rock in his hand. Did the future good fortune of Wandora rest within it? How could he ensure such an opportunity did not just sink into the mire of corruption like so many others? Did he, Kevin Forsythe, have the strength, skills and will to take this forward? Could he be bothered? Life since the tsunami had erupted from the tranquillity that had preceded it. The country was in chaos. He, Kevin, had been landed with serious responsibilities that created a wearying day by day workload. And now there was this lump of rock. Could he really be bothered?

It took a while before he answered his young English friend.

"Invite this fellow Bond here. All expenses paid. Let's have a man to man chat about it."

"Be best if you did it," Pete responded. "Be more official."

Chapter 11

Email to Gene Bond from Kevin Forsythe

Sir. We are aware of your prominent reputation
in matters to do with sustainable development.
We also know that you have been communicating
with a friend of the undersigned, one Pete
Taylor, a student of geology. We are in need
of professional guidance and the writing of a
report which we feel may be within your area of
expertise. To that end, we would like to invite you
to visit this country at your earliest convenience,
with all costs covered by ourselves.

I look forward to what I trust might be a positive
response.

Regards
Kevin Forsythe
Minister for Buildings and
Infrastructure Government of Wandora

Email to Kevin Forsythe from Gene Bond

Sir. I am in receipt of your recent email and intrigued by its content and invitation. I gladly accept the invitation and will be in contact shortly regarding arrangements for this. Matters to do with the material cobalt are developing rapidly and I look forward to meeting Pete Taylor again and for discussions with yourself as to the nature of the report you are seeking.

In passing, I recall some time ago that a UK company, SNEL, undertook some research activity off the coast of Wandora in the aftermath of the tsunami there and had discovered a previously unknown sea anemone. There was some speculation in the media that there may have been beneficial medical properties within it. I have not heard anything about that since but would draw your attention to a recent report from the University of California, published in the Ocean Deeply which is headlined: "How Scientists Use Bioluminescent Deep-Sea Creatures To Fight Cancer." It is a very readable report. It starts by saying "Researchers have developed a new way to test the effectiveness of immunotherapies by injecting enzymes from glowing deep-ocean crustaceans into cancer cells. But threats to the ocean from climate change and exploitation threaten marine life and its medicinal potential."

Regards
Gene Bond

Chapter 12

The President enjoyed driving himself. He knew it customary for a head of state to be chauffeur driven but he relished the freedom of driving his Mercedes. It was a chance to be on his own. Solitude. Escapism. Time to think. Time for simple things like listening to the radio. And, he argued, it was right and proper for a small state like Wandora to show some degree of budget constraint. To be seen to be driven by a chauffeur is a high visibility elitist statement. Ethically vulgar. Not a vote winner. So he drove.

At least, that was what he intended to do when his schedule was supposed to see him drive from his palace to a meeting in the town. But at the turn of the ignition key his world ended.

The explosion was massive. Car parts flew through the air followed instantly by a ball of fire as the tank exploded with a loud boom. The noise was terrifying and echoed off the high walls of the fort and around the town and harbour. People nearby dropped to the ground or fled for their lives. Several ox carts and cows stampeded. It was bedlam.

The explosion could even be heard at the airport, two miles away. By strange coincidence it happened just as Gene Bond was disembarking from the aircraft after his long, 19 hour journey from London via Amsterdam. He had stepped from the aircraft, been hit by the solid wall of suffocating African heat and humidity, and, like everyone else on the steps leading down from the aircraft, was startled by the distant bang. For a moment the world seemed to freeze, brought back into life by the sound of wailing sirens. A cloud of black smoke rose from the direction of Porto Wandora.

Airline staff hustled passengers into the terminal where armed soldiers were already manning all the exit doors allowing nobody in or out. Bond put this down to something of a kneejerk response. He could understand closing the airport down to people entering the building intent upon leaving the country – including possibly escaping perpetrators of the explosion. But why stop people exiting the building who had just arrived in Wandora? It did not seem to make sense. But then nothing seemed to make sense in this moment of mayhem. Nobody appeared to be in command. There was no panic – just confusion and bewilderment. A gloom had descended over the airport. Bond was heading for baggage reclaim when his phone pinged. It was a text message from Kevin Forsythe.

"Chaos in town. Cannot meet you right now. Am sending someone. Book into hotel and I will see you there later." Forsythe.

Bond wondered how he and whoever was coming to pick him up would recognise each other in the cauldron of chaos in the airport terminal. How would such a person get in or he, Bond, get out? With every one of the few seats in the terminal taken, he, like many others, sat on the floor with his back propped against a wall watching events unfold and time ticking by. It was some half hour later when the armed guards decided to start letting people leave the terminal and Bond joined a bustling flow of humanity that eventually exited the building. How whoever Forsythe had sent would recognise him eventually was answered when the young geologist Pete Taylor came into view, searching through the crowds. His face lit up when he saw Bond.

"You've chosen a great moment to arrive!" said Taylor in welcome, shaking Bond's hand vigorously.

"What's happened?" asked Bond. "We heard a bang, saw smoke and a lot of excited military."

"A car's exploded by the royal palace," Taylor told him. "Rumours are flying but it looks like someone's blown up the President."

"Good grief," replied Bond.

"And there's been a shutdown on everything. Kevin – a government Minister – has been summoned to the palace. He told me to use his car but the whole government fleet has been quarantined. I had to borrow this from a friend as I don't have a car."

Bond had already noted the car looked, to put it mildly, a little second hand and certainly more worn than the taxis around the airport.

"Is the President dead?" asked Bond.

Taylor nodded. "If that's who was in the car he must be. I got a quick glance of what's left and there isn't much. Whoever was in it must have been blown to bits. If it is the President, that'll be a terrible loss to the country at a critical moment."

75

They drove in silence through almost deserted streets towards the Palm Trees Hotel. Porto Wandora looked like a ghost town. Only a few vehicles were on the roads and the majority military – Jeeps, 4x4 utilities with fixed gun in the rear, a few armoured personnel carriers. The aftermath of the tsunami was still evident with battered buildings still being rebuilt after the disaster. The place looked a shambles.

"If it was the President then my journey's probably wasted," Bond reflected out loud. "Kevin wanted to brief me so I could write a report to go to the President. If he's dead, is there any point in writing the report?"

"Wandora's in a bit of a mess right now," Pete told him though that was pretty evident to anyone. "That's why the death of the President will be such a disaster. He was trying to hold everything together. As you can see, we're still suffering from the consequences of the tsunami. And there's been trouble in the north with a mining village wiped out by terrorists. Poor old Kevin is having a fraught time at the moment."

"What terrorists?" asked Bond.

Taylor shrugged his shoulders. "Nobody seems to know. They wiped out a mining village – Chinese mine workers and local villagers alike. A massacre. Terrible really. They're still rampaging around the north though."

"But nobody knows who they are?"

"Not as far as I know. Kevin might know."

The lobby of the Palm Trees Hotel was warm and clean but unspectacular. Two palm trees – a sop to the hotel's name – either side of the entrance looked forlorn and jaded. The receptionist, a large middle aged woman, was busy on the phone as Bond arrived, computer case over his shoulder, lightweight case in his hand. She looked up and frowned as if the arrival was an imposition and interruption to her call. But she booked the Englishman into his room with the minimum of fuss and handed him his room card.

Pete Taylor, it was agreed, would leave him to settle in and hopefully join him when and wherever he eventually met Kevin Forsythe.

It was slightly over an hour later when Kevin Forsythe phoned.

"Hope you've settled in, dear boy. What a day to arrive. The place is in turmoil. My life's turned upside down. I suggest you come over to my apartment in about half an hour and we'll have a proper pow wow then. I'll tell Pete to pick you up. I'll have a gin on ice ready for you!"

Twenty minutes later Bond sat in a corner of reception, awaiting the arrival of the young geologist, scanning a crumpled copy of the previous day's newspaper. He looked up as the hotel's front door burst open and, with much noise and gusto, a very large man dressed in colourful, billowing robes entered the hotel accompanied by an entourage of scurrying men and women.

Bond was shocked! He could hardly believe his eyes! His stomach turned and he felt a chill run through his body.

Sum Taeyoung! Of all the people on the planet, the last person he ever expected to see in Wandora was the South Korean. He rapidly raised the newspaper to hide behind it and hoped he had not been seen.

Sum Taeyoung! It was unbelievable. Once the flurry of people had left the lobby Bond busied himself with a text to London.

"You are not going to believe this. Am in hotel in Porto Wandora in Africa. A man you tried to assassinate 18 months ago has just walked past me!"

That would definitely wreck the day for Georgi Patarava!

Chapter 13

The atmosphere was tense. It was early evening and all the staff had gone home. Only the four directors of SNEL remained, sitting in Marcel's office around his oval, glass topped meeting desk. Not a word or glance had been exchanged amongst them as they assembled for the Emergency Board Meeting. Marcel sat where he always did, in what had become known as the Chairman's chair. To his left was Steve Oldbury, slightly older than Gary and not a diving man but an accountant who frequented the bar at the local sailing club where he and Marcel met years ago in the early days of SNEL. They had struck a friendship and Marcel had eventually invited Steve to join the Board to help steer a sound course on financial management.

Charlotte McDonnell, better known as Lotty, had decided university was not for her. She wanted to work and committed to keep knocking on business doors around Southampton until someone gave her a job. Marcel was immediately attracted by her enthusiasm, energy and sense of humour and he applauded her determination to find work. She started on a trial basis as receptionist/secretary/general factotum. In next to no time she had reorganised the company's administrative systems, was promoted to Head of Admin and eventually made a Director a little while ago.

Sitting opposite Marcel was Gary, the only one to be wearing a suit. Whilst the other three had papers on the table before them, Gary had nothing.

"We have an agenda," said Marcel looking up at his three directors. "But I am declaring this an Emergency Board Meeting and am going to take AOB first. I'll ask Steve to tell us what the Board should know."

The finance director nervously shuffled papers before him.

"It has come to my attention," he said in such a quiet voice it was hard to hear, "that a director of this company has launched a company of his own without informing the Board. That's in direct contravention of Article 32 of the Articles of Memorandum of SNEL. I also believe it might be in contravention of the rules of Companies House."

"What's it called?" asked Marcel though he already knew only too well what the answer was.

"Southampton Nautical Expeditions Limited 2050. Apparently known as SNEL 2050. Furthermore, SNEL 2050 has been bidding for research funds using this address."

Silence followed.

"There are explanations due, Gary," Marcel eventually said.

Gary Marchant looked straight at his fellow director and former longstanding friend.

"It's become pretty bloody obvious you're infatuated by the idea of a wild goose chase for the sea anemone in the Gulf of Guinea to satisfy your own ambitions to take a manned submersible down to the Guinea Trench. I've warned you about the problems of that time and time again but you've chosen not to listen. You're throwing time and money at it and while that's happening you're missing real business opportunities."

If Gary considered that an answer, clearly Marcel did not.

"And?"

"As I see it, you're taking SNEL on a path to disaster and dragging everyone else down with you. And it's all because of your infatuated, self-gratuitous, narrow thinking idea."

"So?"

"I've tried hard enough to make you see sense. In the end it's obvious you're not listening to anyone other than those who support what you want to do. So I've been exploring some options."

"By launching a rival company?"

Gary shifted in his chair. "It doesn't have to be."

"But that's what it looks like," said Steve.

There was an awkward silence between them.

"What's your plan then?" Marcel finally asked, a tone suggesting he thought this meeting was going to have a bad end. It was.

"To safeguard the future jobs of people in this company by ensuring we keep commercially focussed. That's a long way off chasing sea anemones!"

"So you've launched a rival?" Steve muttered.

"To give me a vehicle to secure future business," Gary bit back, on the attack now.

"But you work for us – not some new company you've decided to launch without any consultation with anyone. It's quite unbelievable," responded Marcel.

"I've tried to work with you Marcel but you've became impossible. You've got this one-track obsession. It excludes everything else. So what was I expected to do?"

"Remain loyal to the company that pays your salary," said Steve.

"Loyalty! Loyalty!" Gary shot the words back at the Financial Director. "I've bust my gut for this company for years but it's still run by short sighted, narrow thinking, one-track minds. While you mess about trying to raise money for an expedition that won't earn us anything, we miss commercial opportunities. I'm not letting that happen anymore."

Marcel decided it was time to open a new line of attack. "It's a funny sort of loyalty that sees you reading the correspondence of other directors."

"What do you mean?" Gary asked.

"You know full well what I mean Gary," said Marcel. "You read the letter to me from Gene Bond about cobalt. And we know you've been scratching around to see if the story about cobalt in the Gulf of Guinea can be true. We know what you're up to Gary. Do you deny it?"

Gary shrugged his shoulders. "What's the point? If you know, you know."

"But it's not the sort of expedition or line of work SNEL wants to get involved with," Marcel told him.

"Why not?"

"Because deep sea mining has yet to prove it can be undertaken without further damaging the oceans. If mining starts off Wandora it could kill off the sea anemone and that would be a huge loss to medical science."

"But the demand for cobalt is growing all the time," Gary retaliated. "Someone's going to explore it. Why not us? We found The Trench after all."

"Advancing the prospect of the sea anemone as a medical aid is what SNEL is about. Not about further polluting the oceans!" Marcel's voice was raised now, the anger within him blatantly obvious.

"But you can't stop the march of progress," Gary retorted, also in a louder voice.

"You call it progress to further pollute the seas!" Marcel had risen from his chair. "And you expect SNEL to be part of that?"

"I expect to be part of it."

"Not as part of this company you won't," Marcel told his former friend.

"I'll do it anyway," Gary told him, now also standing and staring straight back at the Frenchman. "I'm going to bid for this Marcel, with or without you. If it's without, that's your loss. And you'll be losing more than half the team here."

"What do you mean?"

"I mean I'm leaving and taking more than half the staff with me. They all support what I'm planning. If we can't do it here Marcel we'll do it anyway. Your loss."

"If you're planning to help develop deep sea mining off Wandora we'll fight to stop you," Marcel told him.

"How?" Gary barked back.

"Through the courts if need be," Marcel shouted back. "You can't expect to take half of this company and get away with it."

"Just watch me," responded Gary.

"We'll serve a writ," Marcel threatened.

"See you in court then," shouted Gary, gathering his papers and slamming the door as he left the room.

Marcel slumped back into his chair. "What now?" he asked as if either of the other two had any idea how to answer him.

Chapter 14

"I'm sorry to have arrived with you on what seems a terrible day for your country," Gene Bond said, shaking the hand of the man before him and mindful of the explosion that had apparently killed the President a couple of hours before. He and Pete Turner were meeting Kevin in Kevin's apartment where, as promised, they were welcomed with a large, well iced glass of gin. "And I'm afraid I have some other news which is not good."

"The web of our life is of a mingled yarn, good and ill together," Kevin quoted in response, adding, "but at the moment it's a little out of balance – too much ill and not enough good. What further ill fortune do you wish to bring to my table?"

"You have an international terrorist in your city," Bond reported. "Sum Taeyoung. He seems to have taken over the top rooms at the Palm Trees Hotel. He's a South Korean. Calls himself a chaos entrepreneur. Because of him I've been shot at in London and in Siberia and he's been responsible one way or another for the deaths of people I know."

"Good heavens. Ill news indeed," Kevin agreed. "Though at the moment the whole of Wandora is in a chaotic state and God knows who's in the country. Tell me more about this man."

Gene Bond gave as succinct a reply as he could, telling Kevin about how he had been dragged into various exploits behind which lay the dangerous activities of Sum Taeyoung. He spoke of his longstanding relationship with Georgi Patarava and of the Communications Centre in London of the officially non-existent European secret service. He blamed his friend Georgi for having dragged him into the conflicts with Sum Taeyoung.

"But as Georgi rightly says, things in my daily life like how we're moving away from fossil fuelled power to renewable energy, the pressure on natural resources from water to rare minerals, the impact of climate change – all these things are creating opportunities to be exploited by people like Sum Taeyoung. So I guess as Georgi says, I shouldn't be surprised when I get involved in such activities – even when I seriously could do without them."

Kevin Forsythe had been scribbling notes as Bond spoke. "I need to report this to the right people. I'll phone Moussa Ehouzou as soon as we're finished and tell him about Sum Taeyoung. Ehouzou is in charge of security here."

Kevin would have been astounded and dismayed to know that Moussa Ehouzou was already totally in the hands of the South Korean. Meantime, Kevin was anxious to move on to talk about why he had invited Bond to Wandora. He was keen to know more about cobalt.

Gene Bond told him as much as he knew, much of it being what he had learnt from Professor Slater at the University of Birmingham.

"It seems what young Pete here stumbled upon," said Kevin, nodding towards the young geologist, "could provide an economic lifeline for Wandora. If, indeed, there exists a seam of the stuff somewhere off our coast. It would have to be within our territorial waters for us to claim value from it. There are so many "ifs" to the story at the moment. And explain to me the potential conflict I read about between mining cobalt and extracting health benefits from the sea anemone. In contrast to the issue of cobalt, we do at least know the sea anemone exists offshore Wandora. We just don't know how much."

As best he could, Bond explained how some people have concerns about the potential polluting prospects of seabed mining and its possible damage to oceanic life, including sea anemones.

"So we may have to face the fact we can have one but not the other," Kevin summarised. Bond agreed.

"And tell me more about where cobalt currently comes from in Africa."

Bond told him. Kevin listened intently, only interrupting when Bond talked about the artisan mines and the exploitation of children.

"That's truly shocking," Kevin said. "Sickening and unbelievable in this day and age."

And the more Bond told him, the more clearly agitated and upset Kevin Forsythe became. When Bond finished, Kevin remained silent, deep in thought. In the end, he sighed and shrugged his shoulders.

"I have no idea about the future of this country," he told his two visitors. "Indeed, I wouldn't like to speculate about the long term future of Africa. It's entering a new era with fantastic opportunities but enormous problems. That people like Sum Taeyoung are being attracted here is evidence of the potential wealth of the continent. The dreadful story of the children mining cobalt is a vivid reminder of the gulf between those who have and those who do not have and how the former so often exploit the latter."

"Wandora's in dire financial trouble. If there is cobalt in our area of legal tenure offshore, that has to be of serious interest to us. But so is the potential of the sea anemone. Clearly more research is needed to be able to make proper judgement on these matters. Meantime, I'd like to know more about cobalt. I'd like to see what's happening in the Congo. For me to leave Wandora at the moment will be judged by some to be irresponsible and to be reneging on one's duties. But, to get away from this chaos for a couple of days will help clear my mind. And I can get first hand evidence of what is happening to cobalt in the Congo."

"I propose, therefore, that you, Gene, and I go as soon as possible and before anything else happens that either causes me to change my mind or forces my hand to stay here. As it is, I'm sure the continuing chaos in Wandora will be well able to maintain its momentum with or without my presence."

Chapter 15

Shockwaves went around the world when the UN's HQ in Africa was bombed. Equally disturbing was who claimed to have undertaken it. Of the many people alarmed by the news, Joe was distraught. When the explosion happened, those caught up in the disaster thought they were in the wrong place at the wrong time. Not Joe. From his perspective he was the right person in the right location but he was as shocked and disturbed as anyone about who claimed responsibility. It was not who Joe would have thought of and for this group to be claiming responsibility was extremely worrying. It escalated the African crisis to a new level.

Joseph Wesley Wright II, better known to everyone simply as Joe, fulfilled his ambition some years ago to become a member of the US Navy's Sea, Air and Land teams, better known as SEALs. He was delighting in the role when certain attributes he was demonstrating marked him out and saw him recruited then fast tracked into the darker world of espionage and intelligence gathering. Joe Wright had become a spy.

An oceanic expert by the time he left SEAL, it was seen as a natural progression and highly plausible move for Joe to be assigned to an environmental research programme as Communications Executive at the United

Nations' African HQ in Nairobi based in what is often described as one of the world's 'greenest' buildings. The three storey building opened in 2011 by the then UN Secretary-General Ban Ki-moon, was designed to be a role model of what a state of the art green building should be. It has, amongst other attributes, a North/South orientation to maximise solar and light gain, great use of natural lighting, some 6,000 square metres of roof mounted solar panels and a rainwater harvesting system.

In launching the building, Ban Ki-moon said: "If our growing population is going to survive on this planet, we need smart designs that maximise resources, minimise waste and serve communities. This facility embodies the new, green economy that can usher in a greener future, create jobs and spur economic growth." The building houses some 1,200 people including an eco-research team concerned especially with the green economy opportunities for Africa identified by the former Secretary-General. Joe was concealed within that team as a communications specialist but his real task was to monitor the growing terrorist activity across the continent.

America has increasing concerns about instability in Africa, the world's second largest land mass covering some 11 million square miles and with a population of more than a billion people. Africa is, in the opinion of many experts, in chaos. Those worries include the growing global interest in Africa's natural resources, China's takeover of various African assets, increased drug and gun trafficking, wars ranging from national catastrophes to gang conflicts, the vast number of displaced people now being counted in numbers never seen before on the planet, and the escalation in terrorist activity – all adds up to a dangerous and volatile situation. Only recently members of a US special forces team were killed in Niger, the impoverished state that borders with northern Wandora. In a war most Americans do not even know is being waged, reports told of more than 200 heavily armed attackers swarming towards the soldiers on motorcycles leaving four US, plus a number of national soldiers, dead and not only stripped of their weaponry but their clothes too.

Under the cover of being a communications expert working with the eco-research teams in the UN building in Nairobi, Joe's clandestine task was to track and report on this increased terrorist activity across Africa. The list of active organisations under his surveillance included Al-Shabaab, Ansar al-Sharia, the Lord's Resistance Army, the Movement for Oneness and Jihad, Al-Qaeda, Ansaru, Ansar Dine, Abdullah Azzam Brigades, Al-Itihaad Al-Islamiya, and others. But, worryingly, none of these claimed they had attacked the UN African HQ. It was a bombshell for Africa and the rest of the world when the news broke that ISIS, the self-proclaimed Islamic State of Iraq and Syria, said it was a suicide bomber of theirs who had killed and maimed people in Nairobi. It was well known that ISIS fighters who had fled Syria were now active in the Horn of Africa. It was now becoming obvious they were spreading across Africa like a cancer.

Joe, 34, tall and lean, fit, black and very good looking, originated from the port city of Duluth on Lake Superior in Minnesota. He was on his morning run through the lawns, spectacular trees and shrubs, topiary art forms and variety of gazebos of the parkland adjacent the UN African headquarters when the lone suicide bomber struck. The deadly explosive shattered the tranquillity of an otherwise delightful Nairobi morning. Joe was only some hundreds of yards away when it happened.

His first concern was to offer what help he could to the large number of casualties but at the same time he was in contact with his team.

"Was there any warning?" he asked. "Anyone made any threats?"

"No," came the answer.

It was only minutes later that social media and radio stations throughout the world started running the story that the killer bomb blast close to the entrance of the UN's African HQ had been perpetrated by ISIS.

"Fuck, fuck and fuck," Joe muttered on hearing the news. It was the last thing he needed. As if there were not enough problems in Africa, to hear ISIS was, as some feared it might, widening its activity in Africa as it was beaten back in Syria was very bad news indeed. It could not be worse. His covert lines of communication to Washington leapt into immediate overdrive as they demanded more and more information. The US administration has had nightmares this might happen but went apoplectic when it did.

In London, the Communications Centre of the European Secret Service immediately became caught up in the aftermath of the terrorist act. African/European links are deeply embedded in history and though colonial days are long gone, connections still remain, assets still require protecting, responsibilities continue to be upheld. News of ISIS undertaking such a high profile terrorist act in Africa was very disturbing news.

The Comms Centre, housed in the basement area of the historic former clipper ship warehouses in Wapping Wall, almost in the shadow of Tower Bridge, are, as Georgi Patarava, its CEO explained to his longstanding friend Gene Bond, concealed in the ideal location for an organisation that officially does not exist. Even most MEPs do not know of Europe's secret service operation. "Where else would you locate a non-existent organisation but in a part of a building that also officially does not exist?"

When the warehouses were transformed into luxurious city apartments it was before the Thames Barrier was commissioned. The basement areas of the warehouses were subjected to frequent flooding and were proclaimed unfit for use and sealed off. Later, the Barrier, plus new building techniques, made it possible to open up the previously unusable areas and into these was concealed the secret organisation.

The ISIS declaration from Nigeria saw intelligence agencies across the globe seek more information as government crisis units formulated new strategies to protect their African assets from this latest threat. In Brussels, the European Union's Political and Security Committee (PSC, sometimes known as COPS (an acronym from the French Comité Politique et de Sécurité) met. In London the Prime Minister called an immediate meeting of COBRA, the government's war cabinet so called because it meets in Cabinet Office

Briefing Room A at 70 Whitehall. Both they and their counterparts in America and the UN called for as much intelligence on terrorist activity in Africa as was available. As a matter of routine procedure, Joe Wright was in contact with Georgi's London based European organisation to see if they knew more than he did about the arrival of ISIS in Central Africa.

"I can't say it's a huge surprise to us," said Georgi, responding on a secure line telephone call between the two men. "Nothing ISIS does is a surprise. It's such an unpredictable outfit."

They exchanged what information they could and were about to end the link when Georgi had an afterthought.

"Whilst you're on, I should tell you we know a South Korean terrorist has moved into your neck of the woods. A man called Sum Taeyoung. Nothing to do with ISIS but worth keeping an eye on." And Georgi went on to tell Joe about the skirmishes he had had with the South Korean.

"He's been spotted recently in Porto Wandora which has also had a bomb go off. It killed their President."

"Are you saying ISIS is in Wandora?" Joe asked incredulously.

"No, not at all. We've nothing to link Taeyoung to ISIS or to the bomb in Porto Wandora or to the one in Nairobi," Georgi answered, much to Joe's relief. "And it may be coincidence these terrorist explosions in Africa have happened just as Taeyoung shows up there. But it's almost too much of a coincidence. We've no idea yet what he's up to in Wandora. I've an associate who also happens to be there at the moment and he saw Taeyoung walking into a hotel where apparently he has a long-term let on a suite of rooms. Why he's established a base there I've no idea but I can't help being suspicious that an explosion that may have killed the President has gone off while Taeyoung's in the country. And Wandora is a country in chaos. Taeyoung specialises in chaos. He's a very tricky and dangerous guy."

"Can I ask why you've someone in Wandora right now?" Joe asked.

"He's there in a private capacity, nothing to do with me or the agency," Georgi replied. "Got something to do with the mineral cobalt."

Cobalt! Joe instantly became very interested in what the man in London was saying.

Chapter 16

"I want to sue the balls off the bastard." Marcel's anger was explosive and had been ever since the Board Meeting ended in such acrimonious tones. The normally placid Marcel had been tetchy and short tempered ever since the confrontation with Gary and hardly seen in the office, much to the disappointment of Lotty McDonnell.

"Court action is out of the question," Steve Oldbury told Marcel in no uncertain manner. "As a lawyer friend of mine once told me, if you think the law is about justice, forget it. It's about money. Who can throw the most wins. And you can't afford to throw money at this, Marcel. You haven't got any! So, bite the bullet mate and get on with life and get your own back by ensuring you're successful and Gary isn't."

"But he's stolen more than half my company!"

"That's as maybe and I know it hurts," said Steve. "But to fight it would take a great deal of time in court and money dished out to lawyers. And there's no guarantee you'd win."

"What happened to right and wrong?" Marcel muttered sullenly. "There's no justice."

Events had moved quickly and painfully since the board room bust up. Gary had stormed out and within 48 hours, much to Marcel's dismay and despite his continuing protests, moved three quarters of SNEL's team out of its premises and into offices a few miles away. Marcel was mortified to see people he thought to be as much friends as colleagues walk out. This must, he realised, have been planned for some time. He wondered how Gary had persuaded them. Even more, he wondered how he was funding their salaries and the office.

The question of court action festered in the Frenchman's mind as what he saw as a huge injustice riled him daily. Gary had stolen a large proportion of his business and was getting away with it. It dominated his thinking. His mood became introverted and despondent, not the attitude needed when trying to raise funds for a major project in the Gulf of Guinea. He was sullen and morose and failed day by day to show up at the office. To the frustration of those seeking contact with him, calls to his landline and mobile phone consistently went to voicemail and remained unanswered.

It was the effervescent Lotty McDonnell who took up the challenge. Shocked by the split within SNEL, she realised just how much Marcel meant to her. She was distraught by the hurt caused to the company's founder. She had felt a deep respect and loyalty to him ever since he had given her her first job. Now her feelings quickly developed through sympathy, concern and despair, to – she admitted to herself – feelings for her boss beyond just affection and respect. This was more than just being fond of him. She, with some reluctance, grasped for the first time that she really loved him. It was a preposterous thought. She at 22 was at least ten years his junior.

Perhaps more. She had no real idea how old Marcel was. He was the sort of person to whom age seemed to have no meaning such was his usual gregarious and energetic attack on daily life.

Dismayed to see the founder of SNEL so dejected, and indebted that it had been he who gave her the opportunity to work for the company, she resolved to do something about it, whether Marcel wanted her to or not. Working closely with Steve Oldbury, and picking up on work already well advanced by Marcel, she sought to build a consortium of supporters who would fund a manned exploration off the Guinea Trench with the specific task of capturing more samples of the sea anemone. It was an ambitious goal for someone so youthful and without the knowledge and experience of Marcel. But she had an abundance of bubbling enthusiasm, gritty determination and a naivety that was sometimes helpful. She could get away with saying things that tested people and their thoughts and which she could blame on her inexperience if it backfired. This was an opportunity for her to prove her value to Marcel on a level he had not seen from her before – and to repay a debt. She revelled in the chance and reported back to Steve Oldbury on a daily basis.

It was not as if she was starting from scratch. A great deal of work and a large number of connections had been developed to enable the first exploration of the Gulf of Guinea to happen. Marcel had also secured a number of commitments to a new expedition. These were all Lotty's first ports of call. Her determination was also fuelled by a report from the University of

Plymouth. Lecturer in Marine Molecular Biology, Dr Manuela Truebano, and Professor in Marine Zoology, John Spicer, from the University's Marine Biology and Ecology Research Centre, led the study. Dr Truebano was reported as saying: "Along with ocean acidification and rising temperatures, hypoxia is considered one of the main threats to species within the marine environment – but it is currently the least talked about. As the duration and extent of hypoxic areas is predicted to increase in coastal regions, it is likely that some species will be exposed chronically throughout their life cycle."

Whether or not this would impact on the Gulf of Guinea sea anemone, Lotty had no idea but it sounded like a distinct possibility. It added to a sense of urgency she was already experiencing as she gained more and more understanding of the challenge. She had read reports expressing concern about deep sea mining's potential to pollute oceans and threaten marine life. She added the Plymouth University report to her ammunition being used to encourage support for the manned exploration.

It did not take long before enough people had expressed interest in the project for Steve Oldbury to suggest Lotty call everyone together for a project briefing where each individual organisation could see and speak to others expressing interest. They would, he hoped, be encouraged by the strength in numbers in support. Hopefully, they would sign in there and then. It would also be an opportunity to update Marcel and, rather than invite him to preside over the meeting, tell him he was going to. "If you ask him in the mood he's in at the moment he might well decline. It will do him the world of good to drop him right in it!" Steve told Lotty. "Maybe shake the old bugger out of his present mood."

The meeting took place in the London office of one of the potential sponsors. It was on the 18th floor of a tower close to the Thames and Vauxhall Bridge with a panoramic window giving clear views towards Battersea in one direction and Big Ben and The Eye in the other. Steve, Lotty and Marcel sat together, the latter protesting against suggestions he presided over the meeting right up until everyone was seated. At that moment Lotty pushed all the paperwork she had straight at her boss and company founder. She folded her arms and sat back, looking at him defiantly. The agenda sat on top of the pile. Marcel frowned a look of displeasure at her but realised he had been outmanoeuvred.

As the meeting progressed Marcel, with help from Lotty, grew in confidence and became more like his old self. His enthusiasm and passion for his subject may have been latent recently, stifled by his anger at Gary's actions, but this meeting was reinvigorating it.

"As you all know, there is evidence," he told the meeting, "that what has become known as The Gulf of Guinea Sea Anemone may have pharmaceutical elements of interest to those in the medical profession and especially those engaged in the fight against cancer. The trouble is, the sample we have is minute and slightly contaminated. Unequivocal evidence of its potential powers has not been forthcoming despite extensive laboratory testing within a number of companies and academic institutions. What we need is more samples."

He handed over to Lotty for her to give details of the plan for a two-man sub expedition to The Gulf of Guinea Trench to bring back more substantial samples. As she spoke, Marcel looked at her with growing respect and a totally new perspective. He had always known she was confident, a 'go-getter', and attractive. She had an effervescent, bubbling personality that made her very popular wherever she went. Her rise within the company had been rapid but he had never thought of her performing in such a meeting as this and in such a manner. Her audience was captivated.

Steve followed Lotty with a financial plan for the expedition. As Marcel would have expected, it was thorough, well thought through and well presented. Marcel found his concentration wandering – back to Lotty. Strangely he had never noticed her legs before, shapely, long, currently crossed and thanks to a shortish skirt, showing an element of thigh. Her blonde hair fell over her shoulder, on her left side crossing over to her front so the golden cascade fell over her chest. And her breasts, why had he never noticed them before? They were certainly ample – not excessive but shapely and firm.

Forty five minutes after they had started, the three SNEL executives sat back and invited questions which were directed at Marcel who fielded many of them off to his two companions. Marcel could not have felt happier and more confident about the way the meeting had gone. Clearly Lotty, with Steve's help, had gathered a group of organisations together who were well down the track to supporting the venture before the London meeting took place. However, as experience told him, a deal is not a deal until it is signed. And what he wanted was a set of signatures from the people sitting before him that would commit them to the Gulf of Guinea Sea Anemone Expedition. By the time the meeting closed he had got them – all of them. It was a triumph! He was elated and excited and felt he had left the shackles of his depression and moroseness behind him.

"What are you doing now?" he asked Steve and Lotty. The answer could not have been better. Steve had another commitment. Lotty had none.

"Right," said Marcel in a more positive and decisive mood and tone than the other two had seen for a long time. "You and I for dinner then," he said, putting his arm round Lotty.

They ate in a quiet restaurant not far from where the meeting had been held. To begin with there was an unease between them, both being unsure about the relationship between boss and employee. As the meal progressed and a liberal flow of wine maintained, so the atmosphere warmed and became increasingly intimate. Marcel eventually escorted Lotty in a taxi to the hotel in which she was straying where he walked her into the lobby.

"A great evening, thank you," said Lotty. "In fact, a great day."

"Thanks to you," Marcel responded. "The conference was a massive success and the new expedition is now secured – all thanks to you."

"It was teamwork," she replied.

The moment came for him to leave and he leaned forward intending to give her a polite little kiss on the cheek. But she had other ideas and kissed him firmly and at length on the lips, clasping her hands round the back of his head and pulling them together.

"Mon Dieu," exclaimed Marcel as the lingering kiss ended. "What have I been missing all this time?"

They kissed once more before she turned away and headed for the elevators, giving him a furtive little wave as the doors closed behind her.

Chapter 17

"I want to know why he's in Wandora. I want his emails checked, all social media analysed, his telephone tapped – now! I want to know what he's up to, where he's been lately, who he's been talking to, where he's staying in Wandora and who he's meeting here. I will not have that man and Patarava interfere with my operations in Africa. They have bedevilled enough of my work in the past."

Sum Taeyoung was almost frothing at the mouth with anger. Renowned for his usual self-control and normally placid disposition, he was raging. It had been only the briefest of glimpses as like a one man tsunami he blustered through the lobby of the Palm Trees Hotel with his entourage in his wake. But if Gene Bond thought he had been quick enough to hide behind his newspaper, he was wrong. Eagle-eyed Taeyoung spotted him. It had only been a fleeting, split-second view from the corner of his eye, but the South Korean needed no more. Utterly shocked, Sum did not reduce his stride or give any indication he had sighted his English arch-enemy here in Wandora.

Now safely in his suite of rooms and on his own, he used an encrypted line on his phone to contact his office in Seoul and instigate a full investigation about

Bond and his current activities. His highly competent team in Seoul would, as instructed, feed information back as soon as it was known. No way did he want to wait for a full report. He needed to know what his team learned as they learnt it – immediately. Coded messages quickly started to flow between Seoul and Porto Wandora.

- Bond is in Wandora to meet Kevin Forsythe, a Minister of the Wandoran government
- Forsythe is an Englishman who has lived in Africa for some years.

Why has Bond flown such a long distance to meet Forsythe, Taeyoung wondered? He knew of Forsythe. He had had a message from him organising a meeting with the President before the explosion that killed the political leader. This English member of the Wandoran government could be useful but equally he could be a complication.

- Bond is staying at the Palm Trees Hotel. Duration of stay unknown.
- Bond has links to a young English geologist, Pete Turner. Turner is currently located in Porto Wandora.

Taeyoung asked for a complete profile on Turner.

- Bond is in Wandora to discuss the mineral cobalt with Forsythe and Turner.

- Bond has recently been in meetings and communication with Professor Pete Slater of the Centre for Strategic Elements and Critical Materials at the University of Birmingham in England.

This answered earlier unanswered questions. And – Cobalt! Taeyoung was excited to know it was the mineral that had brought Bond to Wandora. Did it mean there was cobalt in Wandora? That would be incredible. The South Korean was fully aware of its value. If there was, Taeyoung would want some of the action, if not all.

- Bond has been in contact with Sub Nautical Exploration Limited, a company based in Southampton.
- We are assuming if there is cobalt in Wandora it must be in the sea bed, otherwise why would Bond be talking to SNEL?
- There is some trouble at SNEL between the directors.

The intelligence from Seoul intrigued Sum Taeyoung. But it was the reference to cobalt that was dominating his thinking. If there was cobalt in Wandora, the South Korean's control of the port could be a key issue in exporting the mineral out of the country. What with the revenue from the import of drugs and weapons, his percentage cut now on anything the Chinese extracted in the north of the country, and now cobalt the global price of which continues to escalate, Taeyoung's commitment and investment in his new base in Africa looked like reaping great dividends – so long as Bond and Patarava did not interfere.

- SNEL was responsible for the discovery of the Gulf of Guinea Trench and a previously unknown sea anemone.
- Their founder, Marcel Bartoll, is assembling support for another expedition to capture more specimens of the sea anemone.
- Another SNEL director, Gary Marchant, seems to be breaking away to develop a rival expedition but aimed at investigating cobalt off the coast of Wandora.

Taeyoung's immediate assumption had been that if there was cobalt in Wandora it would be inland, possibly in the area where the Chinese were already extracting minerals. The suggestion cobalt might be found in Wandoran territorial waters complicated matters no end. Was it certain the mineral was offshore? If so, where? In how deep waters? Who would own it? And the apparent split between the directors of SNEL was intriguing. Who was this Gary Marchant? Was any more happening about the sea anemone? Had Bartoll progressed his proposed expedition? More questions flew back to Seoul.

- Gary Marchant has launched a new company.
- There's confirmation he is gathering support for an expedition to search for cobalt offshore Wandora.

It did not take long for Taeyoung to understand what Marchant had already realised – that the potential mining of cobalt off the coast of Wandora might, if it were anywhere near the Guinea Trench, prejudice the existence of the sea anemone. The South Korean had already read of concerns by some people about how sea bed mining could potentially harm marine life. If Bartoll was successful in getting his expedition off the ground, maybe it would lead to some sort of ban on mining the seabed. If that were the case, Bartoll had to be stopped, if cobalt did indeed exist offshore Wandora. There were too many 'ifs' in all this thinking for the South Korean's liking. But the stakes were too high for the prospect to be ignored. And what, he wondered, was Bond's role in all of this?

Chapter 18

Gene Bond is horrified and sickened by the scene before him. It reminds him of old black and white films from the treeless, godless, mud dominated countryside of the Somme in WW1, or of medieval times long before civilisation, or perhaps of the Klondike gold rush. What he is looking at certainly has no place in the supposedly civilised world of the 21st century. The landscape is grey – indeed everything is grey except for water, some red tinted, lying in dips in the undulating ground. That apart, there is no colour. It is raining – pouring from a grey, leaden sky. The bleak view from his 4x4 is of a predominantly muddy world bereft of any substantial greenery. Makeshift buildings – temporary structures ranging from tents to mud huts and prefabricated sheds, are scattered – unplanned and chaotic – gold-rush style. Even the few trees are grey. Greenery is as good as non-existent.

Across this alien mud bath of a landscape scurry many scores of people. There is a hive of industry about the place yet these people are labouring and toiling in the most stressful, inhuman conditions. Whilst it is bad enough watching men and women struggling in this frightful environment, it is immediately apparent there are many diminutive little souls here too, children bent double under the weight of the sacks they carry. Some are tiny. Infants.

"Children!" Bond utters. "God help us! Little children."

"Some as young as eight," Mutebar tells him.

"Fucking hell!" Bond responds.

"I think this is hell," mutters Forsythe. "There's been many interpretations of hell on earth but surely none more vivid than this!"

There is much shouting, seemingly mostly by adults and mostly directed at children. As they watch, a man beats a small boy with a tree branch. The lad cannot be more than six or seven years old. He slips and falls in the mud, crying pitifully. His friends gather round, pick him up and help him back towards the mines where he is given another sack to carry. It is almost half his size and filled with rocks. The boy's legs buckle and he staggers under its weight. Close to the mine from which the minerals have been dug, a circle of people, many children but women too, search amongst a pile of stones and pebbles and pick out the precious cobalt. This is the so called artisan mining they have travelled so far to see for themselves.

Without Kevin Forsythe the trip would never have happened or never have been completed. It took diplomatic channels to arrange transport and to have both a guide and a guard for the final road element that took them to where artisan mines could be found in the south of the Democratic Republic of the Congo, normally referred to as the DRC. It was a testing journey starting with a four hour drive in the opposite direction to the one they wished to travel. They had to go west along the coast from Wandora to cross the border into Togo and to the airport at Lomé to catch an ASKY scheduled flight to take them east to Kinshasa, the capital and largest city of the DRC with a population of over 10 million. Ironically it meant the flight across the Gulf of Guinea took them over Porto Wandora from where they had started. From Kinshasa, a further flight south to Lubumbashi took nearly three more hours.

After an exhausting day of travel, they stayed overnight in Lubumbashi and set off early the following morning in a 4x4 accompanied by a government official, Mutebar, who provided the transport. Also on board was an armed member of the Presidential Guard. The road journey was a nightmare, mostly on dirt and mud roads which were far from flat and often severely potholed, many looking to be on the verge of collapse and many cut through thick forest. Bond lost count of the number of times they were stopped and their papers closely inspected. Police, militia, security guards from mining companies, armed mercenaries from various organisations that may well have been any of the terrorist groups active in the country, all contrived to frustrate their progress. Many of the latter wore uniforms, often a motley collection of multi-coloured garments accumulated from a wide variety of sources. Bond found the whole experience very frightening and was thankful for the Presidential guard and his very visible AK15 assault rifle and hand gun in its waist holster.

"I bet many of them wouldn't even be able to tell you the name of the group they're in," observed Forsythe during one paper inspecting stop. "They're mercenaries – just in it for money."

It was quite clear that without the documentation Kevin had assembled from both his own government and that of the DRC, and by the presence of Mutebar who did not seem phased by any threats from anyone, and the guard, they would never have completed the arduous journey.

The destination was an area that has become virtually overwhelmed by artisan mines – many hundreds of them. Now they are parked, watching the scene before them, conscious that even in the ten minutes they have been there a tangible nervousness has overcome the area. The industrious work being conducted as they arrived slowed, then stopped. Men who obviously have some sort of guard function usher the many children away out of sight.

"Obviously some sensitivity about the use of children and us seeing it," observes Kevin Forsythe. "Let's move somewhere else."

They stopped again close by a river where they can see more mines. It looks like a scene from biblical times with vast numbers of people, mostly women, in the water busy washing. But it is not themselves or their clothing they wash but sieved mineral particles being cleaned before being traded. There are even women with babies strapped to their backs standing knee deep in the water, bending perilously forward as they work the pans of rocks in the grey, muddy river. Young children, backs arched under the weight of the burdens they carry, bring sacks of crushed rocks to the women. These diminutive and frail little figures, hardly have the strength to stand upright as they slither and slide across the treacherous mud to the river then back for the next load.

The rain having reduced from a torrent to a more acceptable level, the decision is made to move away from the protection of the 4x4 so they can have a closer look at a mine. A short walk takes them to the top of a vertical hole that disappears into blackness. It is easy to see from the cut marks that the hole has been dug by primitive tools. There are no support timbers, no lights, no ladders. Workers scramble down and out of sight by pressing their backs to one side of the hole then walking down the opposite wall. They move their feet gingerly and slowly. It is a precarious business. There is a dominating smell of mud and human sweat.

"Ask them how deep it is," Bond asks Mutebar.

An excited conversation ensues between the guard and a passing miner, a barefooted man of perhaps mid 20s wearing mud soaked jeans and nothing else, the rain glistening down his mud splattered black torso. There is much gesticulating and fast and animated talk. At last Mutebar turns to Bond.

"He says it's about three men deep. There's water at the bottom. There's no lighting. It's difficult to breath."

"Who does he sell the rocks to?" Bond asks.

More agitated talk.

"He won't say. Too frightened. You must understand they're very nervous you are here. They don't want to talk to you. I've pushed him as hard as I can but he's too scared. But I know he'll sell to a dealer. Probably a Chinese dealer."

Two women sit crossed legged by the side of the top of the hole, each with a rope between their legs. On a signal, one begins heaving and hauling and eventually a sack appears laden with newly cut rocks. A young child, maybe ten years old, heaves the sack onto his back and staggers off towards the river, labouring under the weight and struggling to keep upright as his bare feet try to maintain grip in the mud. As he disappears, an empty sack descends into the darkness. Minutes later the other woman pulls another sack full of rock to the surface, transferring it to the back of a young girl, who sets off on the precarious trek to the river. It is a nonstop process.

"Ask the next child how much they earn from this," Bond tells Mutebar.

They call to a lone youngster, inviting him to come and talk to them. He is a good looking boy with a stubble of black hair. He has a noticeably round and attractive, cheeky face splattered and streaked with mud, some, still dark grey, is wet. Other streaks have dried and are almost white, conspicuous against his black skin. He is reluctant at first to respond to their call but, perhaps through youthful curiosity, eventually draws close to the two white men. He is around ten years of age. It is his eyes that fascinate Bond. They are big and alluring, giving the lad a striking look. But they are never still, constantly and nervously looking around to see if he has been spotted talking to these strangers. He is spattered everywhere with mud. It is on his face. It clings to his thin, unbuttoned shirt and his trousers are saturated and his bare feet caked thick with a mix of both dried and wet mud.

Inexplicably he seems fascinated by Kevin and stares at him through his big, glistening eyes while Mutebar talks to him and translates for Kevin and Bond.

"His name is Divin. He is nine years old."

"His parents are both dead. They died of malnutrition and fever."

"He lives with his aunt in a hut about a mile away."

"He has two siblings – older sisters. They both work here too."

"Ask him how many hours he works here," says Bond.

Divin holds up ten fingers then closes his hand and holds up two more.

"12 hours," translates Mutebar.

"And how much does he earn?"

The answer is translated by Kevin. "It's the equivalent of about eight UK pence a day."

"What does he do with his money?"

"He buys food for the family."

Bond finds it difficult to ask the next question. Emotions within him are running high and the words do not come out easily. "Ask him how he feels. Does he feel OK?"

Mutebar talks to Divin and as he does so, the lad's head drops. Bond is mortified to see his shoulders are shaking. The lad is gently sobbing. He mutters answers to Mutebar's questions. Mutebar has to repeat the questions, not having been able to hear the answers.

"He says he aches. He says his whole body aches. He hates waking in the morning because he aches. And carrying the heavy sacks makes it worse."

115

"Does he go to school?" asks Kevin.

Divin shakes his head and looks up at the Englishman in despair and utter dejectedness. Tears roll down his muddy face.

Bond stares back at the boy, distraught that there is nothing he can do for him. His natural inclination is to try and hold the boy, to hug him – to give some sort of compassion to this diminutive little soul who seems to have no hope, no future, no reason for being.

A man's voice calls out and Divin scurries away towards someone who seems to be in some sort of authority. He holds a five feet long thin tree branch which he uses to lash out at Divin as he joins him. Bond involuntarily twitches as the branch strikes Divin. The lad bows against the whipping and is pulled away by the man into the distance. The desperate scene is interrupted by the arrival of a truck carrying about a dozen men. Some are armed with a motley collection of rifles.

"Time for us to move on," says Mutebar as they climb back aboard the 4x4. "I think we are now not wanted here. We ask too many questions."

Bond would liked to have stayed longer, to talk to more local people but he agrees with Mutebar's plan. It is obvious they have outstayed any welcome they might have had, not that any had been evident.

"They will be from the traders," says Mutebar about the men in the truck. "Protecting their sources of income."

They have agreed to meet an NGO, an Australian called Pete Anderson. He has been working in the artisan mining area of the DRC for some time. They have a set of co-ordinates and a time and nothing else. It is only a short drive and they arrive early, sitting in silence at a crossroads cut into the forest, each buried in thoughts about what they have seen. Eventually a truck arrives bearing the non-government organisation's name hand painted in big white but fading letters along the side of the battered vehicle.

Pete Anderson is tall, with long blond hair and a face weathered from a life of working outside in hot climates. He joins them in their 4x4 to tell them more about the artisan mining of the area. Kevin starts the conversation by talking about some of the things they have seen during the day and especially about the encounter with Divin.

"You have to understand," Anderson told them, "that we may have to accept that artisan mining has to be part of the solution to the world's growing demand for cobalt. And that's not just about securing a supply for the buyers. It's also about providing at least some sort of base income for those involved on the supply side. If you stopped the artisan mining what would happen to the hundreds of Divins? With no money they cannot buy food. Without money they starve."

"The biggest problem as I see it is the insecure state of this place. The DRC is in turmoil. That's no rarity in Africa but it's especially bad here. Many of its provinces are almost devoid of any central control or rule. Corruption is rife. Increasing terrorist activity is destabilising any sense of structure. It's an unruly place and difficult at times to understand who is fighting who. And now ISIS is here. It's not good."

"But if you stop the source of income for these people by closing the mines down, what happens then?" asked Bond. "How does Divin pay for the food he buys his family? It seems like an unanswerable complex and difficult dilemma."

"It is a crazy dilemma," the Australian agreed. "The world is heading away from fossil fuelled vehicles to electric ones. They need batteries. Batteries need cobalt. It's one of the starkest divides I know of between the richness of modern, sophisticated people whose lives are now IT-dependent yet that technology relies on the contributions of people living in some of the worst poverty on the planet."

"Is there a solution?" asked Kevin.

Pete Anderson ruffled his long hair. "God knows. The best that could happen is that somehow artisan mining is officially integrated into the supply chain but with accompanying health, safety and employment rules. But the problem is enormous, complex and downright dangerous. It's reckoned there may be around two million artisan workers in the DRC. And one bit of research found the Congolese army running mines and estimated to be employing 26 per cent of the artisan workforce. The researchers found at least one armed group present at 25 per cent of the mining sites. Add to that the corruption and the smuggling out of the country of huge amounts of the stuff, and you get some idea of the size of the problem."

Putting a hand to his forehead, he sighed. "It's not easy and it's getting worse."

Gene Bond had listened intently to what Anderson had to say but was conscious that Kevin Forsythe had been busy for some minutes, reading and texting messages on his phone. As the Australian finished speaking Kevin announced he had to return to Wandora as soon as possible. "I'm sorry. Apparently a state of emergency's been declared," he told them. "And there's talk of a military coup d'état."

Chapter 19

Reuters Report
Porto Wandora
Wandora
Gulf of Guinea
Africa

A State of Emergency has been declared in the small African state of Wandora following the assassination of its President, the victim of a recent car bomb. I have seen tanks and armoured personnel carriers on the streets of its capital, Porto Wandora, and social media is rife with reports of a military takeover. Minister of Defence, Frederic Gnanligo, appeared on national television to deny an army coup but subsequent attempts by journalists to interview him have failed. Indeed, the current whereabouts of the Minister is now something of a mystery.

Wandora, population four million plus, a former Portuguese and then French colony which gained independence some years ago, and which is located on the Gulf of Guinea, has been badly impacted by increasing terrorist activity. Only months ago a Chinese mining operation in the north of the country was abandoned after miners and Wandoran military personnel were wiped out by a terrorist group, rumoured to be a breakaway faction from ISIS. African nations are becoming increasingly nervous about rising evidence of ISIS activity in the sub-continent.

Who is now in charge of this small former colony is not currently known.

Chapter 20

She lay on the bed totally naked. She was on her side, her long black hair draping down over her white body. Gary Marchant stood looking at her reflectively. She did have exceptionally white skin and she looked so peaceful and contented. She had, unquestionably, a stunning and very sexy body. The early morning sunshine beaming through the bedroom window to declare the start of a new day did not disturb her deep sleep, the sort he wished dearly he had enjoyed. That night they had made love for an age, playing and teasing. Her nipples were hard with passion before, as he lay on his back, she eventually mounted him and, her ample breasts bouncing in carefree abandon, rode him to a crescendo when both exploded in sexual climax. She had collapsed into sleep, exhausted by the physicality of their lovemaking while he sought sleep that eluded him.

Gary's mind was too full of unanswered questions. He was aware of a conference that had taken place in London and that Marcel seemed to have gained enough support to undertake another expedition to the Gulf of Guinea, this time with a manned sub and with the aim of harvesting samples of the sea anemone. At the same time, more and more evidence was coming to light of a growing campaign against widespread deep sea mining.

All this was against a backdrop of him struggling to secure new business.

Gary had raised some funds to enable him to break away from SNEL and to take a large number of employees with him. He had excited them by saying he was involved in securing a project to do with mineral mining on the seabed. It promised significant profits. He had not mentioned the word cobalt to any of them or indeed that the location was the Gulf of Guinea. He sold the story with much exuberance, conviction and significant amounts of sheer bullshit to entice them away from Marcel. Now the problem was maintaining the operation. Hopes he had that many SNEL clients he personally managed would follow the breakaway organisation had not come to fruition in the numbers hoped for. He underestimated client loyalty to Marcel. Cash was becoming a problem. The bank balance was dwindling. His credit cards, by which he juggled with money he really did not have, were not a sustainable answer. He struggled with how he could explore the cobalt opportunity in Wandora – if indeed there was one. It was no surprise sleep was difficult to come by.

Vanessa energised his ego. He was intensely grateful to her for that, for her companionship, for her unwavering support and for her sex. He was aware that she was deeply in love with him. She often tried to explore how their relationship could be better secured. It did not have to be marriage, she had told him many a time. But they had been together long enough now for him to be able to give her more security, or so she believed. In the softest way he could, Gary ducked and dived to avoid any commitments.

He simply did not want to make any. Vanessa was great. No question about that. But she was not the sort of person he could talk to about his business problems or his plans in any detail. Not the sort of confidant he needed. Not the sort of person who of her own volition and initiative could proactively do anything to help. He could ask her to do fairly mundane things and she would deliver to the best of her ability. But beyond that – well, in all truth, not much. He certainly could not talk to her about his current financial plight and the tight rope of uncertainty he was walking.

So a call – out of the blue – from someone who described himself as an agent for an international entrepreneur with interests in certain seabed mineral prospects offshore Africa, seriously excited Gary's curiosity but also rang warning bells big time.

"Gary Marchant?" He did not recognise the voice. Male. English. A refined sort of voice. Well educated.

"Yes," he replied cautiously. "Who's asking?"

"I know you have expertise in deep sea exploration," the voice on the phone ignored Gary's question. "And that you've been involved in a previous expedition to the Gulf of Guinea."

"Yes. But who's calling? Who are you?"

"And you know traces of a particular mineral have been found on the coast of the Gulf of Guinea?"

Who was this? How many people knew about Pete Taylor's find which was what the caller presumably was alluding to? Five? Six, maybe? Gary responded with extreme caution. "That may be. I need to know who I'm talking to before I continue with this call."

There was a slight pause before the caller answered. "I represent an international entrepreneur with many different interests around the world. He's currently especially interested in mineral potential offshore Africa. And he's in need of expertise in deep sea exploration. We believe you have such skills. We also believe you're in need of new business – that you are running out of money. We may be of help to each other."

Gary was intrigued and worried in equal measure. Whoever the caller was, he seemed to know a lot about Gary's business circumstances and his interest in cobalt even though it had not been mentioned specifically by name. That was clearly what the caller was referring to.

"How can we take this conversation forward?" asked Gary. "There's only so much can be said on an open telephone line."

"I agree," responded the caller. "So we propose a meeting. In London. In Westminster. In the café in Central Hall in Westminster."

Gary was taken aback. Clearly the caller already had a clear plan of action in mind. "When?" he asked.

"Tomorrow," came the unexpected reply. "12 o'clock."

"Good grief!" Gary was shocked. "That's short notice."

"My client's on a rare visit to London tomorrow. This is a one and only offer. Take it or leave it. It is my strongest recommendation you take it."

"How will I recognise your client?"

"Oh," said the caller. "Don't worry. He'll recognise you. Just be there."

And the line went dead.

Wesley's Café lies in the basement below the magnificently domed Methodist Central Hall next door to the far more modern Queen Elizabeth Conference Centre and virtually opposite the legendary Palace of Westminster with the Houses of Parliament and Lords within it. The unpretentious café is extensive and spacious and serves a wide range of refreshments, none of it very costly. As a result it is favoured by a cosmopolitan array of people ranging from tourists, business people, students, and even Members of Parliament, some with their PPSs in tow. Scattered around the place will always be found people with their heads in their laptops, busy using the café as a temporary place of work.

Into this diverse assembly of people enters Gary Marchant at 11.45. By 11.55 he is well established at a table, sitting with his back to the wall, surveying everyone before him trying to identify who he is supposed to be meeting. He sips his cappuccino impatiently as the clock ticks onto the hour, then five past, then ten past. A sinking feeling starts to develop as increasingly he wonders if this is all a wild goose chase that involved him making numerous calls to enable him to change his diary and make this unscheduled journey by very early train from Southampton.

In the kaleidoscope of people from a variety of different parts of the planet that frequent the busy café, nobody really stands out in the crowd. Well, most do not. But a tall, six feet four inches, big bodied, long haired, well bearded South Korean who, when he speaks, does so with what might be mistaken as an

Eton accent, is perhaps an exception. The assumption about Eton would be a mistake. Sum Taeyoung was educated at Oxford, the LSE and Harvard Business School. Wesley's café is a venue he selected especially because he feels less conspicuous here amongst such an array of different people than in many other places. So when in London and in need of a meeting place, this is his choice. He had been sitting in the café well before Gary Marchant arrived, watched him enter, buy his coffee and find a suitable table. He kept observing as the appointed time for their meeting came and went. He watched Marchant becoming increasingly anxious, fidgety as nerves set in. This was good. It was all a question of timing. Let the man become increasingly agitated and unsettled but not let him wait so long that he upped and left. So he waited until 12 minutes past the hour before he moved to sit opposite the Englishman.

"How quickly could you put together an expedition to explore the seabed off Wandora?" says the big man. He is dressed in a light grey suit, obviously cut to size and expensively tailored. Underneath there is a bright yellow shirt that many would consider to be too bright – almost garish – which is complemented by a matching yellow silk handkerchief poking from the top of his breast pocket. His open neck shirt reveals even more hair. For someone trying to be inconspicuous the dress code could have been far less lavish but it was conservative in comparison to, for instance, the colourful, loose flowing clothing Nakki had seen him wearing in the aftermath of the massacre on the northern border of Wandora.

There are no introductions. No niceties. No

handshake. Gary cannot get over how much hair the man before him has, and the penetrating eyes that have been fixed on him from the moment the man sat down.

"What sort of expedition?" asks Gary, not sure how much this man knows.

"You know what I am talking about, Mr Marchant. You know what I am interested in. Do not play games."

"I think there are other matters to be resolved before such a step could be taken," replies Gary tentatively, not sure yet how to judge this formidable stranger.

"Such as?"

"Gaining permission to undertake such an expedition in Wandoran territory. And to mine offshore. The seabed is technically Wandoran to 12 miles offshore."

"I know that," responds the big man sharply with some obvious irritation. "Getting such permission is not a problem. Now answer my question."

"But there's also growing opposition to mining the seabed – and that'll be more vigorous if a project to explore a similar part of the seabed off Wandora for a rare sea anemone gains real significance."

"Has that project progressed?" It seemed to Gary the South Korean already knew of Marcel's ambitions.

"It's just been announced Marcel Bartoll has the support and the funding to go ahead," Gary replied.

"And if it does, what happens to any chance of mining for what we want?"

"I think there would be so much pressure from the international community it might stop such activity."

The South Korean sat silent for a moment, his eyes

never leaving Gary's who increasingly found the whole encounter unnerving.

"So can you stop Mr Bartoll?"

"I don't see how," Gary replied. "I have no influence any more over Marcel Bartoll."

Again a pause that seemed to stop time.

"But what if Bartoll's project had to be abandoned? An operation such as I suggest could happen quickly?"

"I guess so."

Sum Taeyoung leaned forward. His face was close enough for Gary to feel the South Korean's breath.

"Don't guess, Mr Marchant. I do not deal in guesses."

"Well, yes. It could be. If funds were available."

"How much funds, Mr Marchant?"

"I need to construct a budget," Gary responded.

"I am astonished you do not have one already," said the South Korean.

"I have a provisional one," admitted Gary. "I can let you have a full one in 48 hours. Where should I send it?"

The big man was still only inches away from Gary. "You have 24," he said. "And you send it nowhere. We will collect it."

And with that, the giant stood and turned to go. But there was one more parting shot.

"You will not let me down Mr Marchant. Letting me down is not good for the health. Not to be recommended."

And with that he was gone.

Chapter 21

Black Bart's Bay is the next inlet east along the coast from Porto Wandora and less than a mile away from the capital. It is named after the Welsh pirate Bartholomew Roberts and is hugely popular amongst locals and tourists alike for the extensive beach bar, sadly utterly decimated by the tsunami.

The Pirates Rest was originally built in the style of a galleon, mostly timber structured with some of the major beams allegedly coming from wrecks of ancient pirate ships. It was a good story and certainly helped advertise the Rest. But it was one that could never be verified. It certainly could not now. Little remains of the old building but even as the rebuild continues the bar is open for business again and serving its wide-ranging menu. It has a legendary offering, especially its unique interpretation of Igname Pilée, a dish consisting of the tuberous vegetable igname pounded energetically to a pulp in a heavy wooden mortar then fashioned into small dumplings and dipped into various sauces. Equally well liked is Djenkoume, a chicken, semolina, ginger and tomato speciality imported from nearby Togo.

There can be few better experiences in life than sitting barefooted under a cloudless, rich blue sky at one of the wooden tables of the Pirates Rest, protected from the sun by a coconut leaved parasol. With toes in the silk-like soft sand, watching silver topped, gentle waves lapping nearby as they make their way up the beach, a vin de palme or one of the other local exotic cocktails being gently sipped – an ice bucket at arm's length containing replenishment Champagne. The aromas of the local cuisine waft across from the Pirates Rest kitchen and drift along the bay.

But today this normally sleepy serenity is being interrupted not only by the hammering and sawing of the industrious rebuild of the wooden restaurant but by the sound of a drone. It is laboriously and meticulously scanning every nook and cranny in Black Bart's Bay and the rest of the coast.

The tsunami that hit the Gulf of Guinea's coastline scraped the seafloor sediments and invertebrates and crashed through seabed rock structures and coastal vegetation. Close to the epicentre from where it originated, waves reached speeds of up to 900 kph. By the time they got to the African coast and the shallower waters off Black Bart's Bay, they had significantly dissipated and were travelling at a mere 40 to 50 kph. But squeezed by the natural shape of the bay, whilst in other parts of the coast the height of the waves was comparatively low, here in the confined space of the bay they hit the beach at 10 meters height and more.

Within the 12 miles offshore political jurisdiction of Wandora, the topography of the seafloor was significantly changed and devastated with ecosystems obliterated and chunks of the seafloor ripped up. The power generated by such happenings is astonishing. Massive amounts of debris can be carried huge distances by a tsunami. It is well recorded that a 66 feet long concrete dock from Misawa in Japan was once swept across the Pacific Ocean in the aftermath of a tsunami and eventually crashed into the Oregan coast – a journey of some 4,700 miles (7600km).

Here at Black Bart's Bay, because the tsunami hit the coast at a particular angle, a large amount of debris was thrown into one corner of the beach forming a new hill some six meters high. Subsequent high winds drifted sand across it so as to make it look like a newly formed dune surrounded by rock and rubble – a completely new feature to the area.

The drone, operated by a small team located near the Pirates Rest, is on the search for cobalt and there, sure enough, on the opposite side of the new dune to the bar and hidden out of sight from anyone just strolling around the beach, a dozen or so examples of the blue/grey mineral are spotted amongst a pile of loose rocks adjacent the dune.

Sum Taeyoung's team followed up the discovery by digging into the rocky sand dune where more cobalt was found. It is the evidence the South Korean has being looking for. Somewhere out at sea, offshore Wandora, there is cobalt. How much and precisely where are the big questions to be answered. Only an expedition to mine samples from the sea bed will prove one way or another whether the precious mineral is out there and in what volume. And then the hope will be it is within Wandora's territory and not in international waters. Despite the doubts, the South Korean is now very excited by the prospect and willing to invest more to progress what could be a very rich opportunity.

Chapter 22

Seventy one people died and 175 were injured on Saturday, September 21st 2013 when what was then considered to be the deadliest jihadi group operating in sub-Saharan Africa attacked the Westgate shopping centre in Nairobi. The memory of that atrocity has never died within the city and a nervousness about terrorism remains embedded within its population. The perpetrators from the Al-Shabaab group died in the attack. The perpetrator of the explosion that killed four and maimed dozens at the UN HQ in the city may never be identified having been blown to bits in the suicide mission. It was only the claim made via various social media channels that attributed the act to ISIS. There was no immediate way of verifying that. Forensic work on the fragments of the bomb and body parts revealed the explosives to have been made from fairly readily available materials and that the person had been female. She appeared to have been carrying a hand gun – shattered to bits by the explosion but providing enough evidence to identify it as a Type 92/QSZ-92, a modern military pistol now a standard sidearm of the Chinese People's Liberation Army (PLA), many police organisations inside China and increasingly finding its way into the illicit arms business.

Joseph Wesley Wright II immediately set about seeking to establish who had been responsible for the attack, whether the individual had come from outside the country, and whether the bomb had been imported or manufactured within Kenya. Based on his own experiences and that of recent African history, he turned to the murky world of drug and weapon trafficking, first calling on some of his contacts who had dealings in both illicit trades. His first port of call was within Nairobi itself, to the vast shanty town of Kibera, home to a huge number of people estimated to be over a million. Recently 30,000 were driven from their shack-like homes to make way for a new highway. This aggressive act sparked more unrest in an area usually controlled by a pseudo-government – the Burnees, a brutal mafia regime renowned for its killing techniques from which its name is derived. Joe found an atmosphere of fear and suspicion prevailing throughout the local population and few were willing to talk to an outsider. But from what he gleaned from contacts here where the big business is marijuana, known on the streets as bhyangi, weed, ndom, kush and gode, a picture started to emerge of traditional routes in illicit goods being distorted by territorial conflicts between rival groups. In the west, the Movement for Oneness and Jihad (MOJWA), a break away from Al-Qaida, was taking an increasing role in drug movement. Boko Haram was also implicated in smuggling heroin and cocaine across West Africa.

A similar situation was happening with armament movement. Africa has long been a gold mine for anyone selling weapons. Conflicts and dictatorships have seen vast amounts of armaments imported into Africa to support aggressive regimes and warfare. But when such events collapse, the weaponry disperses and enriches illicit supply chains. For instance, it is reported that 22,000 man-portable air defence systems (MANPADS) were acquired for Libya's pre-conflict stockpile. Post the collapse of the Gaddafi regime, only some 5,000 were accounted for. Some 17,000 have yet to be found.

To Joe, the link to China via the hand gun of the UN HQ suicide bomber was more than a little interesting. Chinese weaponry was becoming more widespread amongst terrorist groups in Africa. The Type 56 assault rifle, China's version of the Russian AK47 Kalashnikov, is much easier to use than its Russian counterpart, and is fast becoming the killing weapon of choice amongst many groups operating in the sub-continent.

Trying to unravel this jungle was a nightmare made more difficult for Joe by the fluidity of the situation. The constant word back to him was of unnerving instability in traditional supply chains, whether it was for armaments or for drugs. Trying to identify real news from fake news and rumours from fact was almost impossible though the consensus view was that ISIS had indeed attacked the UN HQ.

The word on the street was that traditional east to west drug routes were under threat. New entry points were being established to bring illegal goods into Africa. Activity seemed to be concentrated more centrally, away from Kenya and Nigeria. Rumours were rife that a new organisation had elbowed its way into the already overheated illicit trading business. Niger was mentioned a few times to Joe but checks back to Washington and elsewhere were met with incredulous responses. Niger! No, never. It was well known for its drugs activity but less so for guns.

With the persistence of these mutterings, and just hitting brick walls with all his other enquiries, Joe eventually decided the street chat was strong enough to warrant him undertaking an exploratory visit to Niger, somewhere he had never been to before. Nigeria yes. He had visited the so-called Giant of Africa with its large population and strong economy many times. It was in such sharp contrast to its impoverished neighbour, Niger, 80 per cent of which is covered by the Sahara Desert.

He headed for its capital, Niamey, located in the south west of the country, some 300 kilometres or so north from the border with Wandora. Joe noted that Niger lies between Wandora and Benin to the south with their Gulf of Guinea coastlines, and Algeria and Libya to the north. He could see it as a strategic centre on any illicit drug or armament highway between sea ports and two states renowned for their highly volatile histories.

He also noted that Niger continues to be a country with considerable challenges. To the north, on the borders of the Sahara Desert, poverty and starvation is rife. To the west, MOJWA and the al-Qaida-linked group al-Murabitoun, were, reports said, "piggybacking" on an on-going conflict on the Niger-Mali border that had been rumbling on for decades and was ripe for exploitation. The conflict itself was already being fuelled by climate change which was diminishing usable land and creating unpredictable problems with water supplies. Now terrorist groups were capitalising on the volatility of the area. The MOJWA had been responsible for the small motorcycle army that not so long ago killed four US soldiers and many more local ones. In addition, a breakaway from MOJWA, the Islamic State of the Greater Sahara (ISGS), was now adding to the dangerous situation.

With security much in his mind, Joe chose to stay at the Grand Hotel du Niger mainly because of its high reputation for providing a safe sanctuary by stringently searching vehicles entering the hotel grounds and having metal detectors at the hotel's entrance. A modern, square and chunky looking building, both its architecture and cuisine are a mix of African and Chinese. He particularly liked the peaceful tranquillity of its outside dining area overlooking the bridge crossing the River Niger.

Nearby he found the extraordinary Cap Banga restaurant, an open, wooden structure built on a wooden platform and located on a small island in the middle of the River Niger. For the first few days he used this as a base to meet with local journalists, politicians, NGOs, and anyone else willing to talk to him. Most of the conversation was in French which was hard work for Joe but the consolation was sitting at the end of the day watching the sun go down over the river whilst eating some of the excellent local beef brochette skewers accompanied by the equally acceptable local beer.

These conversations led to contact with people in less salubrious parts of Niamey where information was stimulated by the passing of cash. After four days Joe had a clearer understanding of the magnitude of chaos across the region, extreme factions vying for control, traditional centres for gun smuggling like Agadez in the north of Niger and well into the Sahara Desert virtually competing against new centres and new traffic routes. One such newcomer that kept being mentioned was Wandora with its entry being Porto Wandora and a major distribution centre gaining in significance in the far north of the country, some four or five hours drive to the south of where he now was.

Rumours suggested Chinese activity and influence was growing fast in Wandora. This centred on the mining of industrial minerals including cement, limestone, marble, clay, sand and gravel. But news of gold discoveries in the north of adjacent Benin had apparently excited more Chinese investment in Wandora's fledgling mining operation. Linking this to the evidence of the Chinese hand gun of the UN HQ suicide attacker was tenuous to say the least and a bit like clutching at straws but with nothing else to explore, Joe decided to hire a Jeep, a very second-hand assault rifle, silencer and ammunition and set off on the five hour drive south for the border.

Nearing Wandora he confronted the challenge of crossing the wide River Oti which separates the two countries. Fortunately, at its most northerly point, Wandora is only some fifty miles from the east to west borders. And he knew that here, somewhere close to the river, was the mining activity he was looking for. So, in terms of territory to be covered, it was not too daunting a challenge but one that had to be undertaken on foot. The Jeep had to be abandoned and the river crossed on a long, very narrow canoe-like ferry powered by a very ancient, noisy, smelly and smoky outboard engine. Conversation with the ferry man was almost impossible but Joe managed to extract from him what he thought to be an indication as to which direction the mines were that he was looking for. He also noted wide vehicle tracks which entered the water and, when they reached the opposite bank of the river, emerged from the water. Evidence he thought of some sort of amphibious craft operating in the area and recently because the tracks looked quite fresh.

A savannah-like desert plain confronted him when he landed on Wandoran territory. He ended his first day in the country sleeping under the stars, concealed in one of the few thick clusters of bushes in the area and hopefully hidden from any animals that might consider him to be a meal. His rifle was always at his fingertips. It was a nervous and restless night for the American, one full of animal noises he did not recognise. In his ignorance he treated every one as a potential threat. He was awake before the sun rose but when it did the sky turned a stunning rich red with the huge yellow/red ball gradually climbing from below the horizon. It was a spectacular start to the day. He set off in the direction the boatman had suggested and which corresponded with the still very visible vehicle tracks and was relieved when, after only an hour's trekking, he found what he was looking for.

Warned by the sound of vehicles and voices, Joe was thankful that the desert was giving way to more frequent plant growth offering some concealment. As stealthily as he could, he managed to find a location where he could watch the comings and goings of the mining village which consisted of several white concrete buildings belonging to the mining operation and the mud thatched roofed huts of the natives. Of the people he could see, by far the majority were Chinese. Indeed, the place was surprisingly almost devoid of locals. The village seemed to have recently been rebuilt and some building work was still in progress. Concrete structures were being patched up and the homes of local villagers rebuilt in the aftermath of some disaster not so long ago. In several places there were scorch marks giving evidence of recent fires. And though the mud huts with their thatched roofs were new or significantly rebuilt, few people appeared to be living in them.

Trucks regularly arrived at the site, were loaded up with the materials extracted from the mines, and sent on their way. It was a motley collection of vehicles with no indication on them as to whom they belonged. If, as seemed to be the case, they were from the mining company, Joe thought it strange there were no corporate markings to be seen.

Most of the trucks headed to one area where from what he could hear, Joe realised was where mined materials were being loaded. But, every now and then, a truck would arrive and head in a slightly different direction. Joe had to move to get a view of where they were going. It was another new concrete building, bigger than any of the others on the site. This one also had barred windows, heavy front doors and an armed guard in the form of two burly men carrying light machine guns. Joe watched for some hours and counted four trucks visiting this particular building while a constant flow of traffic continued in the other part of the village. And whilst most of the visiting vehicles were obviously being loaded with mined materials, the four that arrived at this bigger building appeared to be only unloading stuff rather than loading it.

Joe was anxious to see what it was they had delivered to the site. Using his powerful military binoculars got him nowhere. All he could see was a line of men passing boxes one to another and then into the large hut. The only way to discover more would be to try and look through one of the windows. But that would be a night task and a dangerous one. He analysed the risk, considering potential advantage against potential loss. The advantage was having come all this way he would know what was in this building. The loss was potentially his freedom or even his life. But the thought of retracing his tracks without knowing what was being stored here was simply unacceptable. So he resigned himself to just watching while the sun went down and darkness arrived, such as it was because a star studded sky ensured full blackness never came.

The guards seemed only interested in protecting the front doors of the building and ensuring nobody interrupted deliveries when the trucks arrived. During the whole period he watched the building he did not see either of them undertake any patrol around the building or anyone take anything from the building. He assumed that if there was a barred window on the side of the building he could see, the likelihood was there would be one on the other side as well. That far side was less visible to anyone in the village.

Eventually darkness – such as it was – arrived. Activity in the mining village slowly dwindled to a stop and people settled down for the night. The front door guard was reduced to one and he sat at a chair before the front door. He occasionally got up but seemingly just to stretch his legs. He did not go anywhere. Armed with his assault rifle and hunting knife, Joe used as much shadow cover as he could find to creep round to the opposite end of the building to where the guard was and stealthily make his way along the side wall to the window. Having got there it took only a cursory glance to understand what was inside. An armament crate is not difficult to identify and there were scores of them stacked one on top of another. Nearby were large unmarked sacks. It was all he needed to know. Here was a substantial arms and narcotics dump – a warehouse in the supply chain which would see quantities of both illicit products cross the River Oti to be dispersed into central Africa.

He crept back to the bushes where he had been hiding and set about gathering everything together. He would use the cover of darkness to leave the village and start the journey back to Niamey. What he would do with the information that an armament and drugs dump had been established in north Wandora he had at this time no idea. What he did not want was a knee-jerk reaction from his superiors or their associates. Raiding the dump would be a short term win. Joe wanted to track where the stuff was coming from, where it was going, and who was involved. Then they could hit the whole supply chain and create real hurt.

So he went about clearing up where he had spent several hours and preparing to move on. When something made a noise behind him and simultaneously tugged at his trouser leg his heart leapt and he involuntarily jumped. Raw terror engulfed him. His worst fears about being attacked by an animal seemed to have been justified. In a reflex response he spun round, reaching for his gun to confront his attacker. The last thing he expected was to find himself staring into the face of a diminutive, young, frightened, little girl.

Chapter 23

"It's the 21st century, for God's sake! How can this be happening? It's inhuman and despicable. It's utterly shameful and unforgivable." Gene Bond was having difficulty controlling the passion and anger in his voice. "What we saw in the Congo has no place in the modern world. We should be ashamed of ourselves. It's difficult to believe that decent people tolerate using things in their daily lives that so disgustingly and callously depends on abused little children."

Bond was with Kevin Forsythe and Pete Turner in the former's apartment in Porto Wandora.

"And," he continued, "it's incredulous that this bloody awful situation continues when it's so widely known. I've read reports from the UN and Amnesty International about it. I've seen it reported by The Guardian, CBS News, the BBC, Bloomberg, Reuters and others. Companies like Volkswagen, Tesla, Apple, Microsoft and others all say they know about the problem, think it's awful, and promise to do something. But it just goes on. Not only that, it gets worse! Now I've seen it for myself it makes me feel sick."

It was Kevin Forsythe who responded in thoughtful fashion. "There can be no keener revelation of a society's soul than the way in which it treats its children."

"That's very profound," replied an impressed Gene Bond.

"Not my words, dear boy," confessed Kevin. "Very prophetically they were said by none other than Nelson Mandela."

"Good Lord," agreed Bond. "Prophetic indeed! But we all agree it's a bloody disgrace, Kevin. What do we do about it? Seemingly sod all!"

"I've no idea. I feel as passionately about it as you," Kevin replied. "It's an appalling state of affairs. But it's a hopeless dilemma – beyond the capabilities of individual response and mere mortals such as I. And I've so much on my plate here, dear boy, I honestly have to confess the amount of time and thought I can give at the moment is limited – and going to be like that into the foreseeable future by the looks of things."

Gene Bond was fully aware of what was on his friend's plate. On their rapid departure from the Congo in response to the call Kevin had received, they found Wandora almost shut down. It was eerie. They were picked up at the airport in a government car which flew a national pennant on each front wing. The driver, wearing an army uniform, knew Kevin well but talked little as they drove into the capital where people were conspicuous by their absence. The usually bustling streets were more or less empty. Soldiers stood at all the major junctions. They saw a few trucks of armed men and several armoured personnel carriers but little else as they headed to Kevin's apartment. Once there, Kevin busied himself on the phone and talked to various people for a good hour. Pete arrived unexpectedly and together he and Bond sat until Kevin at last ended his calls and could tell them what was happening.

"With the death of the President, the army has declared it controls the country on a temporary basis – 'for the good of democracy', it says. The royal family has fled for unknown destinations and some high ranking officer I've never heard of seems to be in charge. Parliament has been suspended. There's a daily curfew the hours of which I don't yet understand, and the Minister of Defence, Frederic Gnanligo, has disappeared. Apparently he's not been seen for some days. His junior minister, Moussa Ehouzou, who used to be responsible for security – there's an ironic joke in there somewhere – is, I'm told, the 'representative of government' on a new Administration Committee that the army heads. Incredulously, I'm now told I'm on that committee. God knows why! It sounds as though whilst we've been gallivanting around the Congo, the world here has gone bonkers."

"And your problem's the same as most other people," said Bond.

"What do you mean?"

"You're so busy in your daily life that you've no time to give to something like little kids digging up rocks so you can use your iPhone, your iPad, your computer and so on. For most people the problem's too remote for them to be able to do anything about it – even if they wanted to. It's a bit different here. Those kids are just up the road – on your doorstep Kevin, relatively speaking. But even then, it's such an enormous problem one

147

individual can't be expected to be able to do anything about it. So no individual does. Nobody does! And the problem goes on."

Kevin was about to respond when Bond went on.

"And the situation with cobalt is only indicative of a bigger problem. As consumerism continues to devour what critical natural resources we have left on the planet, so those resources will go up in value. The more the value goes up the more the criminal world gets interested. The more the value, the more the corruption. Unlicensed, uncontrolled extraction activity will grow – like the artisan mines we saw in the Congo. But it's not only in mining. I've just downloaded a UNICEF report that says 246 million children are engaged globally in what's called child labour. That includes working with chemicals, pesticides and dangerous machinery. Can you believe that? In the 21st century!"

"It's like sticking kids up chimneys," Pete reflected. "I thought our modern world was beyond that sort of thing."

Bond nodded in agreement. "And UNICEF says more than a million children in child labour will have been trafficked. Children are being used as slave labour!" he added.

"So, what's the answer?" asked Pete.

"Lots of organisations are advocating actions to alleviate child labour by 2025," Bond told him. "There's been enormous conferences around the world on the subject, attended by Ministers from all the major countries. But, quite frankly, when you have greed, corruption and a constantly growing need for stuff to feed our voraciously consumptive appetite, I don't think it can be stopped."

"That's a very gloomy prognosis," Kevin observed.

"After what we saw in the Congo, and what Pete Anderson told us, I think that's the reality. It's unstoppable."

"But what happens if you did manage to stop it?" asked Pete. "If you do, you deny these children money which they use to buy food. If they can't work they can't earn. If they have no money they starve. It's a nightmare."

It was a conversation stopping statement. They sat quietly, nobody knowing quite what to say. Their silence was broken when the phone rang.

The call was summoning Kevin to an urgent meeting of the newly formed Administration Committee. It would be held the following day. He was still muttering oaths about that when the phone rang again. It was Joe Wright on a difficult to hear line.

"Kevin Forsythe?"

"Yes."

"It's Joe Wright. I called you last from Nairobi. I work for the UN there."

"Yes, I remember. It's a bad line Joe. Do speak up."

"I need help Kevin. It's kind of urgent. Right now I'm on the north edge of Wandora, near the mining village. And I've found this little girl. Her parents have recently been killed and she's in a pretty bad way. Traumatised I guess – and starving. Thin as a rake. I doubt she'll survive much longer unless she's looked after. I was just about to head home via Niger when she found me. I can't leave her here Kevin. She's obviously been through hell. I've sent you a picture of her. It's pitiful. Can you help?"

"My goodness!" replied Kevin, taken aback by the call. "I'm not sure how I can help, old son. We have our own challenges right now, don't you know. Can't you take her back with you?"

"No way," the American replied. "I've tried to get my own people to extract us from here but the volatility of this region shuts down that option. You can't let me down, Kevin. Well, at least don't let this little girl down. She's in a pitiful mess."

"Just a minute Joe," replied a slightly flustered Kevin who put the phone to one side. "It's Joe Wright," he told Bond and Pete. "He's an American from the UN in Nairobi. For some godforsaken reason he's in the very north of Wandora in bush land near the mining village. He's found a little girl who seems to have been abandoned. He's supposed to be leaving and crossing the border into Niger. He can't leave her. He can't take her back with him. He's asking for help."

His two friends looked back at him blankly.

Kevin shrugged his shoulders. "I can't do anything. I'm too locked into what's happening here."

"You asking us to?" asked Bond.

"I guess so," Kevin responded, not knowing what he really meant.

A whistling noise came from the phone. Kevin picked it up.

"I can't hang onto this for ever," Joe pleaded.

Kevin thought for a moment. "What are your co-ordinates there?"

150

Joe gave them. Kevin repeated them back.

"Give me two minutes and we'll phone back," he told the American and the call was ended. Kevin took the opportunity to check to see if the photo Joe Wright had said he was sending had arrived. It had. It showed a pretty, diminutive little girl with big eyes and a drawn and shallow face holding the hand of a tall, lean black young man, presumably Joe himself. Clearly no civilised person could possibly abandon such a vulnerable and lost child in the wilderness of north Wandora.

Kevin showed the picture to Bond and Pete who agreed. Such a defenceless little being could not be left to her own fate.

Kevin went to a drawer and pulled out a book of maps. He opened a page which showed the Wandora/Niger border and cross referenced the co-ordinates to pinpoint where Joe was. He stabbed his finger at it.

"It's just north of the mining village. He could just walk in and ask for help. I wonder why he hasn't. But he's no fool. There must be a good reason why he hasn't."

Bond and Pete stood by him looking at the map.

"How far's that from here?" asked Bond.

"About 450 miles, take a few either way."

"A two day drive?"

"Yes."

"Rough territory?"

"It's not bad. They've improved the roads because of traffic from the mines. They send mined materials out of the country via Porto Wandora. Historically, it's always been easier to travel north/south in Wandora than east/

west. Roads going east and west are few and far between, especially in the north."

Gene Bond was agonising over the predicament. His conscience would not let him turn away from a plea for help involving this young girl. Yet the last thing he wanted to do was get involved in yet another Georgi Patarava-type adventure. He had had enough of those to last a lifetime. And a little thought was niggling at the back of his mind. Was Sum Taeyoung somehow involved in this? Was it just co-incidence he had found in Wandora the man who had twice tried to kill him? But the cry for help pulled hard at the heart strings.

"We'd need transport, passes, letters of authority – money," he told Kevin. "And copy me the picture of the girl and Joe."

"No problem. I can fix those quickly. I can do it myself. I could do it now!"

There was silence in the room, broken eventually by Pete.

"I'd come with you."

Bond looked at the young lad. That would help. That was a game changer. There was little appeal in the thought of driving for two days on his own through a militarised country he did not know. To do it with someone else helped swing the balance – a little.

"I've sent you an electronic copy of the photo of the little girl – and one of Joe Wright," Kevin told them.

With a sigh of resignation, Gene Bond took the first step on another unwanted adventure. The reluctant hero was hesitatingly entering the fray again.

Chapter 24

In the months following the London conference, Marcel's life had been transformed. From the blackness of despair came both the delights of a passionate romance and the expedition he so much wanted to undertake.

The relationship with Lotty blossomed in the aftermath of that lingering kiss on the doorstep of her hotel. Taken aback firstly by what she had achieved in bringing together so many people as to make the manned sub project viable, by the way she conducted herself at the conference, by seeing her in a completely different light to how he had seen her before, and then the unexpected passion of her goodbye kiss after the dinner near Vauxhall Bridge, Marcel quickly responded. A generously large bunch of flowers arrived at Lotty's hotel the following morning accompanied by a suitably amorous note. An energetic romance speedily developed. After only four weeks Lotty moved to live with Marcel.

The project to explore the Gulf of Guinea Trench for samples of the sea anemone also moved with good pace until it hit a niggling delaying problem. Getting the expedition up and running initially involved resurrecting contacts and agreements from the previous venture. That, surprisingly, was relatively easy. A lot of goodwill had been won from that first expedition. But a major complication was the securing of permission to undertake an underwater exploration from the Wandoran government. They were to operate in Wandoran territorial waters so such a permit was essential. Refusal would be a game stopper. But the country was in turmoil following the tsunami there and the death of its President. Even communicating with Wandora proved to be a nightmare. The breakthrough came when Marcel discovered a member of the reformed governing body, operating under its new military control, was an Englishman. When eventually Marcel was able to speak to Kevin Forsythe directly, previously seemingly insurmountable and extremely frustrating barriers fell away. Forsythe could not have been more accommodating. He understood the strength of the SNEL project with its endorsements and sponsorship from many international agencies and organisations. For Wandora to stand in its way would be very bad publicity for a country that had enough negative press already. Forsythe was, Marcel found, refreshingly straightforward to deal with in a governmental administration full of people who ducked responsibility, passed any caller onto someone else, and would not take a decision even if their lives depended upon it. Forsythe was different. A friendship quickly developed between he and Marcel even though they had yet to meet. In their conversations, Marcel and Forsythe found they both knew Gene Bond. Though it did not seem important at the time, Kevin told Marcel that Bond was actually in Wandora and heading north to try and rescue an American and a small girl stuck in the northern part of the country.

"That's a very worthy thing for him to be doing," Marcel responded.

"Seems to be a fine fellow," Forsythe said. "We hear the little girl's parents have recently been killed. It's a desperately sad story and when you see the girl – I'll copy her picture over to you – you can maybe understand why Bond agreed to get involved."

"Travel is not that easy in Wandora under military control," Forsythe continued. "In fact, progressing anything at the moment is fraught with difficulties. However, I'll sign the permit for the expedition and that should ensure you're not unnecessarily delayed or interfered with."

To Marcel, Kevin Forsythe's intervention was critical and without it the project would have died. The whole authorisation issue had taken a great deal of time and had been a huge irritant to Marcel. Now he established a regular flow of information to Forsythe who in turn kept Marcel informed of developments in Wandora.

Part of the preparatory activity for the coming expedition included Marcel becoming totally familiar with the small submarine in which he was to journey to the Gulf of Guinea Trench. This ultimately included having to pass the stringent safety and escape tests compulsory for anyone who used the vessel, and to be trained in the use of the telescopic arm by which Marcel would grab samples of the sea anemone.

Throughout, Lotty remained concerned about Marcel's determination to be part of the team that took the submersible deep into the Gulf of Guinea seas.

"The technology is very sound these days," he reassured her. "We're not going that deep. I'm now fully trained and feel very confident. What could possibly go wrong?"

Unbeknown to Marcel and his team, a short distance away from the SNEL offices another group of people had burnt the midnight oil preparing a document for the man Gary had met in London. To draw up a budget for the project, the plan to explore the seabed off Wandora and undertake exploratory drilling, had to be developed with far more detail than anything they actually had. In the end, the proposition had far more 'ifs' and 'buts' than would normally have been acceptable but some intangibles just had to remain as such until more work could be done. That would need more funds. Gary was running out of money.

One uncertainty was gaining a licence to mine from the Wandoran government, assuming cobalt was found within their territorial jurisdiction. There was no guarantee such a licence would be issued. In addition, if cobalt was further offshore than 12 miles, gaining international support and authority to mine might be difficult, costly, and very time consuming. With the current negative press about deep sea mining, the whole project might be blocked – if it was in international waters. So the gamble became quite clear. All investment would be at risk and potentially lost if cobalt was beyond 12 miles. What Gary was also very conscious of but failed to comment on in the document was the danger of the whole exercise being prejudiced if Marcel's venture to recover bigger samples of the Gulf of Guinea Sea Anemone was successful.

Throughout the process of preparing the document, Gary pondered the question – how would he get it to the man he had met in London? The 24 hour deadline could not have been more clearly stated together with the accompanying threat. And as the deadline got closer, so the question became bigger. He even expressed his anxieties to Vanessa. Quite why, he immediately asked the question of himself. The reaction was predictable but unhelpful. She kissed him, pulled his head down to bury it in her expansive chest, and said she was sure everything would "be ok." At any other time it would have been a delightful moment. Under the prevailing circumstances it simply demonstrated her lack of empathy and understanding.

With just one minute to go before the 24 hour period expired, Gary's mobile buzzed to indicate a text message had arrived. It read "I do not trust any sort of communications methodology other than those I control. So, a courier is about to arrive with you. Give him the proposals."

Sure enough, almost simultaneously reception reported a motorcycle courier had arrived to pick up an envelope. With a sigh, Gary sent the document on its way and wondered what would happen next.

Predicting the need to obtain some sort of governmental authorisation for an exploratory investigation of the seabed offshore Wandora, Sum Taeyoung consulted his main political link, Moussa Ehouzou. So far, the South Korean's Wandora plans had worked brilliantly. The President's death and the disappearance of Frederic Gnanligo, the Defence

Minister, had provided a wonderfully engineered opportunity to encourage a senior army officer, Major Moustapha Abass, to see his future life in much the same way as Ehouzou now did. He could either be rich or he could die. It was a no brainer and Major Abass quickly assembled enough support within senior army officials to enable him to declare the country to be under military control "in the interests of the safety of the citizens in the aftermath of the President's untimely death" – as proclaimed by the official declaration of the military take over. The Administration Committee was formed soon after, led by self-declared chairman, Moussa Ehouzou.

Ehouzou and Sum Taeyoung spent some time working out who best should be on the Committee. One by one Ministers from the old parliament were either sent on their way to obscurity or co-opted onto the new controlling body. Eventually they came to the name Kevin Forsythe.

"Who is this man?" asked Taeyoung.

"He's an Englishman. A very experienced civil servant who has worked in Africa for a long time," Moussa told him

"What value does he offer us?" asked Taeyoung.

"I don't know," Moussa did not quite know what to say. What was the South Korean fishing for? "But it might create more problems to get rid of him than to keep him. He is highly respected in African political arenas and still holds an English passport."

Taeyoung thought about that for a while. "Remind me what he does."

"He's in charge of infrastructure – roads and buildings and the like. He is leading on the rebuild in the aftermath of the tsunami. Though he has lived in Africa for many years, he is still very English."

"Does infrastructure mean he has anything to do with the port?" Taeyoung wondered.

"He supposedly controls it – signs licences and permits and the like. But I have more or less taken control of that since you asked me to."

Again Taeyoung paused for thought. He did not necessarily want Moussa to know yet about the cobalt prospect. "You can think how best we can use him – and how best we can control him. And how do we persuade him to sign a permit for an expedition offshore our coast? You think about it – then tell me."

"What sort of offshore expedition?" Moussa asked.

"I will tell you more when you need to know," was the abrupt response.

The document sent through a high security system from London to Porto Wandora gave Taeyoung much food for thought. Gary Marchant's plan was full of holes and uncertainties, some of which the South Korean was able to answer himself. Clearly the big gamble was whether or not there were big supplies of cobalt to be had within 12 miles of the Wandoran coast. Only exploration and test drilling would answer that.

Of more concern was news through his spy channels that Marcel Bartoll was close to launching his expedition to harvest specimens of the sea anemone offshore Wandora. If he was successful, that could end any prospects as far as mining cobalt was concerned. Sum

Taeyoung spent much time deliberating how this could be stopped. Clearly the project had momentum. It had backers. It had the equipment including an expedition boat and crew. It was too late now to stop it getting that far. Without finding answers to his own questions, he made contact with a longstanding ally, Janka Koldun from Belarus.

When Sum Taeyoung first encountered Koldun the Eastern European was heading a highly active gangster organisation based in Minsk and involving a range of illicit activities including extortion, pornography, computer hacking, smuggling and even assassination. Koldun himself had a reputation as a cold and ruthless killer. Good-looking in a rugged sort of way, tall and lean with closely cut hair and sparkling blue eyes, Koldun had expanded his operation way beyond its Eastern European origins. Sum Taeyoung had not been in contact with him for some time and was not sure how far the man's empire now extended and quite what his programme of activity now consisted of.

It was worth a call.

Keeping the conversation as vague as he could, he asked what he proclaimed to be a hypothetical question. If one wanted to 'interrupt' an underwater expedition, had he, Janka Koldun, any ideas how to go about it?

"What sort of underwater expedition?" asked the Eastern European terrorist.

"A small submersible manned by two people," Sum Taeyoung told him. "Could you stop it?"

The answer was a surprise.

"Ah, well, Mr Taeyoung," came the response. "You could not have come to a better place for an answer. I have a new toy that might be just what you need."

"And what might that be?" the South Korean responded, realising the Eastern European terrorist was enjoying the moment – feeling the anticipation of an earning opportunity.

"An ex-Soviet Navy Whisky Class P2 submarine," came the very unexpected answer. "Just the job for solving your problem!"

Chapter 25

The military shutdown of Wandora had benefits and disadvantages to Gene Bond and Pete as they set off north on their rescue mission of Joe Wright and his mysterious little girl. The benefits were lack of traffic. The usual chaotic miscellany of cars, trucks, cycles, hoards of motorcycles and motorcycle taxis, even roaming animals – cows, goats and sheep – was simply missing. It was spooky. The disadvantages were the number of police and military checks right across Porto Wandora which took simply an age to navigate through with a stop seemingly at every major junction for an examination of their papers. Two Englishmen in a 4x4 were conspicuous in normal times and these were certainly not normal. If anyone was going to be stopped it was them.

"Papiers! Papiers!" would be the aggressive demand whether it be from a policeman, someone in military uniform or a gun-carrying, pot-smoking scruffian. Irrationally, one enforced stop could be followed almost immediately by another at the very next junction. It was intensely frustrating. The tension across the city was palpable and these constant interruptions to their journey whoever it was by were anxious moments. But the papers provided by Kevin Forsythe passed scrutiny every time and they made slow and nervous progress out of the city and headed north.

What they had not thought through, even though it was a fairly obvious product of these stops, eventually some official somewhere would decide that news of two Englishmen heading north might be of interest to his boss. His boss told his boss. His boss told Moussa Ehouzou. Eventually Sum Taeyoung himself heard about it, exploded in anger and set various responses into action. But by then Bond and Pete Turner were a long way out of the capital.

Their journey became easier once they left Porto Wandora. As Kevin had told them, the road was pretty straight and relatively newly tarmacked to aid the transport of minerals back from the mines in the north to the harbour. But evidence of the poor state of the country was everywhere. For much of the drive sandy dust drifted across the black strip of road which was often lined with palm or fig trees but more often as not had nothing but sand as far as the eye could see. Occasionally they passed through areas of plantation which they assumed to be tea, but most of these looked rundown, neglected and badly managed.

In the only hilly area they encountered they saw a different type of tree lined either side of the road. They thought they were some sort of large black fruit trees until a truck, probably going to the mines, swayed dangerously off the edge of the road, the driver possibly nodding into a fatigue induced sleep. The temporarily out of control truck kicked up a cloud of sand. Instantaneously, and much to the amazement of the two

Englishmen following close by, the 'fruit' suddenly took flight as a flock of large bats showed that the large fruit was not fruit after all.

The further away from the capital they progressed, the more traffic they encountered though it was still only few and far between and mainly motorcycles and cyclists. It seemed the influence of the military takeover became less the further away they got from Porto Wandora. The only regular vehicles were trucks heading in their direction or back towards the coast, and top of the range 4x4s bearing the letters SDBI and a corporate logo which Gene Bond immediately recognised as belonging to Sum Taeyoung. Every one of these they saw was moving at a conspicuously high speed and leaving a small sand storm in its wake. The trucks were evidence that the military lockdown of the country had not, it seemed, impeded the movement of minerals from the north Wandoran mines.

They passed isolated buildings, some with just a roof and disconnected walls – some just support pillars, sometimes wooden. There was the occasional water tower. Now and then there would be a cluster of mud huts with thatched roofs and a scattering of people. The further north they drove the more voodoo shrines they saw. Kevin Forsythe had warned them about these as he felt it only fair the two should be prepared for when they encountered them. They varied in size and complexity. Some were just simple, carved figures, mostly pretty grotesque. Others were bigger, more elaborate and often dominated by skulls which, depending on the size and complexity of the shrine, included the heads of monkeys, dogs, goats – even elephants and gorillas. They stopped for a closer look at one and made the mistake of opening the car's windows. The smell was appalling. Rotting flesh! It was all a reminder that this part of Africa is where voodoo was born and where it is still much practiced.

The few towns and settlements they encountered were shambolic and busy, showing little signs of being impacted by the military shutdown further south. Perhaps only Porto Wandora was affected? Chaotic arrays of different buildings buzzed with activity and the roads were crammed with people, carts, animals, battered cars and large numbers of motorcycles. On approaching many of these isolated patches of civilisation they would be stopped by a gun-carrying individual – mostly male but sometimes female – often backed up by others standing nearby also carrying guns. A rusty, battered tin would be rattled at them to show it contained coinage and that more was wanted. These, it seemed, were some sort of toll. Whether it was legal or not they never found out – and had no inclination to ask – so simply met the demands rather than face the consequences of not doing so.

They had covered more than two thirds of the distance to the area of the mines before they slept overnight in the cabin of the 4x4 having driven off the main road and up a dusty track to a clump of trees in which they did their best to hide. They had come prepared to be self-sufficient in both food and water.

The following morning they were both awake early and tried to make contact with Joe Wright. There was no response, not even a divert to voicemail. The assumption was that signal strength here was poor. They would try and make contact again as they progressed further north.

The driving was tedious, the road mainly straight and the scenery repetitive. But the time together gave Gene Bond and Pete opportunity to talk about what had brought them together – cobalt.

"What we saw when Kevin Forsythe and I went to the Congo and to the artisan mines was shocking," Bond told the young geologist. "I shall never forget it. I will never forgive the developed world for allowing it to happen. I keep on hearing the words Kevin quoted us in his apartment. Do you remember? 'There can be no keener revelation of a society's soul than the way in which it treats its children'. He was quoting Nelson Mandela. How prophetic. How right. It's beyond appalling – beyond belief what we are allowing to happen."

"I agree," Pete answered. "Who wouldn't? But of course it's not just about cobalt. There are kids mining for tin and gold and lots of other minerals. And as demand in the developed world continues to grow for such stuff so the pressure to extract more goes up. So the opportunities grow. So does the exploitation of child labour."

"Most of the challenges in what Sir Nick Stern called the 'Perfect Storm' seem to me to be getting worse, not better," Bond reflected.

"Not heard of the Perfect Storm," confessed the young geologist.

"It goes back to 2006," Bond told him. "Sir Nick Stern is a leading economist but also someone concerned about climate change. He produced The Stern Review for the UK government. It was an economic assessment of climate change. In it he talked about the 'Perfect Storm' – a raft of major converging challenges including climate change but also the growing global population, the pressure on resources and so on. When I think about it I've got mixed feelings as to how far we've progressed or not since 2006."

The conversation was interrupted as Gene focussed his attention on a large black 4x4 he could see approaching in his wing mirrors. He expected it to overtake and braced himself to be submerged into the sand storm the vehicle was generating. But instead, having caught up with them, it fell in behind them, a few vehicle lengths in arrears.

"Bit strange," Bond explained to Pete what was happening. He watched the vehicle in his wing mirror. It occasionally nearly disappeared in the haze of sand dust they were kicking up in their wake. For the driver following them it must have been quite uncomfortable. Yet the vehicle maintained its position.

Bond and Pete could not help feel nervous and the tension in their vehicle grew as the miles went by and the situation remained unchanged. It was just after they had passed a signpost proclaiming the Wandoran Mines were a mile away that the car behind suddenly accelerated, shot past them and skidded to a halt in a cloud of sand dust sideways across the road in front of them. Gene braked hard, felt the wheels lock up into a skid which eventually brought them to a stop a short distance from the black 4x4. As they stopped and the swirling sand dust subsided, four men, all in identical suits and all carrying machine guns, got out and came towards them.

"Descendre! Papiers! Descendre!" demanded the one who seemed to be their leader. Gene and Pete reluctantly left their vehicle and handed over the collection of Forsythe documents. The man studied them closely. His three colleagues were now standing in a line in front of Gene and Pete.

"You come with us," he eventually demanded in faulting English, handing all the documents to one of his colleagues.

"Who are you?" asked Bond.

"It is of no matter to you. You follow us." The response was curt. It was not a request. It was an order.

"Where are you taking us?" asked Bond.

"It is of no matter. You follow us. Hand me your phones."

"Under what authority are you doing this? Who are you? Where are you taking us?" Despite them being outnumbered by a small gang of armed men, Gene Bond felt as if his blood pressure was rising to near boiling point.

"It is of no matter. Give me your phones." The man was becoming increasingly hostile.

"Are you police?" asked Bond.

"You come. No questions." The leader had stepped forward menacingly.

"But ..." Bond's next question was never asked. The lead man turned his machine gun and stabbed its butt viciously into Pete Turner's midriff. The young Englishman collapsed onto the sandy tarmac, holding his stomach and groaning.

"You come. Now!" ordered the leader as Bond tried to help his young friend. Slowly, with Pete in considerable pain, they re-boarded their vehicle.

"Phones!" demanded the man. There was no point in resisting. Reluctantly Bond handed his and Pete's mobiles through the window.

"Follow us," the lead man repeated. And with that, the four men returned to their vehicle and at a sedate pace continued the journey north, Gene Bond following. There was clearly no choice.

"You OK?" asked an anxious Bond.

"Getting better," Pete told him. "What happens now?"

"God knows," Bond replied.

"They've kept our papers," said Pete.

"So I noticed."

"It also occurs to me," Bond added, "that Joe will wonder where the hell we are. We're leaving him in the shit."

Chapter 26

Being a Minister in a government now under military control was not within Kevin Forsythe's portfolio of experience. In his many years within the British Civil Service, nothing had prepared him for this, even when he was a member of the political advisory team within a British Embassy in Africa. Since the coup d'état was announced in Wandora, apart from being told – much to his amazement – he was a member of the controlling committee, nobody had told him what he could do, could not do, was supposed to do. Without a President there was no higher authority he could call upon to endorse or disapprove any actions he as a Minister might take. He still considered Moussa Ehouzou, now seemingly the self-proclaimed chairman of the ruling committee, a junior politician of limited abilities. Until he was told officially what Ehouzou's role was within the administration, he would continue to do so.

In the aftermath of the meeting with Gene and Pete, Kevin signed papers authorising their journey north under the pretext it was to undertake environmental research around the north border territory. He stamped their documents with his Ministerial seal and made them look as officious as possible. He had also done so with the permit authorising SNEL's expedition offshore

Wandora. He had given much thought to the Marcel project. There were no negative issues about the project that he could think of. He could not believe anyone would accuse him of signing something contrary to the interests of the nation. Indeed, the potential kudos and even revenue accruing from the expedition if it were successful were unarguable benefits. Again Kevin thought his current situation to be ludicrous. He had Ministerial powers but at this moment in time nobody to be answerable to. He had no officials or committees to consult with. No civil servants with whom to discuss matters. It was unnerving and the temptation was to do nothing, just duck everything until the dust settled post the coup. But there was a serious degree of urgency expressed in the expedition's submission not the least of which was the potential of the sea anemone disappearing as marine characteristics changed in the aftermath of the tsunami. On that basis, and with nobody to refer the matter to, Kevin Forsythe signed the authorisation. There was so much to be gained from it. He could see nothing to lose. So why not? He signed his approval.

It transpired that the Administration Committee of the People's Republic of Wandora was composed of just seven people of which he, Kevin Forsythe, was one. He wondered why? Within the seven was one person who had been 'seconded'.

Who he was would presumably be explained at the meeting. They assembled in what had been the late President's main office in the São João Baptista de Wandora, and Kevin quickly noted – as did anyone else entering the room – that the large picture of the former president and the oil painting he claimed to have created himself were no longer. Just areas of slightly brighter paintwork than the rest of the walls gave evidence of what had previously hung there.

Moussa Ehouzou, Minister for National Security, sat in the presidential chair. To his left was Major Moustapha Abass, resplendent in his uniform and trying to look authoritative. To his right was a towering man, tall, very broad shouldered, large in body but with more hair than Kevin Forsythe could recall seeing on any human being. From the man's head, a veritable cascade of it fell to his shoulders whilst a moustache sort of merged into a lengthy beard and made it hard to see a real face. Perhaps, thought Kevin, that was the reason for it. The Englishman sat with three other former members of the Wandoran Parliament and waited with great anticipation to see what was going to happen and to find out who the man with the hair was. The stranger was obviously the seconded body.

"Maybe we should stand and for a silent minute give thanks for the work of our deceased President," said a sombre sounding Moussa Ehouzou.

The small group stood and in what Kevin felt was an embarrassed silence, paid tribute to the recently massacred leader. Kevin wondered what was really in the minds of those around him, some of whom, if not all, had some connection to the killing. Taking the lead from Ehouzou, when he sat the others did the same.

"This," Ehouzou continued, nodding to the man to his right, "is Mr Sum Taeyoung who owns an internationally respected business, Sustainable Development Brokers

International based in Seoul but operating globally. Wandora should already be extremely grateful to our friend here who has been responsible single-handedly for ensuring the continuation of the involvement of the Chinese in mining operations in our country. As you all know, this provides by far the biggest external revenue income to Wandora and could have been lost in the aftermath of the massacre at the northern mines. That would have been disastrous for our economy and hurt us at a moment of great vulnerability in the aftermath of the tsunami and the loss of our President."

Ehouzou paused to take a sip of water. So far, Kevin noted, the conspicuously hairy man sitting next to him had hardly moved though his eyes were constantly checking what was going on around him. Ehouzou had started his statement with some degree of uncertainty, faulting in his speech to begin with but growing in strength and confidence. Kevin did not like the man. He was, he thought, a little, nondescript, low ranking civil servant in a third division African state. It was a travesty that he now sat in the seat of power. A bad joke!

"SDBI provided a fighting force that saw off the terrorists who attacked the Chinese mining operation and nearby village. Only by securing the area and establishing an effective security for the mining operation were we able to encourage the Chinese to continue their investment there. That reassurance extended the length of the route to the harbour at Porto Wandora, and the port itself, so the Chinese could feel reassured their investment was well protected. The government of Wandora has, therefore, contracted with SDBI to provide security at the minerals extraction site, the harbour and the route between the two."

Kevin wondered who had authorised the contract.

"I have, therefore," continued Ehouzou, "invited the President of SDBI to join the Administration Committee as the role of his company is now so bound into the future prosperity of Wandora."

The self-proclaimed Chairman of the Administrative Committee paused, stared at each of the men before him as if to challenge them to say something. Nobody did.

"In the sad and shocking demise of our President," continued Ehouzou, "which threatened to send this country into a state of total anarchy, the decision was taken to place control into the hands of an Administrative Committee, supported by the army represented here by Major Abass. For the time being, the committee is the senior point of authority for Wandora and Major Moustapha Abass is part of that controlling body because of the essential role the army is providing. SDBI's Security Division will work closely with the army but because of the contractual arrangement established with the Chinese will be primarily responsible for all security issues in the north of the country, in the harbour area of Porto Wandora, and the route between the two. In these areas, the army will be subordinate to SDBI."

Kevin was shocked. Moussa Ehouzou was passing military control of a strategically vital part of the country to the South Korean. He looked at Sum Taeyoung but the big man sat impassively alongside the Wandoran politician who Kevin now realised was his puppet.

"You," continued Ehouzou looking at Kevin and the three men sat with him, "will more or less continue in the Ministerial roles you had before. However, all major decisions will be brought to me for final approval. Is that clear?"

Which, in essence, makes Moussa Ehouzou a dictator, thought Kevin, but one who jumps when Sum Taeyoung pulls the strings. Wandora was now being controlled and manipulated by the South Korean! What, he wondered, would Gene Bond make of this?

Ehouzou went on to explain in more detail how the administration would now function. Throughout it all, Sum Taeyoung remained silent and indeed had not spoken a word by the time the meeting broke up. As Kevin headed for the door with the rest of the 'minions', Ehouzou called to him.

"Mr Forsythe. You will stay behind. We need to talk further with you."

Chapter 27

There was much interest around the world about what happened to the former Soviet/Russian Navy's Whisky Class P2 submarine after it was sold. Few, including the specialist agency responsible for its sale, knew who had bought it and where it now was. Rumours suggested it was being modified to be used for 'adventure tourism' and many agencies waited for it to appear somewhere in that or any other capacity. As it still had military capabilities, the defence and intelligence agencies of several countries were more than a little interested in its future use.

Janka Koldun was to later tell Sum Taeyoung that once the sub was purchased it was sailed down to the Colombia Pacific coast and up one of the many wet mangrove tributaries of the area. "The dense jungle there creates such a stifling heat it distorts the view from above", Koldun told him. "Spy satellites can't see through it. That's why it's become the centre for the manufacture of drug smuggling submarines. It's quite unbelievable but there's a whole industry there."

It transpired the ex-Soviet/Russian sub was sent to its temporary Colombian hideaway for a refit to be made suitable for its future career which, as the Eastern European terrorist explained, had little to do with adventure tourism. Drugs and weapons movement were to be its bread and butter workload, sometimes towing another craft which, if they were detected and looked like being arrested, could be released to rid themselves of any evidence. But the craft was fully armed and could be called upon to undertake far more than illicit smuggling.

"You own it?" asked an incredulous Sum Taeyoung. He knew the Eastern European's business interests had expanded but this seemed extraordinary. They were meeting in the Culinaire Bazaar restaurant close by Charles de Gaulle airport in Paris. The South Korean refused to meet in the terminal itself. Koldun had flown in from Minsk. Taeyoung was on his way from London back to Africa. It was an inconvenience to both of them to have to meet but what they wanted to talk about neither trusted to do so across any telephone line however secure it may have claimed to be.

"I have a share in it," Koldun explained. He clearly did not want to expand on that. "And in the revenue it might generate in the future."

"And it's fully operational?"

"Oh yes," Koldun assured him. "It can do over 10,000 mile journeys and dive to 200 metres. It does nearly 20 knots on the surface and a little over 10 when it's submerged. It's very effective. It was very expensive but a good investment."

"Does it still have its armament?" asked Taeyoung. The whole story seemed preposterous.

"Oh yes," said Koldun. You could hear the pride in his voice. "Four torpedo tubes at the front and two at the back."

"They work?"

"Of course."

"And you have the torpedoes?"

"Yes."

"Where is it now? Could it be off-coast the Coast of Guinea in the near future?"

"Can't tell you where it is now," replied Koldun bluntly. "The truth is – I don't know but if I did I still couldn't tell you. What is the nature of the business you want to call on it to do?"

"I need to blow up another submarine." Taeyoung told him in a matter of fact way – as if this was a routine requirement.

The Eastern European terrorist paused. "I need to know more. Where is this to happen? At what depth? What sort of submarine is the target. And now I know you want to fire torpedoes, the cost goes up. There's a scale of charges for the sub – from simple smuggling the cost varies depending on where on the planet it is and if armaments are to be deployed. It's a lot to do with how big a crew is needed for each task."

Always on the lookout for a deal, Taeyoung dealt another card into the negotiations.

"I can see a way of offsetting some of my costs of hiring your no doubt extortionately costed submarine by doubling up its use. I guess there would be no objection from you if I were to hire your submarine to convey an assignment from South America to Africa as phase one of my project?"

"What sort of weight would you be thinking of?"

"Just for the sake of this discussion, if we were to say a tonne?"

"That would be possible," Koldun told him.

"So how do we take my business forward?" asked Taeyoung.

"I need a full specification of the task so we can respond with a proposal and quotation," Koldun told him. "We need to know where and how we would take delivery of your assignment, where it is to be delivered to, dates of the shipping, then all the details as I said earlier about the attack element of the project."

The business-like nature of the conversation surprised the South Korean but it was also reassuring. Janka Koldun had matured greatly as a businessman since they first worked together. This assignment was going to be a costly affair. The movement and subsequent sales of drugs would counter that expense but it was good to know that the matter was being dealt with properly and professionally.

"OK. And how fast can this happen?"

"You can have a quotation within four hours of giving me the specification," said Koldun.

Chapter 28

The crisis meeting of the Committee on Cooperation, International Relations and Conflict Resolution of the Pan-African Parliament assembled in Midrand, South Africa. Consisting of 250 members representing 50 African states, the PAP, as it is commonly known, is funded by the African Union, the European Union, the World Bank, the International Monetary Fund, and the United Nations Development Programme. It was established in 2004 "to ensure the full participation of African peoples in the development and economic integration of the continent." Five years after its formation it was planned that a conference would be staged to "review the operation and its effectiveness." Such a review event has never been held. Its members are not directly elected and the organisation has no binding legislative powers.

The crisis meeting was called by the World Bank. The spread of ISIS across Africa was causing serious concern. The continent was already beset with conflicts and huge numbers of people made homeless. Oxfam, for instance, was reporting fighting has forced four million people to leave their homes in the Democratic Republic of the Congo making it the largest displacement crisis in Africa. It is also home to nearly 500,000 refugees from Burundi,

Central African Republic and South Sudan. Over seven million people are in dire need of humanitarian help.

Now the spread of ISIS was fuelling the disaster. Typifying the news that had especially disturbed the World Bank, in Burkina Faso's East Province a police escorted convoy returning from the Boungou gold mine had been ambushed. Four gendarmes and a civilian died in the attack. Apparently the lead vehicle exploded after driving over an improvised explosive device after which the convoy came under intense fire from unidentified armed individuals. The Burkinabé defence ministry was treating this as a 'terrorist' attack. Similar attacks were reported on an almost daily basis from Ethiopia and the Democratic Republic of the Congo to Nigeria, Niger, Burkina Faso, Benin, Wandora, Togo and others.

The destabilisation of an already volatile situation was mainly attributed to the increasing activity of ISIS in Africa as its operations in Syria ended. In the DRC, reports were emerging of attacks on artisan mines from which gold, cobalt and other valuable minerals were extracted. The situation had become sufficiently serious for the World Bank to sponsor a survey of the situation. The results were very disturbing. In some areas, mining had been totally interrupted by infighting between ISIS fighters and local terrorist groups anxious to protect their territory and traditional revenues from the mining operations.

The report even suggested the disruption of the flow of cobalt from the mines could compromise IT development in the advanced world and had the potential to slow or even stop the move away from combustion engined vehicles to electric cars. In their research activity, the World Bank spoke to BMW, Apple, Microsoft and others, all of whom expressed extreme concern about what the bank was telling them. One part of the World Bank report stated; "electric cars are gaining ground, with about one million EV sales predicted in China per annum as that country invests in them as an industrial strategy and for better air quality. Not all Li-ion batteries need cobalt, but most do, which explains why cobalt's price has shot up from about $25,000 per tonne to $90,000 per tonne in two years. This matters for electric cars, because up to half their cost is made up of the battery and ingredients account for 50 to 80 per cent of the battery itself. The higher the cost of cobalt, the more people will have to pay for an electric car. Compromising the availability of cobalt will slow the automotive industry's move towards electric cars, increase the price of electric cars and be counter-productive in stimulating consumer interest in buying electric cars."

Bloomberg was reporting "a burgeoning risk of a supply crunch in cobalt – a key battery metal that's more than tripled in price in two years – poses one of the biggest threats to forecasts for rising electric vehicle adoption." Bloomberg New Energy Finance analysts said shortages of cobalt are "likely earlier than previously forecast and the issue poses a potential challenge to EV sales over the coming five to seven years."

By co-incidence, the World Bank had turned to the same expert as had Gene Bond. Professor Pete Slater at the University of Birmingham in the UK in a written response to the Bank said "this is potentially a very serious issue (although the price of cobalt is still much lower than Au, it can only keep going up in price). One of the fallacies commonly put forward is that this won't be a problem due to reductions in cobalt in the battery electrode. Previously NMC-111 was commonly used: this is essentially 33% cobalt on the transition metal site. There is a move currently to NMC-622 or NMC-532 to reduce the cobalt (now 20% cobalt). And then ultimately (when the issues surrounding it can be solved) NMC-811 (10% cobalt)."

"So commonly car companies put forward the message they are reducing cobalt so the supply chain can be maintained. However with the forecasted rapid growth of electric cars it is clear that even with this cobalt reduction (even with complete change to NMC-811, just selling three times more electric cars would lead to the same amount of cobalt needed as today), the amount of cobalt that we would need would dramatically increase."

The World Bank also called upon Washington for a view of the situation, mindful that the commander of US Special Operations in Africa had recently warned of "the growing African terror threat."

The Major General was reported as saying; "ISIS and Al-Qaeda represent major threats and are growing in strength in West Africa. The Al-Qaeda and ISIS inspired threats in Lake Chad Basin and in the Sahel are very real and continue to grow in strength. Both ISIS and Al-Qaeda franchises here should be taken seriously. They both have either carried out, or attempted, attacks on western interests in Africa, and they both have aspirations to continue attacks on western interests."

World Bank and American officials were also concerned about ISIS affiliates in Libya, the Sahel, the Lake Chad Basin, and Somalia, particularly the prospect of foreign fighters leaving Iraq and Syria and joining these newer affiliates. The two groups in the Lake Chad Basin, which involved Nigeria, Niger, Cameroon and Chad include Boko Haram and ISIS West Africa. The US military told the World Bank they believed "Boko Haram fields approximately 1,500 fighters and ISIS West Africa approximately 3,500."

The Major General concluded his report to the World Bank by saying; "As the physical caliphate collapses, where those fighters go is a question. There are already sub-pockets again both in the Sahel, in Libya, in Lake Chad Basin and a small one in Somalia where those ISIS fighters could find themselves. The threat is increasing at different rates and different volumes depending on where you are at in the theatre in Africa."

The Midrand crisis meeting of the Committee on Cooperation, International Relations and Conflict Resolution of the Pan-African Parliament concluded that the growing terrorist activity in Africa, fuelled in part by the westward movement of ISIS groups, generated a real threat to the economic and social well-being and stability of increasing numbers of African nations. It recognised the precarious economic situation of tens of thousands of people linked to artisan mining and the disaster that would result from their loss of earnings, meagre though they might be, if the mines were closed down.

It acknowledged the despicable use of child labour and children trafficking in the supply chain but warned that denying earning opportunities could lead to increased widespread starvation.

An embryonic thought emerging from the meeting was sparked by the existing Great Green Wall project. Approved in 2007 by the African Union, this ambitious project plans an almost 5,000 miles long, 10 miles wide, wall of trees to be established across the African continent – from Senegal in the west to Djibouti in the east. Such a wall would lessen the prospect of further desert encroachment, provide shelter from the sun, hold water in root structures and generally improve the standard of life of people living in the drylands on the borders of the Sahara. Though this project has become bogged down in political bureaucracy, it has made some progress, notably in Senegal.

While the sub-Sahara Great Green Wall was about the creation of new forest areas, the DRC had an abundance of them. It has the second largest and most intact area of contiguous rainforest in the world covering over 75 million hectares (three times the size of the UK). But it was the multi-state, multi-organisations co-operation that could be learnt from the Great Green Wall project. At the Midrand meeting, a growing number of people were supporting the idea of something similar but based on the comprehensive use of the resources of the existing forests – but for local communities. This could be developed in the Congo and even extended as a southern version of the Great Green Wall right across the continent from Liberia in the west to Somalia in the east, an Atlantic Ocean to Indian Ocean project of some 4,000 miles length. The objective would be a co-ordinated, multi-agency, NGO delivered project aimed at encouraging and educating local communities in, for instance, the utilisation of forest waste, local food production, providing water and cooking facilities to tens of thousands who had no access to such things, and providing local employment and income. It would pay for the education of local children and offset income streams that would die with the demise of artisan mining. Though massively ambitious, if taken in "bite-sized chunks" involving perhaps a few start-up projects in three or four countries, over time a second Great Green Wall could be delivered.

The meeting ended with a project task force being formed to undertake a feasibility study for a Great Green Wall-type project to be established first in the Democratic Republic of the Congo with the prospect of it being extended east and west if successful. A call was extended to the US, Europe and private enterprises across the planet, led by the Pan-African Parliament, to urgently develop a strategy to combat the growing terrorist threat and to consider alternate economic models to those currently in place. Cynics suggested no progress would be made until corruption was eradicated and the "forces of evil" – ISIS – now already degenerating an already deplorable human catastrophe, eliminated.

Chapter 29

It was a glorious, cloudless, rich blue sky day and the expedition's boat swayed gently as it made steady progress through a gentle swell. Charlotte McDonnell lay prostrate on the poop deck, her youthful and curvaceous body clothed in the scantiest bikini she had. She glorified in the sunshine. If she had less inhibitions she might have exposed her naked body to the elements. Lovely though that thought was, she was content with what the moment had to offer. The mildest of breezes and the lapping of a gentle sea against the expedition's boat created an idyllic place to be. For someone who not so long ago had virtually nothing but was given a chance which she grasped, to be here was close to a miracle. Despite her meteoric climb within the company, Lotty never lost sight of how fortunate she had been to be given such a chance – by Marcel. Now they were an entity, two people entwined by love, and she could still hardly believe it.

They were heading towards the Gulf of Guinea Trench and while they did so Marcel was utterly preoccupied ensuring he was one hundred per cent ready for the task that lay before him. Lotty could offer nothing to help him and saw little of him. It was to be expected and in no way upset her. The forthcoming dive niggled at her and she could not escape a sense of trepidation. The few times she had raised the matter with Marcel he had dismissed it out of hand. To raise it again would, at the very least, irritate him and she did not want that. So she kept her concerns to herself and tried to enjoy the voyage.

Once Marcel was installed in the submarine, Lotty would be the main communications link between him and the expedition team. The sub's pilot, Karl, would be linked direct to the expedition's technical team. But, until then, there was little for her to do except enjoy the sun – and worry. She might have been even more troubled had she, or anyone else on the expedition craft, been conscious of a small fishing smack that remained within their sight throughout their voyage. Their concerns would have been seriously heightened had they known that on the small boat a certain man from Belarus maintained a constant watch on their progress and reported it to the captain of the submarine he partly owned and which tracked astern of them at a discrete distance.

Interest in the expedition had continued to grow as soon as the concept was launched. The long-term prospects of the Gulf of Guinea Sea Anemone providing value to the medical fraternity also gained increasing amounts of support. It seemed to Marcel and his team, Lotty included, that the whole project was critically time-balanced – a race against the threats to the sea anemone's existence caused by changes to the oceans of the planet – and the prospect of sea bed mining. Marcel knew only too well that traditionally it takes a long time for the pharmaceutical industry to respond to the potential of newly discovered maritime species having some value to them. But recent research into the group of creatures known as cnidarians – including sea anemones – had opened up a new channel of opportunity. Such animals are the only ones that inject venom via sting cells. There was growing belief that the formation of sting cells in sea anemones could inspire a new way of delivering drugs into the human body. How venom and the way it is produced in animals might, according to world leading authorities of the subject, potentially be used to create life-saving treatments for humans. It is, Marcel discovered, a rapidly growing area of research. It was reported that Dr. Kartik Sunagar at the Centre for Ecological Sciences of the Indian Institute of Science in Bangalore, India, in his investigations into the origin of venom-delivery systems, was saying that "science is just starting to grasp which genes encode the production of deadly toxins. Little is known about how venomous creatures evolved the arsenal needed to discharge venom into their prey." It was hoped that capturing more specimens of the Gulf of Guinea Sea Anemone might help this line of work.

The urgent need to capture such samples was further stimulated by more concerns being published by the University of Exeter and Greenpeace scientists about sea bed mining. Mining on the ocean floor, they said, could do "irreversible damage to deep sea ecosystems. Deep sea (depths below 200m) covers about half of the Earth's surface and is home to a vast range of species." Their report says "little is known about these marine environments", and their researchers were saying mining could have "long-lasting and unforeseen consequences"– not just at mining sites but also across much larger areas. This seemed to imply that the Gulf of Guinea Sea Anemone could be terminally damaged by any mining activity within its vicinity. "Our knowledge of these ecosystems is still limited, but we know they're very sensitive," said Dr David Santillo, a marine biologist and senior Greenpeace scientist based at the University of Exeter. "Recovery from man-made disturbance could take decades, centuries or even millennia, if these ecosystems recover at all."

Marcel used all this growing evidence to secure funding for the expedition. Lotty had been carried along by his passion and excitement. And as the expedition's craft closed on the area of the Gulf of Guinea Trench, so, tangibly, a tension of excitement could be felt throughout the vessel.

Reaching the location where the dive was to take place, the support vessel dropped its anchor and preparations were made for the submersible to be launched early the following morning. That night, Lotty and Marcel made love in the confined space of their bunk, their passion stirred by the inherent dangers, however low, both knew any dive into the deep carried with it. The limited space of the bunk and the close proximity of other people separated by wafer thin walls constrained their normally exuberant – and often noisy – love-making but did nothing to minimise their lust for each other.

The following morning the weather remained calm and the sea gentle and welcoming. They were blessed with the ideal conditions for the expedition. The launch of the sub went like clockwork and soon Marcel was easing himself into its tight confine and the seat alongside Karl. Divers were soon locking the top of the small vessel. Even in these calm conditions the sub bobbed around like a cork and Marcel felt a queasiness developing in his stomach. The last thing he needed was to be seasick and he was thankful when they were released by the support vessel and their descent started. Though he had done such dives many times before, it was always an adrenaline pumping moment. One minute he could see the aft deck of the support ship and its A-frame standing tall against a light blue sky. Then the waters were swirling around them in a crazed cauldron as they sank below the surface and into the calmness below the waves.

"It's like diving into a washing machine," Marcel joked to Karl who smiled but said nothing. Karl was not renowned for his social chat. Marcel concentrated on the view outside, the wondrous colours of the sea below the waves and the occasional passing fish or small shoals. But as they dived deeper, so the light from above quickly dimmed and they increasingly became reliant on the powerful lights of the sub. The hum of its engine and the intermittent hiss of gas being exhausted from the vessel's ballast control were the only sounds to penetrate their otherwise silent world.

Soon they were deep enough to be utterly dependent on the sub's searchlights and the on-board computer screens to see anything. The eventual sighting of the parallel scrape marks on the sea bed reassured them that the computerised navigation systems had brought them to the right place. They tracked the marks until the edge of the oceanic trench came into view, a moment of excitement for them both. The wall of the trench dropped down sheer and quickly out of sight but as they passed over the top of it they had the briefest glimpses of what appeared to be flowers – orange centred with white tentacles waving in the current. In an otherwise colourless world they created a startling display of colour. Then they were gone from view and Karl busied himself trying to turn the sub through a sharp, 180 degrees U-turn against an extremely aggressive current. With the nose of the vessel now pointed at the cliff face over which they had just passed, the sub's powerful beams of light illuminated dozens of what Marcel continued to think of as plants. These were, he kept reminding himself, predatory animals. It seemed incredulous. Those captured in the beams of light looked so beautiful – so floral.

With every minute of the dive being precious, Marcel was already starting to extend a grab arm with which to home in on one of the sea anemones as Karl's U-turn manoeuvre was completed. Now all Karl needed to do was to keep the sub as stable as he could – no mean task in the exceptionally strong currents. It had taken less than a minute to swing the craft round in the fast running current over the Gulf of Guinea Trench so it now hovered close to the top of the cliff face of the Trench. Marcel started to extend the grab arm. It was the last act he was to undertake in the sub-sea expedition.

The explosion blew Marcel's underwater world asunder. On the surface, all hell let loose as those on the support ship heard a very loud thud followed almost immediately by a massive eruption in the sea nearby.

A huge column of water gushed 60 feet towards the sky then crashed downwards like a massive, out of control, fountain. The ship rocked violently as angry waves hit it. Crew members, the scientific crew and unsecured equipment were sent flying in all directions. Pandemonium and chaos consumed the vessel. Some individuals escaped with bashes and bruises. Others had broken limbs. The radio operators were in agony and totally deafened. Lotty was on the floor, hands to her head, screaming in pain and fright. SNEL Project Leader Maria Cummings regained her feet in the wheelhouse but was dazed and bewildered, blood trickling from a gash on her forehead.

The ship's captain, with no idea what has happened except that their submarine and the two men in it are in dire trouble, grabbed the microphone of the ship's radio. With his two sub-mariners' lives in peril he did not hesitate in calling "Mayday" "Mayday" and adding their co-ordinates. He prayed someone might be listening.

Fortunately, people were. In Lagos, the Nigerian coastal patrol craft Alibori set off immediately at its maximum 30 knots into the Gulf of Guinea. Benin also scrambled one of its French-made OCEA coastal patrol vessels. A US helicopter on a UN patrol off the coast of Wandora diverts to respond to the Mayday call. A variety of commercial ships of varying sizes and from different nations alter their routes to join in the search and, hopefully, rescue.

On board the expedition support vessel, order starts to emerge from the chaos. The injured are assembled, assessed and helped where help can be applied. Some will have to be lifted off the boat and sent to the nearest hospital, Lotty amongst them. She remains in a bad state and continuously sobs. She cannot hear a thing and is having difficulty speaking. The only word she utters that anyone can understand is 'Marcel.'

None of the team's divers were hurt. Thankfully they had been on board at the time of the explosion. As soon as practical they are sent off to see if they can find the sub, Marcel and Karl. They join the growing air/sea search now in full swing.

Standing at the very bows of the support vessel, Maria Cummings scans the view before her through powerful binoculars and prays for any sign of life or the craft in which life was once sustained. She sees nothing.

Chapter 30

The attack came without warning though with no surprise to people monitoring the spread of ISIS west across Africa. It happened in the southern corner of the Democratic Republic of the Congo in the strip of that country that stretches to the coast and lies between Angola to the south and the Republic of the Congo to the north. The area has a concentration of artisan mines and much of it resembles the hell-like conditions of the mud-swamped Somme killing fields of WW1. As in the area Bond and Forsythe had witnessed, children are widely used here to dig stones from the ground, carry them to where they are cleaned and segregated and where agents purchase their backbreaking labouring for paltry sums. The agents, allegedly independent, assemble what they buy and sell it on in volume to specialist buyers who in turn sell to mineral processors, mostly of Chinese ownership.

In a motley battle fleet of armoured vehicles, Toyota gun trucks and heavily protected, fighter carrying vehicles, all flying the familiar black flag of ISIS, more than 100 combatants descend on the poorly protected mining operations of the area. The disorganised protection supposedly defending not only the mines but the income they generated for local terrorist organisations, is pitiful and quickly collapses. Those to whom the mines mean wealth try desperately to respond and money is rapidly deployed to organise resistance from local terrorist organisations. The ensuing terrorist against terrorist fighting bedded in so it was no longer just a skirmish but a protracted and bloody battle. It disrupts the flow of mineral extraction from the mines and leaves communities dependent on the mines without their vital capacity to earn, a pittance though it might have been. NGOs in the area report a rapid increase in incidents of starvation, malnutrition and general health problems, especially amongst the young.

The fighting also interrupts an important supply chain for the developed world's hunger for cobalt. Though representing only a fraction of the artisan mining industry of Africa, the incident sounds alarm bells across the planet. Expert observers of African politics and economics rightly interpret what has happened as being ISIS seeking not only further territorial gains in Western Africa but, for the first time but probably not the last, securing for their own benefit the wealth to be gained from the cobalt supply chain.

To those reliant upon the supply of the critical mineral, the need to mature the extraction industry into a more dependable and secure supply source is even more obvious than before. Western news sources quickly headline stories about how the ISIS attack underlines the vulnerability of the supply of cobalt and how that could thwart the developed world's move away from fossil fuelled vehicles to electric ones. The scale of the move to electric vehicles has been reflected in a new economic report that says: "Traditional carmakers are scrambling to retool their businesses for the electric vehicle market. Ford said it is doubling its investment in the sector to $11 billion over the next five years. French carmaker Peugeot said it is returning to North America with an entire fleet of electrified vehicles by 2025 while Volkswagen is targeting a 300-model battery-powered lineup by 2030. Volkswagen will invest more than $40 billion in the next five years as part of a push into battery-powered vehicles and autonomous-driving systems. Daimler AG is spending 10 billion euros on 10 battery models by 2022."

The boom in electric cars could more than quadruple demand for cobalt to in excess of 450,000 tons by 2030 from less than 100,000 tons, according to Bloomberg New Energy Finance.

Whilst the world looked to the DRC government for some sort of response to the aggressive ISIS move to take ownership of artisan cobalt mining operations, its unexpected reaction was to announce a new generation of taxes on minerals extracted from the country including copper, cobalt and gold. Industry observers noted that the annual production of cobalt was primarily a byproduct of nickel and copper mining but that more than 60% of the world's supply came from the DRC. Longstanding fears about political instability in that country and the challenges of 'ethical sourcing' appeared to be well evidenced by the ISIS activity but the imposition of a new tax regime was an unexpected development.

The immediate impact on the global metals market was to push the price of cobalt even higher. In recent times its value had increased by more than 150% and the ISIS destabilisation of the supply chain plus the new taxes pushed that even higher as the boom in demand from electric vehicles, most of which will be powered by nickel-manganese-cobalt batteries, continued to increase.

In Wandora, Sum Taeyoung noted these developments with considerable interest. His ambitions were excited by the rapid escalation in the price of cobalt and the seeming long-term reliance on the mineral by the world's automotive industry for its revolutionary switch to electric power. It certainly enhanced the necessity for an exploratory expedition to provide evidence of the prospect of mining cobalt from Wandora's territorial waters. Any immediate development of that project had to be shelved temporarily in the aftermath of the explosion that interrupted the SNEL hunt for specimens of the sea anemone. That disaster and its associated loss of life attracted significant media interest. It meant being extremely discreet about progressing his own project though he would always be keen it attracted as little attention as possible.

With Taeyoung pestering to accelerate the development of Gary Marchant's plan to explore the sea bed for evidence of cobalt, the Englishman started to identify the various people and equipment needed. As had been the case with Marcel Bartoll's expedition, Taeyoung too would need Wandoran government approval. To achieve that he needed to inform Moussa Ehouzou which he did without going into any great detail. The word cobalt was certainly avoided.

"Authority for any mining operation offshore Wandora and in our territorial waters will need to be signed off by the appropriate Minister for it to be able to stand any external scrutiny or audit," Ehouzou told him.

"Is that Forsythe?" asked Taeyoung though he was certain it would be.

"Yes."

"Well see to it he signs off the permit. I'll give you a full set of proposals."

Which Taeyoung did. But instead of being a hunt for cobalt the expedition was, so the proposals from Gary Marchant's company stated, for copper. Kevin Forsythe was immediately curious to know more about the evidence that suggested such an expedition was appropriate. He was well aware of the growing concern around the world about deep sea mining. The supportive evidence in the proposal documentation and permit application was, to put it mildly, flimsy.

"You will sign it." It was not a request from Ehouzou. It was an order and despite Kevin Forsythe's objection that he was authorising something he did not know enough about, his dictator-like master gave him no option. He signed it.

Chapter 31

When the line broke the telephone connection to Kevin Forsythe in Porto Wandora it was more than annoying to Joe Wright. He now has no idea whether anyone was heading his way to get himself and his diminutive girl companion away from whatever was going on here in the north of the country. They had moved some way away from the mining village for security sake while Joe continued to try and make contact with Gene Bond or Kevin Forsythe. He eventually raised an answer from the former English civil servant, now a Wandoran politician.

"I'm sorry Joe. I haven't heard from Gene for a while now. I've been trying to contact him and I must admit to being quite concerned."

"It causes me one hell of a headache," Joe admitted. "This little girl and I are stuck out in the wilderness. If I don't hear soon I'll have to trust my luck and try and get us both back to Niger. It's not an option I like."

And that is as far as the telephone conversation progressed. The line went dead and as much as Joe tried to re-establish contact it was without success. Mobile signals across Wandora are unreliable at the best of times and these times were by no means the best! Joe was unsure whether lack of contact with Gene Bond and now with Kevin was just because of poor signal strengths or for more sinister reasons. He suspected the latter. Whatever, the American now felt utterly isolated.

Back in Porto Wandora, Kevin was also more than a little concerned about loss of contact with Gene and Pete and now Joe, particularly since his encounter with Moussa Ehouzou and Sum Taeyoung. It had not been a pleasant experience but was not one he felt he needed to share with the American. Joe Wright had enough problems on his hands.

"We need to re-establish the terms of reference with you," Ehouzou told him after instructing him not to leave with the others when the meeting of the Administration Committee broke up. The self-proclaimed leader of the committee still sat with the large South Korean on one side and Major Moustapha Abass on the other. Kevin realised he had not heard Abass utter a single word. Ehouzou he continued to consider with distain. Taeyoung he found simply curious. He remained unsure what he was seeking to achieve. At the moment the South Korean was just sitting there, holding Kevin in a fixed and penetrating stare that would unnerve most people. There was no invitation to sit and Kevin found himself standing with some trepidation in front of the other three as a school child might stand in front of the headmaster and senior teachers.

"We recognise the experience you bring, Mr Forsythe, and particularly your connections to the UK government, the European Commissioners and various important organisations in Africa. Your management skills and knowledge about the workings of governments are greatly appreciated and have been very helpful and effective in the aftermath of the tsunami."

Such flattering words did nothing to allay Kevin's fears about what was to come. He waited for the word "but" and it was not long coming.

"However, we work in unusually challenging times. Conventional ways of conducting government have had to be reviewed and changed in the aftermath of the tragic death of our President. Your responsibilities for the rebuild of buildings and our infrastructure will continue as before but you will report to me before any major decisions are made or contracts signed off. Is that understood?"

Kevin nodded. The question did not warrant anything more.

"The area of the mining village and the port of Porto Wandora will be excluded from your portfolio. The security branch of SDBI will be responsible for those and for the protection of vehicles transporting extracted minerals. Anything of any substantial consequence you will bring to me before any decisions are made. Understood?"

Again Kevin merely nodded.

"So we understand what has been happening lately, an update on recent activity is required."

Ehouzou waited for Kevin to respond. Kevin, feeling increasingly petulant and rebellious, was not sure who Ehouzou meant when he said 'we'. He was not sure if he was supposed to say anything in response to what Ehouzou had said. So to be bloody-minded, he said nothing. He assumed the 'update' being requested would be in the form of a report. An uneasy silence followed.

"An update," Ehouzou eventually said again.

"I expected you'd be referring to a written report," Kevin answered.

"No, you tell us – now," came the response.

Kevin was taken aback.

"To respond so spontaneously endangers the accuracy of any such report. How much detail do you want? Do you need dates? I am not confident my memory will be adequate."

"Just the headlines will do," Ehouzou told him, increasingly agitated by the Englishman's attitude.

With a great deal of reluctance, Kevin told of his work on buildings and road repairs especially in Porto Wandora. He reported authorising various actions and projects including that from SNEL in the UK for a second expedition to the Gulf of Guinea Trench.

For the first time, Sum Taeyoung spoke. Kevin noted the almost aristocratic English delivery, tinged with a hint of American. "On what authority did you do that?"

"On my own authority. The President had taken a personal interest in the first expedition and would most certainly have supported this one. But someone blew him up so I could not count on his endorsement." Kevin chose his callous words with care mindful of his previous thoughts about who might have been linked to the death of the leader. Two of the men sitting before him were high on his suspect list.

"I have had nobody to refer to. No civil servants to discuss the matter with. No experts to give their judgements. No appraisal committee. Nothing. And with there being urgency attached to the application which came supported by a myriad of international, worthy, highly respected organisations, I approved it."

"Why was it so urgent?" the South Korean asked. He sounded a little aggrieved but Kevin was not to know of his invested interests in the coastal waters of Wandora.

"There was supporting evidence with the application that advised of reduction in the quality of sea waters in general. In the case of the Gulf of Guinea, this was accentuated by subterranean turmoil that provoked the tsunami. The implications on marine ecosystems are matters of conjecture but there is a degree of probability that the longevity of the sea anemone might be prejudiced. As you will recall from the outcome of the first expedition, the medical fraternity has been excited by the potential benefits the sea anemone might provide. Samples from the first expedition were too small and sufficiently contaminated to compromise unequivocal results. The new expedition is primarily tasked with recovering more samples for further examination. That is why so many worthy medical and oceanic organisations supported the application."

Sum Taeyoung was clearly seriously interested in the SNEL venture. Kevin started to wonder why. "So what is the status of this new expedition you have sanctioned?" the South Korean asked.

"I believe they're currently undertaking trials offshore Wandora and will be sailing to the Trench in the next few days."

Kevin thought Sum Taeyoung frowned. It was impossible to be certain as so much hair concealed so much face.

"I think such authoritarian judgements and decisions as demonstrated by your actions on this matter are a prime example of processes that in future you will bring to me," Ehouzou told Kevin before turning and holding a whispered conversation with Sum Taeyoung.

"That will be all," the self-proclaimed chairman eventually told Kevin who turned and walked towards the door. He was in the act of opening it when Sum Taeyoung spoke out again.

"Mr Forsythe. Before you leave us. I believe you know an Englishman called Gene Bond."

Kevin paused, hand still on the door handle. "To say I know him is something of an overstatement," he responded. "I've met him."

"You met him?"

"Yes."

"Where?"

"Here in Wandora."

"And do you know where he is now?"

Kevin's mind raced. Gene Bond had told him about his encounters with Sum Taeyoung and what a dangerous man this South Korean was. His initial immediate reaction was to tell Taeyoung nothing. But he, Kevin, had signed a variety of authorisations for Bond and Pete Turner to journey north and that surely would soon come to the attention of Ehouzou who would no doubt tell Taeyoung. Any cover up was futile and would compromise his own already fragile position and that would be unhelpful to Bond. The truth – or at least part truth – he decided was best.

"I believe he's heading towards the northern part of the country," he told them.

"Why's he going there?" asked Taeyoung.

"He's on an environmental and geological exploration with a young English geologist called Pete Turner," Kevin told them. He felt a sickness swelling in his stomach. He was seriously worried about the consequences of what he was saying but felt he had no option.

"How do you know this?" probed Ehouzou.

"I signed travel papers for them, as you know," Kevin answered.

Again the two men held a whispered exchange.

"This is," said Ehouzou, "clearly another example of actions which in the future will not happen without you conferring with me and seeking my approval. Is that clear?"

"Abundantly," Kevin assured his master – and his master too.

"You are dismissed," Ehouzou told him. Relieved it was over, Kevin completed the action of walking out of the room, closing the door behind him.

Chapter 32

Transcript
BBC Central African Correspondent
Nairobi

An extensive search has been launched for a leading British marine explorer missing after a mysterious explosion in the Gulf of Guinea. French-born but British-naturalised Marcel Bartoll was one of two men in a scientific submarine exploring the sea off the coast of Africa. The other was the German pilot of the vessel. Mr Bartoll is the founder of SNEL, the Southampton based marine research company that recently discovered an oceanic trench off the coast of Wandora. Samples of a previously unknown sea anemone found at the top of the trench indicated there may be significant pharmaceutical benefits from it. Mr Bartoll's latest expedition was seeking to bring back more samples.

A spokesperson for SNEL told us they had no idea what caused the 'substantial explosion' in the sea where their submarine was operating. So far, despite a large search programme involving boats and aircraft from many nations, there has been no sign of the submarine or the two men within it.

Chapter 33

With the abrupt ending to the telephone conversation with Kevin Forsythe, Joe Wright felt cut off and isolated. He now has no idea what is going on in Wandora. Though he can no longer speak to Kevin or Gene Bond, surprisingly and suspiciously he can make contact with his team in Nairobi. It supports his belief that some serious limiting control of communications has been applied in Wandora. Kevin and Gene's phones have, he suspects, been blocked or cut completely. However, any sense of delight in being able to talk to his people in Nairobi is short-lived. His request that he and his young companion be extracted out of their predicament hit an instant brick wall. He suggested if they crossed the river into Niger, could an airlift be better organised from there?

The answer was an emphatic no! He was told skirmishes between various terrorist groups had broken out across central Africa. ISIS, it seems, was squeezing other groups out of what they considered their controlled territories and disrupting established revenue streams especially those of illicit drugs and weapons movement. In the latest incident, six people had been killed in Burkina Faso's East Province when a police escorted convoy returning from the Boungou gold mine was ambushed. Four gendarmes and a civilian had died in the attack. Apparently the lead vehicle exploded after driving over an improvised explosive device after which unidentified armed individuals opened fire. The Burkinabé defence ministry was treating this as a 'terrorist' attack.

Whilst this was north and west of where Joe was, his office also reported similar action in the southern area of Niger, north of the River Oti. The whole area had become, he was told, "very volatile" and too risky to send any help to lift out Joe and his young companion. It was recommended he "evacuate to adjacent territories" and if he could do that then the situation would be reviewed.

The two of them had now been together for more than a full day and night. Talk between them was minimal though by now he knew her name to be Nakki and she knew him to be Joe. They had survived hidden in the desert, nibbling away at the high energy commando food Joe had brought with him plus what little greenery, berries and water Nakki could scavenge using skills handed down to her then developed on her own. When Joe first encountered her she was timid and half starved, a frightened little being still traumatised by what she had seen of the massacre of her family and the village community. The longer she was with the American the more a glimmer of confidence emerged from within her. From the outset it was obvious she was scared of everyone, Joe included, but as the hours passed and he tried talking with her, so her confidence flickered back into life.

Despite the advice from his office, Joe decided they needed to move north and to try to cross the river back into Niger where, hopefully, he might locate his Jeep. The cross country options east or west to adjoining nations seemed too formidable, especially with the young Nakki as an added responsibility. There was no road as such between the village and the river, more of a well-defined track established by the passing of vehicles. The only break in the monotonously sandy terrain was where the track crossed a short wadi, a rock-strewn depression in what could become a fast flowing tributary of the Oti in the short rainy season.

When they eventually arrived at the river at the point where Joe previously made his crossing, they could see on the far bank the wrecked remains of the long canoe-like ferry. Its charred hull still smouldered. Of the boatman there was no sign. Indeed, there was no sign of any life but as they explored the edge of the river the sounds of gunfire from the north became more regular. Some was not far away. Clearly the report Joe had had was unfortunately more accurate than he had hoped.

Heading back to Niger was now no longer an option. The borders to the east and west were too distanced to contemplate with the youngster now to care for. The mining village held no hope. The discovery of the arms and drugs cache meant they could not expect to be welcomed there. The thought of stealing a vehicle and heading south was quickly dismissed. They would not avoid capture for long. The only positive inkling of an idea was for them to somehow hide in one of the mineral trucks and journey that way back to Porto

Wandora. He had little faith in his plan and no idea what would happen next if they got to the coast. But apart from giving themselves up to the Chinese, he could not think of anything else. Had the Chinese mining operation been just that, he would not have hesitated in simply walking into the village. But knowing now that a large illicit arms and drugs dump was there changed the whole situation.

So they walked back across the desert towards the mining village which they approached after darkness had fallen. Joe found what he considered to be a relatively safe hiding point a short distance from the village and left Nakki, giving her, as best he could, strict instructions not to move while he was away. He prepared for a further visit into the village, leaving the gun behind but taking a knife. He wore black from top to bottom and, not for the first time, gave a mental note of thanks for the colour of his skin which helped him further merge into the darkness. With only the vaguest of plans in his mind, he headed closer to the village with the intention of watching the movement of trucks to hopefully identify an opportunity for the two of them to climb aboard one and gain a lift back to the coast. It quickly became clear that truck movements were significantly reduced during the hours of darkness but they certainly did not stop and Joe watched three vehicles arrive, load up and go on their way back to the coast. In between this activity the village fell back into a sleepy silence.

Because all the trucks had arrived from the south, when another vehicle entered the village from the north, passing close to where Joe was hiding, it took him completely by surprise. Joe immediately recognised it as an ex-military six-wheeled amphibious cargo vehicle. It was accompanied by an SDBI 4x4. Their arrival stimulated a buzz of activity around the building where Joe knew the arms and drugs to be. With a significant armed guard now present, the front doors of the building were opened and crates and sacks moved from within the building into the cargo vehicle. It took half an hour before the building was locked up again and the cargo carrier sent on its way – north again, another SDBI 4x4 leaving with it as some sort of escort. This was, Joe realised, the missing link. This was how arms and drugs were being transported through Wandora then further into Africa across the River Oti. He had wondered how they were crossing the river on the narrow, precarious and now wrecked ferry. Now he knew they were not. They had a quite sophisticated amphibious vehicle available to them.

With the two vehicles departed, Joe turned his attention back to the mineral trucks. Though security appeared to be pretty lax, there seemed always to be sufficient people around or close to each truck as to make the prospect of climbing into the back of one a highly unlikely prospect. Joe had just reached this depressing conclusion when a detail of uniformed and armed men appeared, this time not by the building with the arms cache but another one nearby. Why they had arrived was soon answered as two 4x4s entered the village at speed, coming to a stop in a cloud of dusty sand. The second bore the logo of SDBI. As they stopped, armed soldiers surrounded the first vehicle. There was much shouting and gesticulating which eventually encouraged two men to exit the front vehicle. Though he had never seen them before, Joe immediately concluded they were Gene Bond and the young geologist Pete Turner. His would-be rescuers were now themselves prisoners. Joe wondered when his rotten luck was going to change.

He watched as the two Englishmen were escorted under heavy armed guard into one of the administrative buildings. Whatever illicit activity was going on here, it was obvious to Joe that both the SDBI and the Chinese mining company were deeply involved in the arms and drugs cache and their movement into Africa. For more than an hour there was much coming and going to and from the building into which Bond and Turner had been escorted. It was now late into the night and eventually the village settled down into its routine, presumably allowing both captors and captives some sleep. Joe hoped Nakki was still safe and not too worried by his continued absence.

By the middle of the night the temperature had dropped to just belo rt w 20 degrees C. There was not a breath of wind and a star-filled sky ensured there was enough light to still cast shadows. Joe watched and waited, sometimes momentarily alarmed by the apparent closeness of animal noises which penetrated a night that was otherwise still and silent. That was broken each time the occasional truck arrived for another load of extracted minerals. Just one guard was positioned at the front of the building in which Gene Bond and Pete Turner were held captive, a giant of a man with wide shoulders and big torso and armed with an automatic rifle. He had a cartridge belt slung diagonally across his body and a pistol stuck into his belt by his left hand. He spent most of the time on a simple wooden chair by the front door, legs extended outward before him and body leaning back. To all intent and purposes he looked asleep. Joe doubted he was. Every now and then the man would rise from the chair, stretch, then take a short walkabout apparently more to exercise his muscles than to undertake any sort of security check.

This particular building had one window in each side wall but none at the back. So when Joe crept towards one of the side windows there was some risk the guard might spot him if on one of his walkabouts he chose to walk around the side of the building. It was a gamble but Joe waited until the man settled back in his chair after his latest walk. He made his way down the side of the building, hugging himself tight to the wall. On reaching the window he peered in but could see nothing except his own reflection. He tried to open it but, as expected, it was shut and probably locked. Joe tried a gentle knock on the glass, hardly audible. He wanted to draw the attention of those inside, not the guard. With a total lack of response he tried again, this time a little louder. Would the guard come? Or would there be a response from inside? He waited, nerves jangling, heart pounding. Then, at last, there was a face at the other side of the glass. He instantly recognised the man he thought to be Pete Turner who approached the window from inside with a mix of curiosity and extreme caution.

Joe breathed heavily on the glass then quickly used his finger to write backwards in the haze he had created.

"draug eht tcartsiD. thgirW eoJ m'I"

Turner hesitated a moment then disappeared. Joe wondered what he would do – if anything. To be ready to respond to whatever might happen, he crept along the side of the building towards its front corner, combat knife now in his hand. He dared a quick look to reassure himself the guard was still there, sitting in his chair, legs stretched out before him. A few minutes later he heard a groan from within the building, followed by another then another. Then the sound of someone heaving, then more groaning. Shortly afterwards he heard Pete by the front door trying to talk to the guard. Though the man had no idea what Pete was saying, it was fairly obvious from the accompanying gesticulations and the noise coming from within the building that Pete was asking for help because his friend was ill. The guard was standing now, facing Pete who remained inside the building but imploring the man to help. With no real response from the guard, Pete disappeared but was soon back dragging Gene Bond along who appeared to be near fainting and was groaning in some sort of pain. It was hardly an Oscar-winning performance but it was enough to encourage the guard to look more fully into the doorway, enough of a distraction for Joe to move swiftly round and thwack him on the back of the neck with a karate blow. The giant sank to the floor.

"Get him inside," Joe urged and Pete and Gene Bond, who had made a remarkably swift recovery from his apparent illness, responded. The guard was unceremoniously hauled into the building and the door shut.

"This has to be fast," said Joe. There was no time for any introductions. "No telling how soon anyone might spot the guard is not there."

"How do we get out of here?" asked Bond.

Joe scratched his head and embarrassedly admitted he did not know. "The best we've come up with is to try and get into the back of one of the mineral trucks. But I've watched a lot of them and there's always numbers of people close by. That was my plan A. Bad news guys is I have no plan B."

"And we have to go and get Nakki," he added as an afterthought.

Nobody said anything for a couple of minutes. It seemed to each of them like eternity. It was Gene Bond who eventually broke the silence.

"I've got an idea," he told them. "But I've no idea how to execute it!"

"Tell us later," it was not a suggtestion from Joe. It was an order. "We've got to get out of here now, before anyone misses the guard."

They crept from the village through the African night. Any concerns they had about a search party being sent out to find the perpetrators of the attack on the guard and the escaped Englishmen were unfounded. The people in the village were obviously also worried about searching the African scrubland at night where hungry animals searched for meals. The same thought was very much in the minds of the escaping group and they were thankful when they re-established contact with Nakki and set their temporary camp complete with a lookout roster. Once settled, they turned their minds to Bond's incomplete plan of action.

Chapter 34

In Marchwood, on the opposite side of the River Test to the city of Southampton, two companies sharing the same initials and located less than a mile and a half apart were adjusting to the consequences of the massive explosion offshore Wandora in the Gulf of Guinea. Marcel Bartoll's Sub Nautical Exploration Limited was struggling to reorganise after the tragic loss of its founder and leader while Gary Marchant's Southampton Nautical Expeditions Limited 2050 was getting nowhere in its ambitions to launch its cobalt hunting expedition.

In the aftermath of the mysterious explosion, an intensive air and sea search for the submarine and two crew members continued for two days without anything being found. Surprisingly, and a puzzle to everyone, there was the complete lack of any debris from the wrecked mini-sub. It – and the two men in it – had simply disappeared! Speculation as to what had caused the explosion was rife and mostly just imaginative. Nobody really had a clue. Divers who examined the area around the top of the Guinea Trench reported extensive damage to the sea bed and to the lip at the top of the Trench but there were no signs as to what had caused it or where the sub was. There was growing consensus to a theory that it, its crew and whatever had been the cause of the explosion had all sunk into the Trench and were now deep within it. As nobody had yet been to the bottom of the Trench there was no way of knowing what depths everything might have reached. For that theory to be explored a major deep-sea expedition into the Trench using highly specialist equipment was needed. It would involve seriously expensive resources. There were no signs of anyone rushing to put such an expedition together. Even the directors of SNEL reluctantly realised that such an expedition was way beyond their own capabilities.

As for what had caused the explosion, from the accounts of those who witnessed the way the sea erupted, it was as if a mine had been detonated. The prospect of the mini-sub encountering an old WW2 mine seemed implausible but was the best of a bad bunch of theories. There was even speculation somehow linking the disaster to the ever present and notoriously dangerous modern-day pirate activity prolific in these seas. How and why that might have happened also remained adventurously speculative.

Back in Southampton, Steve Oldbury was left trying to maintain some sort of business momentum. He was also the key person to whom anything related to the disaster was directed which meant fending off an initial fury of media interest. And then there were the difficult decisions and actions to be taken in organising something of a funeral event even though there was no body to dispose of. Lotty remained in hospital. She was still ill but also seemingly without any will to live. Lack of news about the fate of Marcel mortified her. The more time moved on the more everyone resigned themselves to the inevitable conclusion. Lotty's heart was truly broken. It was also very apparent to Steve that the corporate heart of SNEL had also been taken from them and though there was an avalanche of messages of condolence about the devastating loss of Marcel, business quickly started to drop off as the absence of the lynchpin of the company became fully felt. Still shocked at the loss of his friend, Steve also started to realise the future of the business was looking very doubtful.

At SNEL 2050, the day after the explosion in the Gulf of Guinea, Gary returned home from a hectic business trip to London to find Vanessa waiting for him in the most revealing of dresses and a bottle of champagne on ice. It was the first time he had seen her since the news from Africa that an explosion at sea had ended Marcel's expedition and Marcel was missing. As he walked into his apartment Vanessa threw her arms around him and kissed him with irrepressible eagerness. Despite any real reaction from Gary, her kiss lingered on. He could feel her sexually charged body hard against him, urging his response. But he was exhausted from a long and difficult day, the ever-present challenges of his troubled business, the continued pressures from Taeyoung, and now the news from the Gulf of Guinea. It all rested heavily upon him. He just wanted to collapse into a chair with a large whisky.

"Why the champagne?" he asked, eventually prising himself away from her kiss.

"Your mining project," she said, surprised he was not also in celebratory mood. "It can go ahead now. You've got the permit from the government and now any threat from Marcel's project is gone. I thought it a good reason to have some bubbly!"

Gary was dumbfounded. He was still getting used to the death of a man he had known for years and had worked with for so long. And he had been deeply involved in what had happened. It amounted to murder – and he had helped plan it! And Vanessa wanted to celebrate! As far as he was concerned it was another example of her lack of empathy and understanding.

While the days passed without any news of Marcel, his pilot or the mini-sub, the pressure started to grow on Gary to progress the exploration for cobalt off the Wandoran coast. Sum Taeyoung, his expectations flying high as the price of the mineral continued to climb on the world's markets, was applying massive pressure to get his expedition on its way. Gary Marchant's problem was that even though Taeyoung had, to Gary's surprise, secured from the Wandoran government a permit for the expedition and exploratory drilling of the sea bed within its territorial jurisdiction, essential suppliers were showing reluctance in supporting the venture until the aftermath of the loss of the miniature sub in the Gulf of Guinea died down. Not that Gary had a huge number of potential suppliers to go to. Companies with the ability to undertake marine seismic surveying and exploratory drilling are still few and far between in what is a fledgling industry. Those few specialist companies are concentrating their activities on parts of the world where the biggest deposits of iron, copper and rare-earth elements were thought to be – in the middle of the

Pacific, certainly not offshore Africa. Trying to encourage anyone to explore a prospect in Wandora's territory was proving to be extremely difficult – as Gary constantly reported back to Taeyoung.

In Wandora, most people were oblivious to the disaster that had occurred to the Gulf of Guinea Sea Anemone expedition. The military controlled the media throughout the country and the accident that had befallen the English explorers was further bad news Wandora could do without. So it was supressed. The very act of blocking the news stimulated some English journalists to try and pry further and, for a while, interest in what was happening in Wandora, now under military control, was rekindled. That there was an Englishman in a high-ranking role within the government was significant to reporters and motivated their curiosity. Kevin Forsythe's office fended off an initial barrage of enquiries. In the immediate aftermath of the tragedy Kevin posted a statement of regret and condolence but the government refused to comment further on anything to do with the incident.

Wandora's involvement with the search for survivors had been limited and was called off after a few days, as was that of everyone else. However the incident had put the country in an unwanted spotlight for a while and journalist interest rumbled on. Some were keen to understand how the country was now being governed post the death of the president, the departure from the country of the royal family, and the instigation of military control. For a while Kevin was well occupied in responding to the more determined members of an inquisitive media pack. He found his long experience in diplomacy invaluable. Ultimately, with no new developments from the site of the accident at sea, the lack of bodies and the continual news blockage by the Wandoran government, media attention fizzled out.

Taeyoung, of course, knew precisely what had caused the incident at sea though he was no wiser than anyone else as to the actual fate of Marcel Bartoll and his pilot. His only concern now was to see his own expedition make some progress and, hopefully, discover a cobalt seam in Wandoran territorial waters. Now the prospect of ongoing sea anemone harvesting had been killed off, and with a government permit in his hand, as far as he was concerned there was no reason for delay. The market for cobalt was rocketing. The quicker he could capitalise on it the better. So he became increasingly agitated when Gary Marchant kept reporting that, for one reason then another, assembling the expedition was taking longer than he had hoped.

"My patience is not unlimited," Sum Taeyoung warned the Englishman. "And you should seek to avoid the consequences of it becoming exhausted," he threatened.

Chapter 35

A few miles north of the mining village, Joe, Pete, Bond and Nakki lay under a starlit sky waiting for the arrival of their target. It was a calm and still night. Every now and then a wispy movement of air gently lifted sand dust from the ground, often in little spirals or miniature whirlwinds. Gene Bond thought the sheer depth of silence was phenomenal and made it impossible to judge whether the occasional animal noise was originating nearby or from a distance. He felt slightly sick with apprehension as the time to implement his plan crept slowly ever nearer. There was no sense of excitement in his anticipation, just a nauseating awareness that the fate of the four of them depended on whether his idea worked or not. He felt a slight irony that someone of his family name should take such a subservient, back seat role in simply looking after Nakki while Joe and Pete exposed themselves to real danger. But in matching tasks to be done against individual skills, he knew it was right. Anyway, it made a change from his previous, often precarious reluctant hero ventures involving Sum Taeyoung. It was time to let others be at the forefront of danger.

Pete Turner was certainly anticipating with massive trepidation the oncoming exposure to danger. He was perspiring freely in the relatively coolness of the night. It was sheer nerves. If he fouled up his role their plan collapsed.

Joe Wright now lay some distance from the others in a small shallow trench he had scraped out of the sand using bush branches as a tool. Now, like the others, he waited for the action to happen and prayed he had got it right and that what he lay in wasn't going to become his own grave.

"When the 4x4 stops it'll be the passenger that gets out," he had told the others. "It's standard practice. The driver stays put in case of trouble. If there is any he floors it and is away."

Earlier Gene Bond had sown the seeds of the plan.

"I think the hope we can all climb aboard one of the mineral trucks without being detected is highly unlikely," Bond had whispered to Joe and Pete in the hut where they had overwhelmed their guard and pulled his unconscious body into the building. "There's just too many people around each truck as they're loaded. We'd probably encounter the same problem at the other end – at Porto Wandora. I've been thinking a lot about this. I think it would be better if we could somehow hijack an SDBI 4x4. They fly around this country with impunity. If we could get hold of one we could drive unchallenged out of the country – maybe go east towards Benin. I guess that's the closest border unless we go north but Joe's already told us there's too much trouble in that direction."

The others looked at him as if expecting him to say more – to complete his solution. Joe was relieved that someone else agreed with his own conclusions – that smuggling themselves onto a mineral truck was an unlikely prospect to say the least.

"The bad news is I've no bloody idea how we make my idea work," Bond admitted.

Joe responded. "Whatever we're going to do we need to do it fast. But first we must get out of here now before someone notices the guard isn't on duty. Let's get out of here and go find Nakki."

They crept undetected out of the village and into the scrubland where Joe was relieved to be able to guide them in the semi darkness to where Nakki was still hiding. She looked pitiful, frail, vulnerable but big-eyed and with a smile that denied her frailty but clearly showed how pleased and relieved she was to see Joe again. She greeted him like a long-lost father, hugging him and settling down close to him. Joe did his best to introduce her to the others now with him and to explain who they were and what they were going to do next – such as he knew. It was not easy and he was by no means convinced she had a clue as to what was going to happen. It had been a long and tough night for them all and they settled down to get what sleep they could.

The following morning they gave more time to developing Bond's idea. "I've been thinking more about where we might hijack an SDBI 4x4 – or at least try," Joe had told the others. "I think I've got an answer. I don't know how often it happens but I suspect it's every evening. An ex-military six-wheeled amphibious cargo vehicle arrives from the north and is loaded up with all the guns and drugs that have been delivered into the village during the day. It then heads back north to cross the River Oti into Niger under the cover of darkness. It's escorted by an SDBI 4x4 which turns round when they get to the river and returns to the village. The 4x4 I saw do this had two men in it."

"Just south of the Oti there's a wadi. It's a rock-strewn dried-up river bed and vehicles have to slow to weave their way through. It's a weak point in their journey. I suggest we hit the 4x4 there as it heads back to the village."

"How? What do you mean by 'hit'?" asked Gene Bond.

"I've got a rifle and silencer with me. I could take out a front tyre as they cross the wadi. When they stop to change it, we deal with the crew."

"How?" Bond repeated.

"I haven't a fucking clue!" Joe replied, annoyed about the demands on him for details of a plan he was making up as he went along. "Give me credit for thinking it through this far!"

They talked the problem through over and over again until their plan eventually gained some shape and detail and tasks allocated. By late morning and with what little confidence they could muster they trekked off to the wadi where Joe instructed them to collect more small boulders and where he wanted them positioned. They were to be located in enough numbers to ensure the 4x4 was slowed but not too many as to make the trap obvious.

It took them until late afternoon to satisfy Joe. Then they hid and waited. They had no idea what time the cargo vehicle and its escort might come. Indeed, there was no guarantee one would come at all. As time monotonously crept on, doubts began to grow within each of them that the plan was going to work. It was dusk before anything happened. It was an enormous relief to them all when the first sounds of vehicles came to them. Shortly afterwards, an SDBI 4x4 with roof mounted spotlights blazing arrived with the bulky armoured amphibious carrier behind. Their speed had been limited by the bigger vehicle but still they slowed to a crawl as they reached the wadi and started to pick their way through the boulders before accelerating and disappearing out of site. Once they had gone, Joe and the others emerged from their hiding points, excited now that their plan was likely to work and the 4x4 would return soon. With much patting of backs and "good lucks" all round, they scattered back to the respective positions.

The adrenalin rush from the passing of the convoy soon dissipated and as time slowly ticked on, Pete Turner's anxieties grew. Had he made a mistake in telling Joe he was "quite good" with a rifle? Originally Joe talked about doing the shooting. But it quickly became apparent the American could not do everything. So the sophisticated gun now nestled against Pete's body. It was like nothing he had ever seen before let alone shot. It was true that rifle shooting was something he did every now and then. It was not often enough to call it a hobby. But he knew how to shoot and was normally way above average in his accuracy. Him taking on this role released Joe to spring stage two of their trap, the killing by knife of the driver. Pete could then shoot the passenger who Joe anticipated would have left the vehicle on the offside to walk round it to confirm the puncture to the nearside front tyre.

The planned sequence of events ran through Pete's mind time and time again. The responsibility lay heavily on him and the thought of actually killing someone was horrendous. He had not dared tell Joe he was not sure when the moment arrived he would actually be able to pull the trigger. He could hear Joe telling them what would happen.

"Gene. You look after Nakki."

"Pete, you shoot the front tyre."

"The vehicle stops. I approach it from behind, crawl down the side and take out the driver."

"As soon as I hit the driver, you shoot the passenger."

"Easy!" Joe had concluded.

As the evening wore on Pete became increasingly anxious. He had agreed to do what Joe had asked of him but only because there seemed to be no alternative. But saying he would do it and actually undertaking to shoot someone were two very different matters. As he lay waiting so his apprehensions grew. Would he be able to pull the trigger when the moment came to do so? Could he actually kill someone – end a life! Whoever he was to shoot – whatever he was – he was, when all said and done, a human being with a life of his own – maybe with a family somewhere. Pete was by no means certain he could do it. And as for Joe knifing the driver? He tried not to think about it.

But if this plan did not work, what else could they do? And lying behind a small mound of sand and earth away from the others, a loneliness and feeling of vulnerability set in alongside his doubts. As time passed, he felt he wanted reassurance the others were still nearby. It was ridiculous to think they would not be but his mind would not stop playing tricks on him, spurred on by his self-doubts as to whether or not he could deliver what he had been tasked to do. In his solitude, under the brilliantly star-studded desert night, fatigue finally got the better of him and he found himself nodding into sleep. Each time it happened he jerked back into alertness, worried stiff he might have missed the arrival of the 4x4.

When he actually heard the approaching vehicle it was miles away and long before it actually arrived. SDBI 4x4s had a reputation of driving at speed everywhere and this one was no exception though speed was relative to its environment. It was travelling far quicker than most drivers would have thought prudent as it picked its way through the desert scrubland in the soft light of the moon and stars, following the tracks established over time by the few vehicles that passed this way. Nowadays that was mostly the two vehicle convoys delivering arms into the rest of Africa. The noise from the high revving vehicle and the powerful beams of six spotlight swinging though the darkness meant that Pete Turner was well alerted to its arrival at the wadi where it slowed rapidly in a dust storm of its own making and started picking its way cautiously across the boulder-strewn dried-up river bed.

Lying on his stomach, Pete wriggled forward so he could just see over the low hump in the ground before him, rifle at the ready. He looked down its sights and established the 4x4 in the centre of the cross hairs. The vehicle had only just driven down the slight incline onto the dry river bottom and was now gingerly navigating round the numerous rocks and boulders some of which Pete and the team had deposited there only a few hours ago. He could see quite clearly there were only two people in the vehicle, just as Joe had predicted.

Now his moment arrived. He could delay no more. He moved the rifle so the front wheel was now dominating the view through the sights.

"Get the cross hairs at a point towards the front of the tyre," Joe had told him. "Steady yourself. Take a deep breath in and hold it. Then gently squeeze the trigger. Don't pull it. Just a gentle caress."

Pete found the trigger with his forefinger. He felt that somehow very reassuringly. Now he was ready to take the shot. He lined up the sights on the front edge of the tyre, took a deep breath and applied the slightest of pressure to the trigger. The rifle snorted and recoiled and the view of the wheel through the sights disappeared. In almost a panic, Pete regained sight of the vehicle and saw it slowing to a stop. Now he dared lower the rifle and look over the mound to see what was happening. In the middle of the dried-up river, the driver, obviously immediately aware that something was wrong but not totally convinced his tyre had punctured, slowed the vehicle to a stop. Again as Joe had predicted, the passenger disembarked from his side of the vehicle to investigate what had happened, an automatic rifle in his hands. Instantly Pete saw Joe run to the back of the 4x4, his body bent low. He reached the back of the vehicle as the passenger got to the front. Clearly, if the passenger moved round the corner of the vehicle he would see Joe. This was the part of the plan Pete utterly dreaded but the moment had come and he had to shake off all doubts and inhibitions. Joe's life and all their futures now depended upon him. He lifted the rifle into position again, found his target in the sights and aimed at the man's torso. For a second time the rifle jumped in recoil and momentarily Pete lost his view through the sights. He looked towards the 4x4 in time to see the passenger stagger backwards, blood pouring from his chest.

Pete rolled over in the sand and was violently sick. He was shaking throughout his body and his legs weakened. He thought he might pass out but he did not and the moment of faintness passed. He eventually summoned up enough courage to look back at the scene in the wadi. The man he had shot was now lying in front of the 4x4, his legs at a strange angle in his collapsed heap on the floor. The driver was also lying on the ground near the driver's door. Pete was thankful his moment of sickness meant he missed seeing Joe strike. It had been bad enough to shoot a man dead. To watch someone else slit another's throat would have been ghastly.

Joe called the others to him, Bond leaving Nakki where he had cared for her during their ambush.

"I'm not sure if the driver got a radio message off before I got to him," he told the others before suggesting that Pete and Gene buried their two victims best they could while he changed the wheel on the 4x4. They needed to head off as soon as they could.

The decision had been made. It was, they all agreed, pointless to head towards Porto Wandora. What would they do when they got there, if indeed they succeeded? So they headed east towards Benin but as Kevin Forsythe had told Bond and Pete, roads running west to east in Wandora are few and far between and that especially applies in the north of the country. So the three of them plus the young girl in their care, headed off into the half-light of a desert night and the savannah-like wilderness that is the largely uninhabited area of northern Wandora. It was, they reckoned, about 50 miles or so to the Benin border. Would they be able to cross unhindered into Benin when they got there? Or, maybe, if the driver of the 4x4 had made a radio call, could they expect to be hunted?

In the event it proved to be a relatively unadventurous drive. There was no chase. No helicopter gunships. No ambushes. Indeed they did not see a single person as they threaded their way east across the flat savannah. After less than two hours of monotonous driving and unchanged scenery, they at last encountered more fertile country with trees and bushes and a distinct track which became more defined the longer they drove along it. Dawn had come and gone and the new day was well established by the time they encountered increasing numbers of dwellings, mostly mud-structured and then, quite surprisingly, something resembling a sign post which said TANGUIETA.

"We're in Benin," said Joe with a sense of triumph in his voice. They drove on and eventually entered the town which, Joe told them from information off his phone, has a population of some 50,000 people. The fact his phone was working again was a relief to everyone.

Contact with the outside world had been restored. As soon as they were able they stopped and using the delay on the camera on Joe's phone, took a group picture of the four of them and sent it to Kevin with a message saying "Mission accomplished. Now in Benin. Speak soon."

Chapter 36

By sheer co-incidence, and before anyone became aware that one of the SDBI's 4x4s was missing, the day after the Joe and company's ambush, an assault group of heavily armed fighters in vehicles flying a familiar black flag attacked the Chinese-run mining village in north Wandora. Sophisticated, well-trained and well-equipped though the SDBI guards were they were significantly outnumbered and no match against the intruders though the battle for the mining village was intense and bloody on both sides and took a whole day before the ISIS brigade finally secured it.

The fighting was at its ferocious peak when news of it reached Porto Wandora. Minister Moussa Ehouzou heard about it at roughly the same time as the news got to Kevin Forsythe. Kevin was acutely aware that Gene Bond and Pete were on their way into that area to rescue Joe and the girl. He prayed for their safety. He had not heard from any of them for ages but knew that mobile phone services across Wandora had been cut by Ehouzou as a way of stifling any opposition uprising.

As soon as he heard the news, Kevin demanded an immediate meeting with Minister Ehouzou.

"Has the army moved against this new threat?" the Englishman asked his boss. There had been no niceties between them. No greeting. No handshake. There was a tension between them from the outset.

"Not yet," Ehouzou replied.

"Why on earth not?" This was alien territory for Kevin. In his entire career he would never have dreamt of talking to a superior in the way he was now doing. "You could assemble a fighting force from the armoured and infantry squadrons and back them up with tanks. I'm sure you could assemble far more firepower than the insurgents have."

Ehouzou thought before responding. "You know better than most that the army is scattered across the country helping in the rebuild after the tsunami. You should know. You're managing the process. We haven't the manpower to repel the intruders."

"Even Wandora can muster some firepower when it needs to," said Kevin. "You could use tanks and airborne commandos. It's not just a matter of individual numbers. You'd have far more firepower than they've got."

Ehouzou did not respond.

"So if you're not going to do anything, why not?" Kevin challenged. "Surely you can see we mustn't let ISIS develop a strong base in Wandora."

"But the village is in the northern territory," said Ehouzou.

"So?" responded Kevin.

His boss shuffled nervously. "Because the northern territory is not the responsibility of the army."

Kevin was horrified. He knew the reason. "Because of SDBI?" he barked back.

"Yes," responded Ehouzou in discomfort.

235

"Because of Sum Taeyoung," added Kevin as a statement, not a question.

"It's the arrangement we have agreed – as you know," Ehouzou muttered, now no longer looking at Kevin but at a spot on the floor.

"Because of your personal arrangements with the South Korean – and for whatever you're getting out of it," Kevin's anger was growing but he let slip this last comment and immediately regretted it. It was a step too far. It infuriated his boss.

"How dare you say that to me," Ehouzou shouted at Kevin. The Minister was going red in the face." Repeat that in front of anyone and you'll face severe consequences."

"But both you and I know it to be the truth." Despite his discomfort, Kevin was determined to probe further. "So what are you going to do? You cannot possibly just sit by and let ISIS secure a foothold position in the north. That's insanity! They'll spread everywhere. You've got to send the army in!"

"I'm considering it," responded Ehouzou.

"Well," said Kevin with much sarcasm. "May I recommend the Minister considers it with all haste!"

"You need to remember your position," Ehouzou barked back at him. "I'll handle this as I see fit. Recommendations from you I do not need."

"But you'll need Taeyoung's approval," countered Kevin. "He got you into this mess."

"What happens in the upper echelons of decision making of this country has nothing to do with you," Ehouzou retorted. Kevin had never seen him behave like this. Normally he was a passive, subservient little person. Of all the words that described Ehouzou before he became influenced by Taeyoung, the one Kevin thought mostly summed up his boss was – wimp. But Kevin had egged him into an explosive temper.

"Decision making is nothing to do with you. You are a civil servant. A servant! You just do what you are told."

And with that Minister Ehouzou trounced from their meeting leaving Kevin seething. The Minister did not need Kevin Forsythe to spell out the problem. It was blatantly obvious to anyone. And in any other circumstances he would have immediately ordered the army to respond. It was not a question of jeopardising the large fees Sum Taeyoung paid him. More it was question of staying alive. Taeyoung could not have been clearer. Obey and be rich. Disobey and die.

As it was, Sum Taeyoung was already thinking Ehouzou's future was in the balance. With more and more problems mounting on the South Korean, Ehouzou was proving to be little more than worthless. Taeyoung considered taking direct control but worried how much time that would consume. So, for the time being, it was prudent to let Ehouzou live on. While Kevin Forsythe was concerned about the political and security ramifications of the ISIS attack in northern Wandora, Taeyoung was worried that now ISIS had hit his arms and drugs dump his fledgling route into Africa was compromised. Fast action was needed. Supplies kept arriving at Porto Wandora but the trucks had stopped running. There was no point at all in just handing more and more arms and drugs straight over to ISIS. Fortunately the amphibious cargo carrier had not got caught up in the attack on the mining village and was now in hiding on the Niger side of the river. Mining had basically stopped which meant Taeyoung's fees from China had dried up, accompanied by demands from Beijing that SDBI fulfil its contractual obligations. The South Korean wished he could. Taking on ISIS was not something he had planned or budgeted for. It was, he admitted to himself, even beyond his abilities.

On top of the problems in north Wandora was a bigger irritation – lack of progress with the exploration planned to find cobalt off the coast of Wandora. As if to compound his frustrations, daily he read about the escalation in the price of the mineral. It was as if the opportunity was slipping through his fingers. He totally blamed Gary Marchant and wondered what to do. He had sent him messages. He had spoken with him. But the response was always the same. Assembling everything to explore the sea bed offshore Wandora was proving to be a slower than usual task – because of the aftermath vibrations of the mystery sinking of the SNEL sub. They kept reverberating throughout the industry. Stopping Marcel's project had seemed imperative at the time. Now, ironically, it was a serious hurdle.

With problems mounting in all directions, Sum Taeyoung wondered if it was time to cut and run from Africa? Wandora had been a perfect opportunity. Now it was becoming a liability. But the revenue from drug and arms dealing was enormous and the potential staggering. And the cobalt prospect was tantalisingly within grasp. It was time, concluded the South Korean, to start applying pressure.

Chapter 37

Pete Anderson's angry and frustrated thoughts were interrupted by the ringing of his mobile phone. He was driving his battered and dilapidated truck away from one of many similar meetings held across the DRC. With one hand on the steering wheel, the other held a much needed can of beer held in a somewhat scruffy and elderly VB stubby holder. If he could not drink his favourite beer at least the holder provided a reminder of his staple drink from his Melbourne home.

The event he was driving away from was held as part of a programme of localised consultations following the meeting in Midrand of the PAP's Committee on Cooperation, International Relations and Conflict Resolution, led by the World Bank. It was hoped to gauge how field operators of the many NGOs in the DRC responded to ideas from the Midrand meeting, especially those related to a new Great Green Wall to be built across the DRC. Based on the similar wall in the sub-Sahara, this would be a far smaller version albeit one that stretched right across the Republic and especially through the areas in which artisan mining is concentrated. It would, the meeting was told, bring together key delivery partners such as leading international charitable organisations, world-renowned benevolent individuals and businesses, universities and other research institutes, and the DRC government to create a co-ordinated delivery of low-tech renewable energy, water provision schemes, and affordable and fuel-efficient wood stoves for cooking.

The line-up of speakers came from the UN and the DRC government. They told the audience that the project would, over time, increasingly employ local people in its delivery and maintenance. A comprehensive training programme would be instigated aimed especially at youngsters. Ultimately a new economy would be generated which would provide an alternative income for those impacted by changes in artisan mining. As youngsters were taken out of the mining process, so they would be able to earn from this alternative employment. As for the mining and extraction of cobalt, the aspiration was to create secure and properly run supply chains with well executed contracts between the mineral's extractors and the world's automotive and IT companies which were increasingly clamouring desperately for the mineral. The eradication of child exploitation in the mining process was a priority objective of the proposed scheme. New licencing and control methods would, the meeting was told, seek to ensure proceeds from mining were not feeding corrupt organisations or terrorist groups but would be used to pay for the education programmes and subsequent re-employment of children currently dependent upon the mines.

Pete Anderson listened intently as speaker after speaker enthused about the plan and gave different perspectives about its delivery. Much was repetitive but there were a lot of vested interests in this idea and they all wanted to be seen to be involved. Despite their enthusiasm, authority and seemingly total conviction in the idea, what was said could not shake off Pete's cynical views. The plan was, he thought, riddled with problems starting with the biggest – corruption. But now he also had growing concerns about the activities of ISIS. Nothing had been mentioned about either in the meeting. He saw corruption as the proverbial elephant in the room. In his opinion and experience, Africa was diseased and riddled with corruption and until that was dealt with there was little or no prospect of achieving the aspirations of the PAP or the World Bank.

When it came to the open debate, Anderson, a man with a reputation for not holding back in saying what he thought, was one of the first to stand and speak. "There are too many interests – many of them severely corrupted – invested in the current situation. They'll ensure the proposed scheme won't work," he told the meeting and noted quite a lot of nodding and supportive muttered comments around the audience. "They won't let it happen. They will vigorously defend the status quo. They won't let anything divert revenue from their own pockets. You must tackle corruption otherwise your ideas will fail."

The lady from the World Bank tried to reassure him.

"The government of the Republic is one of the members of the multi-agency partnership committed to making this happen," she responded. "I hear what you are saying and it is obviously a concern to us all. But with the government's commitment and with the support of all the other agencies I'm convinced we can make this happen."

Anderson was quickly up on his feet again. "That the government has just raised taxes on mining processes shows they are singularly interested in only one thing. Money!" Again the audience reaction suggested his was not a lone opinion and he felt encouraged to say more. But nobody else stood and endorsed his viewpoint or took issue with the officials. Not being the authorised voice of the organisation he worked for, he felt he could not test the matter further. It was beyond his remit. And the ISIS issue was also too politically contentious. So he backed off and mentally kicked himself for doing so. He was, by not saying any more, demonstrating his own self-interests prevailed.

"You bloody hypocrite," he thought. "I'm as bad as all the others."

It was the ringing of his mobile phone that brought to an end his analytical thoughts about the meeting and his self-crucifixion. He could see the call was from his local base.

"We've a guy here," the depot receptionist was telling him. "A European. He's just walked in. Says he's looking for work. He's a bit odd. Not threatening or anything like that. Just a bit odd. Think you should see him."

Anderson drove on, reflecting back on the meeting rather than thinking about the telephone call. So when he walked into his office he had not thought at all about the man he was to meet.

"Hi. I'm Pete Anderson," he said, extending his hand to the man before him who wore jeans and a ragged sweater, had an unkempt beard and tangled hair and a weather-worn face. "Who are you?"

"I wish I could tell you," the stranger answered.

Chapter 38

He stood sipping his iced South African artisan gin cocktail looking out towards the sweeping bay with its silver sand, palm trees and rich blue sea and reflected that the contrast between this environment and his office in his home city could not be more extreme. One end of the lounge in the palatial suite in the Palm Trees Hotel, Porto Wandora consists of a picture window and balcony. It provides a phenomenal view of the richly colourful coast. Within the luxurious environment of the balcony he could relish the vision before him, smell the sea and an air filled with heady aromas from the nearby forest. He even delighted in the slight breeze that provided a freshness in marked contrast to the manufactured, sanitised, air-conditioned, cocooned environments in which he conducted most of his daily business.

His relatively small, practical and austere office with its one smallish window offers only a limited view of the concrete jungle that is the city of Seoul and the somewhat sterile River Han. Yet he felt some sort of yearning to be home and away from what was troubling him. Maybe he needed to go home. Maybe he was missing the double harmony tea which, when in Seoul, he consumes daily in the Flying Bird Tea Shop in the Insadong district. It was something of a religion for him to visit there every morning. He loved the quaintness of the strange establishment with its creaking narrow wooden stairs, rickety tables and chairs, knick-knacks everywhere, the pervading aroma of exotic teas, and the startlingly colourful little birds that have the run of the place. But most of all he believed his continued good health and long life would be more likely if he regularly consumed the tea room's infamous double harmony tea. Allegedly containing dried roots, ginger, ginseng, cinnamon bark, and other medicinal ingredients, its aroma, let alone its bitter taste, convinces most people of its potent powers.

Maybe, that was what was missing in his life. Or maybe it was time to turn away from Africa. Africa had dominated his business world now for perhaps too long yet the sheer size and scale of opportunities here were intoxicating. Few people realise the enormity of the place – bigger than China, India, the USA and most of Europe combined! A place of opportunity for sure but also a place often overwhelmed by corruption and with many of its 50 plus countries in disarray or permanent or semi-permanent conflict. It should have been the ideal environment for someone who proudly proclaimed himself to be a 'chaos entrepreneur'. For someone who harboured ambitions to add to his wealth by draining the income from mining cobalt from the sea bed, such wealth would make the frustrations bearable. His control over Wandora was beyond anything he had ever really expected to achieve but the country was desperately poor and in chaos. Cobalt would change all of that. Cobalt plus the revenue from using Wandora as an entry point to Africa for his drugs and armament trading and from the commission and fees from the Chinese when their mine was operating, made Wandora still an attractive if difficult proposition. It would not take much to achieve complete control of the country, to in essence privatise it to his total advantage. History had seen this before in Africa. King Leopold 11 of Belgium took personal ownership of the Congo in the late 1800s and exploited its rubber, copper and other assets. Sum Taeyoung thought he could do the same with Wandora. Ownership of the Congo had made King Leopold the biggest land owner in history. There was no way Taeyoung could emulate that in Wandora but it was, nevertheless, interesting to see a precedent in African history.

But all his initiatives here were currently experiencing challenges. It was very frustrating. The cobalt opportunity especially was niggling but one he would not abandon, not that he was accustomed to turning his back on anything he initiated. Sum Taeyoung had a reputation for making things happen – so long as they were to his advantage.

Analysing the troubles that were besetting him and identifying remedial actions, the South Korean felt there was still much to be gained from the position he had engineered in Wandora. It would not take much more to achieve total control. The ISIS attack on the mining village was more than annoying and a real setback. He had lost two revenue streams in one go – the commission from the Chinese mining operation and the fees the Chinese paid for protecting the operation. As far as the mining itself was concerned, as far as he knew all work had stopped. That was a loss not only for himself but for the Chinese too. It now dawned on him as he sipped his gin cocktail it was also a loss for ISIS. Its fighters had surely attacked the village with the hope of taking over whatever revenue streams the mines generated. If the mines were not now functioning because the Chinese had withdrawn after the attack, that negated any value ISIS might have hoped to have gained. Which gave rise to the idea that maybe a business approach to the local ISIS group might be a way forward? They would surely be interested in any proposition that generated funds for them. However, that could only relate to the mining operation. If he could do a deal, the Chinese would hugely welcome it and his fees would be reinstated, albeit shared with ISIS.

There was no way he would talk to ISIS about his smuggling activity. That was not to be shared – with anybody! What he needed to do – and do quickly – was find an alternative place south of the Oti for a depot. That was not going to be easy but he felt better having identified a course of action. Maybe there were some government facilities he could take over. He would talk to Moussa Ehouzou about it.

But cathartic analytical examination of the real sources of his unease, frustration and general negative disposition clearly identified cobalt and lack of project progress as being the principle reason for his dejected mood. Was there a seam offshore Wandora or not? The evidence from Black Bart's Bay was compelling. And the sky-high value of the stuff – and forecasted future demands for it, left it as a prize worth going for. Gary Marchant had seemed like the perfect delivery agent bearing in mind his diving experience and his knowledge of offshore Wandoran waters – and the discovery of the Gulf of Guinea Trench. But the man seemed incapable of delivering anything at speed. It was intensely irritating and irritation was not a state of mind Sum Taeyoung cared to tolerate.

He rolled the liquor round in the large crystal glass bowl and contemplated this source of annoyance. How could he influence Marchant? How could he hasten the project? What pressure could he bring to bear?

He walked into the apartment and to his study, sat at his desk and opened his computer. The file 'Gary Marchant' had no great content but as he browsed through it he came across a photograph and introduction to Vanessa Sambrook, apparently Marchant's assistant but who was, from various photographs and other material in the file, far more than that. The pictures, some taken at a distance on powerful telescopic lenses, showed the relationship between the two was significantly more than just business. There as a click through to a video taken from a hidden ceiling spy camera in a hotel in Spain showing the two of them naked, he on top of her and the two indulging in what was clearly not mere business activity.

Taeyoung pondered over the file and wondered. Was this a lever by which to speed up the cobalt expedition? Was it time to again call on the services of Janka Koldun?

Chapter 39

It had been Karl's violent 180 degrees turn of the mini-sub plus the particularly high speed currents around the Gulf of Guinea Trench that caused the torpedo not to hit its target square on. It was the nearest of misses and the weapon actually scraped their craft a glancing blow. A second later it was hitting the top of the Trench's cliff face over which they had just passed. It exploded near to but astern of the sub. A miss though it was, the effect was catastrophic. The intense explosion sent the mini sub hurtling forward into the opposite lip at the top of the Trench, hitting it with such force that the top of the craft split away from the bottom as its whole structure disintegrated. In moments such as these, fate often plays strange games and it did so on this occasion. The blast instantly shattered various elements within the sub, including the seat in which Marcel sat. Instantly unconscious from the impact of the crash and stunned by shock waves from the explosion, Marcel was thrown from the craft and caught in an upward surge of water and air bubbles. Meanwhile, what was left of the torpedo, vast amounts of rock from the top of the Trench, the distorted and broken wreck of the sub itself and Karl – still strapped to his chair – slid into the Trench in one mangled chaos and down into its fathomless depths.

Marcel was thrown around like a rag doll in a washing machine but eventually reached the surface where, though pretty well still unconscious, he instinctively gulped in air so as to breathe again. His seemingly lifeless body was swept along at speed by ferocious currents and appeared to be heading to a watery end out at sea when it was spotted by two men in a small, ancient fishing smack. It was the younger of the two who saw the lifeless body floating by not far away. He shouted to his father, pointing at what he could see. The older man saw Marcel but told his son to get on with the fishing. The argument that followed continued even while the younger man steered their small craft towards the floating body. Eventually, and with a great deal of reluctance from his angry father who saw this as an interruption to their vital daily work, they hauled the body aboard and propped it up against the deck house.

"If he lives we'll take him to land," the gnarled ancient fisherman told his long-suffering son. "If he dies, we'll throw him back again."

And with that they continued the essential daily toil of trying to catch a living from the sea, oblivious to the events that had brought Marcel to them though conscious of the couple of helicopters and a military aircraft heading west some way off their port side.

Rather than have Marcel with them when they reached their home port, the old fisherman decided to land him on a secluded beach. "If we take him all the way with us the authorities will know who brought him ashore," he told his son. "There will be lots of questioning. And more. It will take time. Nobody will pay us for that. Best we just get rid of him."

So they dragged Marcel across the sand and propped him up in the shade against a palm tree. The older man searched through Marcel's pockets, finding his wallet and some lose coinage. The wallet contained paper money which he did not recognise and which he discarded as he did the coins.

"Too much trouble to trade," he muttered to his son as the notes fluttered away across the sand. But he pocketed all the credit cards. Those there might be a discrete market for. He could find nothing else of apparent value and eventually threw the wallet onto the sand alongside the propped-up Marcel. They tried as best they could to make him drink some water before they departed, leaving a couple of fresh water-filled bottles with him.

It was hours later that Marcel started to regain consciousness. He was utterly bewildered and confused. After not moving for some time, trying desperately to understand anything, he gently tested his limbs to see if they were functioning properly. His head pounded and he wondered if it was damaged in some way. He felt his skull and could not detect any serious injury though there was a large lump. He could see he was lying on the edge of a forest and that to the left and to the right a silver-sanded beach stretched out as far as he could see, deserted in both directions. It curved round in a wide bay with the sea some way away from him but getting closer as the tide came in.

A wallet – he assumed it was his – lay open nearby close to two water bottles, one full, one open and partly consumed. He drank from the open one. The first question he failed to find an answer for was why was he where he was? He had no recollection of arriving on the beach. How did he get here? Where had he come from? How long had he been here? Slowly a far bigger question emerged. Who was he? He was startled to realise he did not know. As he lay there on the beach, however much he tried, nothing about his life before now came to mind. His memory had completely gone. He assumed the knock to his head must have triggered amnesia. He hoped it would pass quickly. The wallet lying open on the beach gave no clues. There was no maker's name – nothing. He stared at the only thing in it – a tightly folded picture of two people – a man and a little girl. He had no idea who they were and there was nothing written on the photograph or on the back of it to tell him anything. The few coins he found lying around were English. He found that strange. He was thinking in French and assumed he was French. So why the English currency? Why was there nothing in his meagre collection of belongings in French? The beach on which he lay was certainly not English. It was semi-tropical. Maybe Equatorial?

Puzzled and exhausted, he slid into more sleep.

It was early morning when he next woke. The sun was just appearing over the horizon out to sea. The day was still and virtually silent. The only signs of life were a few birds on the wing and one or two searching for food along the water's edge.

With some effort he stood and stretched. His legs were weak. He felt dizzy. He had to hold onto the tree for support. His head was pounding. He felt it again and found a considerable lump and an area of stickiness, presumably dried blood. He had no idea what had caused the damage or how he came to be on the beach. He guessed someone must have helped by propping him up against the palm tree. Presumably whoever it was also left the water bottles. But who? He had no idea. Maybe whoever it was didn't want to get involved. Perhaps they were afraid of becoming involved with the authorities. Perhaps they were the reason for him being here? Perhaps they had given him the lump on his head? So many questions. And no answers.

His pockets contained nothing but a comb, some coins – English – and a handkerchief. There was the wallet in the sand and he guessed whoever had brought him to the beach had looked through it for valuables. There were a few bank notes lying around – English but obviously of no value to those who had left him here.

He slept a lot under the palm tree. It was thirst and hunger that eventually drove him to move. Shocked at how very weak he was, it took him an age to stagger and crawl along the sand until he came to the outskirts of a village. Hardly surprisingly, villagers looked at him with great suspicion and his efforts to beg for food and water had very limited success. Though he had no idea what their native language was, most people he met spoke French to one degree or another. He thought of trying to find someone in authority – the police maybe – but one villager, a bit of a hobo, warned him this was not a good idea.

"You don't know if authority is friend or enemy," he said. "Keep away until you know."

It seemed like sound advice. So Marcel retreated into the forest.

The next few days saw him scrambling around the edge of the tree line, occasionally hitching a lift but to nowhere in particular and stealing and begging for food and drink. He slowly worked his way along the coast, avoiding big conurbations and by now realising he was in Africa. He did not know where. He did not know why. And he still did not know if officialdom was his friend or foe. So he avoided it in whatever guise it showed itself. Eventually he hitched a lift from an English-speaking driver of a truck parked in a forest café stop. The name of an NGO was painted on the side of the truck. It seemed to strike some accord with Marcel but he could not be sure. What he knew and what he did not know was a complete confusion to him.

"Where you want to go?" asked the driver.

"Anywhere," the stranger answered. "I need work. I need to earn. I need food and drink."

The driver hesitated. The man looked dishevelled, in bad need of a thorough clean-up yet the way he spoke – in English but with a distinct French tinge to it, hinted at someone who did not fit the image being presented. So the driver decided to give him a lift and to take him to his depot where his superiors could decide what to do with him.

When Pete Anderson met him he did not know what to think.

"I'm sorry. I don't know," the man said when Anderson asked him who he was. The Australian was taken aback. Nobody had ever said anything like that to him before. It was hard to know how to respond. So he led the stranger into his office, sat him down and fixed a coffee for them both.

"You'd better try and tell me what this is about," he said, settling into his chair and looking at the man who sat the other side of his desk. He had a bewildered look about him.

"I seem to have lost my memory," the man said. "I haven't a clue who I am or where I've come from – or how or why I'm here."

"Have you been to the authorities?" asked Anderson.

"No," the man was hesitant and nervous. "If you mean the police – someone suggested they would either not be interested or would lock me up as they didn't know what else to do with me. I didn't relish that prospect."

"What's the last you can remember?" Anderson probed.

"Em," the man ran his hand through his raggedy hair. "I can remember the last few days with great clarity and in detail. But nothing before that. The first I remember is being on a beach but I've no idea how I had got there or where I was. I had the clothes I was wearing and a wallet. Oh, and a few coins in my pocket. They're English and I obviously speak English. But, strangely, I think in French. I seem to have got a gash in my head and that may explain the loss of memory. There's a few more cuts and bruises around. So maybe I've been in some sort of accident. But where? And how?"

Anderson asked if he could look at the man's head and sure enough found a large gash matted with dried blood. It could well have sparked the insomnia.

"How did you get from the beach to here?" Anderson asked. "And why are you here?"

"It's all a bit fuzzy – a bit, er, déroutant," the man shrugged his shoulders in apology for slipping into French. It was, Anderson thought, a very Gallic gesture.

It was a strange story and Anderson was not sure how to respond or how to help. The next port of call surely had to be the police to see if they had any missing person notifications that might be this man.

"What's in the wallet?" he asked.

The man shuffled on his seat and retrieved it from a trouser pocket. He handed it over to the Australian. It was brown and folded into two halves.

"Mind if I look?" Anderson queried.

"Help yourself," the man replied.

There was nothing in the compartments in which money would normally have been stashed and the credit card section was empty.

"No credit cards?" Anderson commented.

"No. I guess if there had been any they've been stolen."

Anderson opened the wallet. There was a crumbled piece of paper. He took it, unfolded it to reveal a picture of a man and a girl.

"Who are they?" he asked the stranger.

"I haven't a clue," answered the man.

"But it could be a clue," Anderson suggested. "Mind if I circulate it?"

"Help yourself," said the man.

"Wouldn't hurt if I sent a photo of you with it," Anderson added.

"Whatever," the man replied.

Chapter 40

The weather across the Solent estuary had been particularly vile for some days, thick grey clouds overhead, gusty winds off the sea and squally rain that was lashing when it arrived. Everything and everywhere – even everyone – looked grey and miserable. Vanessa Sambrook normally relied on Gary Marchant for her transport but reverted to taxis when he was not available. She did not have a driving licence having given up trying to pass the test after her third failure. She was good business for taxi services around the Solent estuary and she had got to know many of the drivers by first name. Without exception, they were all only too willing to chat to the vivacious, curvaceous, attractive woman who seemed to attack every day with huge gusto, enthusiasm and energy whilst exuding a sensuous personality.

Her monthly shopping spree always culminated in high tea. And for Vanessa this truly meant high because the ritual was conducted with friends in the tea room of The Spinnaker Tower, the 170 metre high observation tower in Portsmouth. That meant a round trip of more than 60 miles up and down the M27 – welcomed business for taxi drivers. And, routinely, on finishing tea and saying farewell to her friends, before she entered the lift she phoned for a taxi and hoped she would not have to wait long for it once she reached ground level. On this occasion it was a good five minutes before a car arrived. She did not recognise it or the driver and noted he was conspicuous in his lack of conversation. Eventually she also noted the glass or Perspex divide between the front of the car and the rear, something she was accustomed to seeing in black cabs but not in private hire cars. She assumed it was nothing more than a security precaution. She settled back and tried to relax, reflecting on the recent tea with her friends.

When the car turned off towards Woolstow rather than crossing the River Test as she expected, alarm bells started to ring within her. Wherever they were going they were the wrong side of the river to Marchwood. The first inclination was to say something to the driver but now she realised that, as distinct from the divides found in black cabs, this one had no holes in it, no way for the passenger to talk to the driver or vice versa. She looked for any sort of intercom. There was none. She knocked gently on the glass divide. No response. After three attempts she tried hammering the glass with her fist. She could see the reflection of the driver in his rear mirror. He was clearly looking at her every now and then and knew perfectly well she was distressed and seeking some sort of response from him. But he did nothing. Indeed, there was even the suggestion of something resembling a smile though it could easily have been interpreted as a smirk. Whichever, it revealed a mouth short of several teeth. If it was a smile it certainly was macabre and only accentuated Vanessa's growing panic.

She reverted to hitting the glass screen with a shoe but that only resulted in the heel snapping off which added to her distraught, now tearful and near-frenzied state. Without thinking of the consequences of flinging herself from a moving car, she pulled on the door handle to open it. But it was locked. So was the door on the opposite side. She was well and truly trapped.

In driving rain and the half-light of a late afternoon prematurely darkened by the thick black clouds, the car drove into an area she had never seen before, an old and abandoned dockland of narrow, unlit streets and mostly derelict buildings but with early signs of site clearances preparatory to new development. The car slowed alongside a tall security fence and the driver sounded the horn twice. Nearby two men flung open a double gate and the car drove through into a small compound and on into a dilapidated garage the doors of which were closed as soon as it had come to a stop.

A terrified Vanessa was hauled from the back of the car kicking and thrashing about as much as she could. Her screaming and shouts were abruptly ended when a wide tape was stuck over her mouth. She was part carried, part dragged into a room lit by a single bulb hanging from the ceiling. She was quickly tied with rope to a simple wooden chair and the tape across her mouth painfully ripped off. The room, she could see, was once an office but had obviously not been used for some time. A few wooden chairs stood around the place on a threadbare, colour-faded and dusty carpet. There was one small table, again a simple wooden item, with a black bag on its top. Four men, burly, with virtually bald heads, all wearing well-worn donkey jackets and jeans, did nothing to hide their identities. When they spoke, unless it was to her, it was in a foreign language she did not recognise. She was never to know that these were Janka Koldun's men who roamed across Europe doing dirty work for people like Sum Taeyoung.

Vanessa was exhausted from her fight with the men who had carried her here from the car. She was terrified. For most of the time she kept her eyes tightly closed in some form of defence. She was close to fainting. Of the four men, one she recognised as the driver. But it was another who seemed to be their leader. He pulled the small table close to Vanessa and grabbed her hair, pulling her head back so she was forced to look at him. She could smell his vile breath. It was repulsive.

"So pretty," he said softly to her in English but with a pronounced accent. "So sexy!"

He laughed and ran his hand over her breasts. He said something in his own language to the other men and they laughed. She kicked out at him, catching him just below the knee bone. He yelped at the sudden pain and slapped her across the face with such power she was sent flying, chair and all, onto the floor. She was quickly hauled back to a sitting position, one side of her face reddened from the slap and blood now trickling down from a wide cut.

One of the men quickly bound her legs to the chair to stop her lashing out again.

"Now, little lady," the leader of the group said to her, his face close to her. His breath filled her nostrils. It was utterly foul. She felt as if she would heave. "No more nonsense. We need a piece of you to send to your boyfriend. He needs to be encouraged to work harder for us. So we send him a bit of you."

Eyes big in terror, she looked back at him in horror.

"But what bit?" the man pondered as if enjoying and savouring the moment. "A tooth maybe? A finger?" He turned to the other men. "What do you think?"

And then back to Vanessa. "And, of course, if your boyfriend – he does not respond. We send him another bit – maybe tomorrow."

He looked long at her as if undecided what to do. Then, mind made up, he felt into the bag on top of the table and pulled out a large knife and a wooden mallet.

"A finger, I think," he said.

Vanessa fainted.

The A5 sized brown envelope was delivered by hand to Southampton Nautical Expeditions Limited 2050 and marked private and confidential for the attention of Gary Marchant. He slit open the envelope and shook out its content. Out fell a note and a photograph of a battered and bloody Vanessa tied to a chair, her head held up by a burly figure behind her and her clothes in shreds. And then there was the finger – incongruously with painted nail. At first his brain refused to comprehend what he was seeing. Time froze as the whole sickening reality took seconds to sink in. When it did he dropped the envelope in horror and vomited across his office desk. He gulped for air and grabbed a nearby beaker of water, downing its contents and spilling some down his shirt. His head was swimming. His legs felt weak. It took a while to regain enough composure to eventually read the note. It said;

"This is an incentive to accelerate the progress of the cobalt expedition in Wandora. This can be delayed no longer. The expedition vessel must arrive at Porto Wandora seven days from now. It will then leave for test drilling eight days from now. You will advise your client when these actions are happening. If you do not, you will receive more body parts. You will text the number at the bottom of this note to confirm you have read, understood and agreed to the actions demanded. If we do not receive such a text another body part will be despatched tomorrow. Also be warned we will know if you take this matter to the police. Be assured if you do you prejudice the life of the asset we hold."

Gary pushed the note to one side. He could not look at it any more. He strode up and down his office in anguish. "What to do? What to do?" The question kept repeating. The image of the battered Vanessa was etched onto his mind – as was the finger. "How could people do such a thing?" "Who were they?" "Where were they?" "Poor, poor Vanessa." His thoughts were in a whirl.

The one team in the UK with the capabilities of providing what he needed had not long returned from another expedition. They had quoted for the Wandora cobalt expedition. It was very pricey and their turn-round time from their previous project to a new one was at least two weeks. They had quoted only yesterday!

He picked up the phone and stared at it – as if it would provide answers. He thought of phoning Sum Taeyoung. He had a number. But what could he say. There could be no clearer signal. The South Korean needed action, not a telephone call. There was no action Gary could report.

He could say nothing the South Korean wanted to hear. And unless he said something possible – something tangible – poor Vanessa would suffer more. After much pondering he phoned Ken Burlington, CEO of the UK company that had quoted for the Wandora project. He spoke to Burlington's secretary and in a garbled way virtually demanded a meeting that day. The secretary, bemused by both Gary's manner and his disjointed conversation, tried to say her boss was unavailable. But that only accentuated Gary's eccentric call which now had a clear element of desperation about it. His sheer persistence won the day and late that afternoon Gary met Ken in the latter's offices in Plymouth but not before he had sent a text confirming he had received the message from Vanessa's kidnappers.

Ken Burlington was greatly puzzled by the man before him. They had met before and Ken had assessed Gary as being a smart, determined, perhaps arrogant and ambitious business man. From his initial assessment he did not necessarily like him. Now the man was standing before him and blabbering like a maniac. He was having difficulty in stringing a coherent sentence together.

"The expedition. It must arrive in Porto Wandora seven days from now," Gary told him. He had not even said their quotation had been successful. "It then needs to leave for diving eight days from now."

Utterly confused, Ken Burlington did not want to prejudice winning the order but some practicalities had to be acknowledged.

"We said in our quotation we could not assemble an expedition for at least another two weeks."

"I know. I know. I know," Gary Marchant was agitated, almost incoherent, and had all the makings of a man in the middle of a nervous breakdown. "I can't wait. The timetable – it's not mine. It's how it has to be."

"Then I am truly sorry, Mr Marchant, I don't think we can help you. Your demands are beyond our practical capabilities," Ken Burlington told his visitor.

Gary leant over Ken's desk and grabbed his hand. "I can't wait. It's got to happen. I'll pay whatever you want. I've nobody else that can help me. But we have to be in Porto Wandora in seven days."

Ken extracted himself from the other's grip. "What's causing this pressure? Are you under some sort of threat?"

Gary stared back at him, big-eyed, a dribble of saliva trickling from the corner of his mouth. He looked demented. "You've got to help me! Please!"

Ken did not know what to say. Did he actually want to do business with someone so deranged?

"It's a matter of life and death," blurted Gary.

Ken was taken aback. "What do you mean? Whose life?"

Gary wished he had not said that. But he had and the cat was now not quite out of the bag. "I can't say any more."

"If you're under some sort of threat perhaps you should go to the police," Ken suggested.

"No! No!" Gary pleaded. "No police."

There was a short silence between them before Gary almost whispered "I just need your help."

Ken Burlington's mind was racing. The Wandora project had been of great interest to them. Coming in straight after another major project it would be welcomed new revenue. But there were serious practicalities and his mind raced to consider them one by one. None seemed insurmountable. By throwing more resources at the turn-round it could be done quicker, even potentially quick enough to meet Gary Marchant's demands. But it would cost and he needed some guarantees, especially from a man who looked totally out of control and hardly in a position to make serious business decisions.

"The cost will go up and I will need 50% of the bill up front and in cash," he eventually told Gary.

Gary looked at him as a drowning man might look at an arriving lifeguard.

"We can do that! Yes, we can do that."

Ken Burlington was unsure if Gary was offering an answer or trying to convince himself he could meet his demands.

"50% cash up front," he underlined to Gary.

"Just a minute," Gary said. "Just – just wait a minute." His flustered brain was trying to think out the consequences of what he was saying. He was saying yes to Burlington but in reality had no idea where he would find the cash. He had none. There was nothing in the bank. The business was close to being bust. It had no materialistic assets he could sell.

"Just a minute," he said again and busied himself on his mobile phone. First a text. Yes, that would be quickest – he hoped. If Sum Taeyoung wanted fast action he would have to pay for it. Only the South Korean's money could save Vanessa.

Chapter 41

Cobalt! The children Bond and Pete saw scraping the stuff from the ground. The Mandella quotation – "There can be no keener revelation of a society's soul than the way in which it treats its children." Despite his mind overburdened with daily pressures, Kevin Forsythe could not shake these things from his head. However much he did not want further loads on his shoulders, he seemed not to be able to stop thinking about the much sought after mineral.

In rare moments of escape from his now daily grind of work, he increasingly wondered what the hell he was doing in this godforsaken corner of Africa. In total disarray were his dreams of gentle days sipping cocktails on silver sanded beaches whilst occasionally giving instructions to subordinates who would keep the ship sailing in the right direction and ensure a flow of income, enough to pay for the lifestyle he deserved.

In reality, the amount of work piled up day by day. Managing all the clean-up and rebuild after the tsunami was a prodigious responsibility made more difficult by the lack of a proper civil service structure, administrative backup or even staff of any sort. Of the latter, considering the tasks confronting him, the number of people allocated to him was quite pitiful.

The army, NGOs, the UN, the US army and navy, contingents of volunteers from all over the world, specialists in this, that and the other, Wandora's own army of workers – all looked to him for direction and instruction. It was as demanding and taxing a role as any in his long career as a civil servant. And for whatever reason – maybe because people could find no sensible alternative – he increasingly became involved in activities outside his portfolio of responsibilities. Health and medical, food provision, even security and general policing – all somehow seemed to find their way onto his chaotic desk.

"Chaos is come again." The quote from Othello was almost right. But the truth was, chaos had never gone. Chaos in Kevin Forsythe's world had become the norm. He hated it.

Now he was also a politician – so called – and a member of the elite committee managing a country under military control. How, he pondered, had he got himself into this crazy mess? Why did he not just walk away from it?

"To be or not to be?" To stay or go? To some degree he felt trapped. Home? Shakespeare again came to mind – "I rather would entreat thy company; To see the wonders of the world abroad, Than, living dully sluggardized at home, Wear out thy youth with shapeless idleness." To Kevin, shapeless idleness was becoming quite an attractive proposition! Oh to be at home and sluggardly!

In his office, pandemonium continued to prevail as much as it had done when Pete Taylor had tried to talk to him about a stone he had found. God! That seemed like a lifetime ago. He wondered how the young geologist and Gene Bond had got on. He was worried about them. Had he not missed a telephone message from the latter reporting they had escaped northern Wandora and were now in Benin his fears for their safety would have been relieved. Their message – in a stack of messages waiting his attention – said they were now waiting instructions from Joe's lords and masters and would let Kevin know as soon as possible what they planned to do. Such was the turmoil of daily life, not only did Kevin miss the message from Benin but he also failed to see an incoming email from Pete Anderson in the Congo.

Minister Moussa Ehouzou continued to be a pain in his side though, thankfully, was away from the country at an international conference in Montreux. Out of curiosity that bordered on being mischievous, Kevin's discreet detective work found the event lasted a mere three days which raised a question – unasked – as to why the Wandoran Minister was going to be in Switzerland for virtually a month – no doubt in luxurious accommodation and all that went with it. Prior to his departure, Ehouzou had been particularly bothersome, pestering Kevin about what depot-like facilities Wandora had in the north. Why he needed to know Kevin had no idea. He thought of asking but when he did Ehouzou avoided the question and demanded Kevin provide an answer.

"Buildings and such assets come within your jurisdiction," his boss reminded him.

"Diminutive little shit," thought Kevin and asked one of his team to divert from important tsunami work to research an answer for the Minister.

That ISIS had a foothold in Wandora continued to niggle at the Englishman. Why it should so bother him he had no idea. It was not something he should get concerned about but he could not help doing so. It was a dangerous situation and should be nipped in the bud. But Ehouzou would have nothing to do with it. Clearly Taeyoung instructions prevailed.

And then there was cobalt. The application for a research expedition offshore Wandora had been granted and now there was daily pressure for the venture to start. That included a request for space at Porto Wandora for the main expedition vessel but also an array of secondary craft of one sort and another plus shore space to accommodate things like provisions as they were assembled and prepared. That alone was a challenge because the port was becoming crowded, the latest problems being imported goods from SDBI which normally would be shipped north but because of the difficulties up there were now accumulating around the harbour.

Meantime, Kevin's interest in the mineral continued to increase. The latest report he read had a headline – "Cobalt prices are up 148% over last year. Might just be getting started." The report, from PRN Newswire in Palm Beach said; *"In the past 8 months, the electric vehicle conversation stopped being about whether or not Tesla Motors had the ability to scale, and started being about how the legacy companies are going to supply the growing EV market that Tesla opened up. Audi, BMW and General Motors are adjusting to put themselves in position to keep up with a changing auto market and are causing the undersupplied cobalt market to undergo a shift of its own. Runaway cobalt price (+148% Trailing Twelve Months) is fueling an aggressive push to create new supply. Companies like First Cobalt, Pacific Rim Cobalt Corp., Lithium Chile(LITH), and Katanga Mining continue to explore potential cobalt sources. The demand from automakers is expected to exceed the increasing supply."*

"The supply deficit in the cobalt market that is being brought on by the EV scale-up is causing a runaway cobalt price similar to the lithium supply crunch that came early on when the EV boom was just a market projection."

There was no doubt about it in Kevin's mind. If cobalt was found in Wandora territorial waters it could transform the nation's teetering economy. But that assumed the revenue would come into the country and with Sum Taeyoung's involvement that was by no means guaranteed. The South Korean was the common denominator to the three significant and strategically important problems – the control of the nation through the Administration Committee, the mines of the north now in ISIS hands and the offshore minerals exploration.

How he wished he had Pete and Bond here in Porto Wandora to talk to. And now there was Joe. Joe's advice and guidance would be invaluable. With an inkling of an outrageous plan in his mind which he kept putting aside because it was too audacious, Kevin turned to someone else he knew, not well, but well enough hopefully to test some ideas. Adrian Rego, a major in the army's armoured division, was born in Wandora but of an English mother. Largely educated in England, he did his military training there. On the few occasions Kevin and Rego had been together, Kevin found him to be a very likeable and straightforward sort of man. Kevin decided to invite him to lunch.

Adrian Rego was taken aback to receive an invitation from such a senior person as Kevin Forsythe but was keen to accept and find out why he had been invited. It did not take long. Kevin was keen to get to the point.

"I've been thinking – and worrying a lot – about the ISIS situation in the north. I'm very concerned. They now have a foothold in the country. Unless they're stopped they'll spread further and further south and eventually arrive here in Porto Wandora. That would be catastrophic. In my mind it's a problem that should be nipped in the bud – now, so as to speak."

Major Rego nodded in sympathetic agreement.

"I've talked to Minister Moussa Ehouzou about this but to no avail. I've suggested an attack by us using what heavy weaponry we could bring to bear should be more than a band of ISIS bandits could cope with. What is your view of that?"

"With tanks and artillery support it's something we should be able to do," the major agreed.

"What about air support?" asked Kevin.

Major Rego shrugged his shoulders. "If only. The Wandora Air Force has no strike power. And all its resources are currently involved in the aftermath of the tsunami."

"Could tanks and artillery be brought to bear on the ISIS insurgents quickly – say within the next two weeks?"

"I don't see why not," the major responded.

"It's all much as I thought," said Kevin. "But Ehouzou seems to have an agenda that stops anything like this happening. I can only guess what that might be and I'd be shot for treason if I said what I thought – even though I've more or less said it to his face. So, if I can be frank and open with you, I've an idea."

Kevin was fully aware of the risks he was taking. If Major Rego reported this conversation to Moussa Ehouzou, Kevin's time in Wandora would be at an end. Indeed, so might his life! But carefully he opened his thinking to the young major, testing his reactions as he progressed. He had, it quickly became apparent, found a sympathetic ear. Indeed, the young major revealed there was much unrest within the armed forces. That was significant intelligence for Kevin and he mentally filed it for use in the near future. His plan, he told Major Rego, capitalised on Ehouzou being out of the country, living it up at the expense of Wandoran tax payers. And though Kevin was unsure what the ultimate outcomes might be from the actions he was promoting, they would, he was utterly confident, send a cat running among the pigeons.

It was late afternoon when Major Adrian Rego left Kevin's apartment. Kevin, his mind still racing with the embryonic scheme he had shared with the young military man, poured himself a stiff drink, settled down in front of his computer and decided to spend some time catching up on emails. Two of them would change his life!

Chapter 42

The immediate reaction from Sum Taeyoung to Gary Marchant's plea for cash – a lot of it and immediately – was to ridicule the request and instruct Janka Koldun to send another body part to accelerate the cobalt seabed exploration. But on further reflection he concluded that Marchant was only responding to the pressure being put on him. If cash was the only thing needed to kick-start the expedition, Sum Taeyoung had succeeded in doing what he had set out to do.

He sent a text message back with a chilling kick in its tail.

"Provide bank details and the necessary cash will be transferred immediately. Our guarantee will be held until the expedition has left Porto W and will be returned to your safe keeping only if you have complied with our requests. Meantime, failure to do so will result in more parts being delivered."

A relieved Gary immediately contacted Ken Burlington who confirmed that if money was in the bank that day or the day after, he would ensure the cobalt seabed mining expedition was ready to go from an operational base on Porto Wandora within seven days. A thankful and relieved Gary sent a text to Sum Taeyoung assuring him that his deadline was going to be met and pleaded that no further harm be inflicted on Vanessa. Despite his reservations and irritations about her, Gary was horrified by what had happened and desperate to see her safe release. Now he was torn between flying out to Wandora or staying in England to ensure Vanessa's safety. In the end he concluded he could do nothing to directly help Vanessa – he did not even know where she was – but needed to be on location with the exploration team to ensure they complied with Taeyoung's demanding timetable. So he arranged to fly out the following day and booked himself into the Palm Trees Hotel in Porto Wandora.

Chapter 43

Two messages he had not answered were to have a momentous impact on the future life of Kevin Forsythe. One was an email, the other a missed telephone call from Joe Wright. The email, from Pete Anderson, set actions rolling that were to influence chains of events in Africa, the UK and South Korea. But it was the second message that was of truly monumental proportions. It came from a source he did not recognise. It simply asked Kevin to urgently find a 'secure telephone line' and to phone a number he also did not recognise. Puzzled, more than a little suspicious, and very cautious because he smelt a trap, Kevin put the phone call aside for further consideration.

Pete Anderson's message attached photographs, one of a man and a little girl and the other of a man who seemed to be peering vacantly at the camera. In his message Anderson asked if anyone knew these people. Kevin was dumbfounded to see the photo of Joe and Nakki. He had, of course, seen it before. Indeed, a little while ago he had sent it on to a few other people. His mind drifted back to when that happened and he checked back to see to whom he had sent it. Slowly, very slowly, Kevin Forsythe began to put two and two together and, through a process of ellimination, came up with a startling conclusion, so startling he initially disbelieved his own logic. Of the very few people to whom Kevin had forwarded the photo one had been Marcel Bartoll. He could account for everyone else to whom he had sent the photograph. Only one could now be with Anderson. Marcel! But he was dead – or at least had long been considered dead after the explosion at sea and the disappearance of the submersible craft he was in. His body had never been recovered. No bodies had been found. Now Kevin looked at the picture of the man. According to Pete Anderson this copy of the photo came from the man without a name who was now with him. Incredulous though it might seem, was this, he wondered, the missing Frenchman? Not having met Marcel he could not immediately tell. But a quick Google took him to Marcel's LinkedIn page and his obituary. And there, staring back at him from his computer, was Marcel Bartoll, the same man as in the photo Pete Anderson had sent!

Shocked at his finding, he quickly emailed the Australian.

"I think the man you have with you is Marcel Bartoll who has been missing, presumed dead, since an explosion off the coast of Wandora some weeks ago. If you Google his website you will see I am right."

And then there was the second message. Warned he needed to find a secure telephone line upon which to respond, and despite inner cautions that this might be at best a fairly harmless scam or worse a career or even life-ending trap, after much deliberation Kevin turned to his new ally and confidant, Major Adrian Rego. Rego was only too pleased to try and help and invited Kevin to use a military phone he believed to be as secure as anything could be in Wandora.

Kevin thought he recognised the voice that answered but could not bring to mind who it was.

"Please confirm you are Kevin Horatio Forsythe."

Horatio! Kevin nearly dropped the phone in shock. He never – never – used his second Christian name, embarrassingly hoisted upon him by his highly patriotic parents. He never used it under any circumstances.

"Yes," he confirmed almost shyly but with considerable uncertainty as to who could know this well-kept secret.

There followed a short, concise but positively explosive conversation that amazed, humbled and severely frightened the Englishman in equal measure. Never in his wildest dreams would he ever have expected to have become central to a plot such as now entrapped him. Any hopes that life might become more peaceful were blown asunder. Living a 'dully sluggardized life in shapeless idleness' was, indeed, wishful thinking!

Still reeling from the shock of the call, Kevin decided to take advantage of Major Rego's hopefully secure line to phone Joe Wright back to find he and Bond, Pete and Nakki were still in Tanguieta in Benin. Joe was distraught at the news the US Embassy in Nairobi had been closed as a precaution against the threat of an attack from an ISIS splinter group. His natural reaction, he told Kevin, had been to return to his base with Bond, Peter and Nakki. But he was told by his seniors that it was important to trace the source of the supply chain of drugs and weaponry apparently entering Africa via Wandora. He, Joe, had little idea how to tackle this and wondered if he could turn to Kevin for 'inspired guidance.' Ideally, he would welcome the opportunity to meet and talk it through.

Kevin's immediate reaction was to think this was just one challenge too many in his extraordinary life, especially having been tasked to do what he was still in shock about. But a whim of a plan came to mind. It would bring together all the pieces of a jigsaw that he was now confronting. That could be extremely helpful – if it could happen. It was indeed a very big 'if'.

"Could you get to Porto Novo by nightfall tomorrow?" he asked the American.

There was a pause. "That's about as far from here as anywhere in Benin," Joe replied. "But I guess so. If we start driving now and don't stop. Why?"

"A boat will be leaving for Porto Wandora from Porto Novo. It is a very private matter – highly illegal. Its cargo has to be the best guarded secret of all time and must not become known to those who currently control Wandora. But – and it is quite an enormous 'but' – I have an adventurous plan others will have to agree to. It'll smuggle you and your party into Wandora and to my home apartment. To have you and Gene Bond and the cargo on that boat all with me at the same time would, I believe, be extremely helpful to all our mutual ambitions."

Joe was intrigued. What was the secret cargo Kevin Forsythe was alluding to? Such subterfuge and illicit dealings seemed out of character for the stiff upper lipped, pink gin civil servant, epitome of an old-fashioned British embassy diplomat that he took Kevin Forsythe to be.

"What happens next?" he asked.

"I need to get permission for you to join the boat," the Englishman responded. "I'll seek to do that immediately and will come back to you with further instructions. Meantime don't go anywhere and don't tell anyone what I've told you. All right?"

"Fine by me," Joe responded. "We'll head off towards Porto Novo and await your instructions."

Chapter 44

Pete Anderson was dumfounded when he received the message from Kevin Forsythe. The Englishman's revelation that the man who had turned up at his depot in the DRC was the missing marine explorer, Marcel Bartoll, seemed incredulous. But, as Forsythe had done, Pete found himself seeking confirmation on the Web. And there it was – unequivocal evidence. The man who had lost his memory was indeed Marcel Bartoll.

Not quite knowing what to do, he phoned Forsythe in Porto Wandora to thank him for the information and to confirm that the stranger without a memory was beyond doubt Marcel.

"Have you told him yet?" Kevin Forsythe asked.

"No," said Anderson. "He's not here just now. When he gets back I'll break the news to him. Going to be a weird thing to do."

"Rather you than me," said Kevin. "Going to need a fair degree of tact and diplomacy."

"I'm not renowned for either of those," quipped the Australian.

"And what happens after that?" asked Kevin.

"Don't ask me," Anderson responded. "I've no idea."

"I wonder if you'd consider bringing Bartoll over to Porto Wandora?" Kevin ventured. He too was making this plan up as it developed. But bits of the jigsaw were perhaps starting to fit together.

"Why?" asked Anderson.

"I'm sorry, dear boy," said Kevin. "There's things happening I can't tell you about at the moment but a number of people are all heading here at the moment. I think it would be beneficial if both of you were here to be included in that group. You'll have to trust me, Mr Anderson, but I just think it would be helpful."

Pete Anderson agreed to give it some consideration and to let Kevin know. His number one priority was to jump the first hurdle – breaking the news to Marcel Bartoll. The Australian had sent the stranger out on a site-clearing mission with another member of his team. It was late afternoon when he welcomed him back into the depot and suggested they have a beer together in his office.

"I think I know who you are," Pete told the man sitting the other side of his desk. He had pondered all day how to break this news as compassionately as he could. Without being able to consult psychiatrists or other professional advisors, he decided to tell it how it was in good old, straight-talking, old-fashioned Ozzie style.

"You are Marcel Bartoll. You're a Frenchman but you've lived in England for years." He paused, waiting for a reaction. There was none. "You've been missing since a small scientific submarine got caught in some mysterious explosion at sea in the Gulf of Guinea. You'd been given up as dead."

He paused again. The man opposite him was staring at him intently, seemingly devouring every word but

281

not saying anything. Pete was already finding the whole experience very disconcerting and unnerving.

"I've checked the Internet," Pete continued, struggling as best he could to maintain this strange conversation. He tried to adopt as sympathetic and gentle a voice as possible. From a tray of papers on his desk he pulled a print taken from Marcel's web site. "This is you – from your own website," he said, pushing the photograph and short biography across his desk.

The man stared at the picture and text and still said nothing. He just stared at it.

Pete Anderson watched in fascination. He did not know what to expect – had no idea how the man would respond.

"You live on the south coast of England," he eventually continued in not much more than a whisper. "And run your own business – Sub Nautical Exploration Limited. SNEL."

Still the man opposite did nothing but stare at the photograph. Pete was finding the situation very difficult – highly volatile. The man could, he thought, do anything in response. Anything was possible.

"Ring any bells?" Pete asked after what felt a long enough silence between them.

The man looked up from the photograph. "It's all – all very odd," he replied hesitatingly. "It's weird and very disconcerting. I hear what you're telling me and I see the photo and I read the words. Now, all of a sudden, I don't know what I really know as distinct from what you've told me. It all blurs together. And there are other things tantalisingly in my mind that I can't quite grasp."

He rubbed his hands vigorously through his unkempt hair as if in an attempt to reawaken his brain. "What else can you tell me? What was the accident you mentioned?"

Pete told him what he could recall from what he had read about the mysterious explosion in the Gulf of Guinea after which all trace had been lost of the scientific submarine and its two occupants. As the Australian talked, flimsy, transparent images started to come to Marcel Bartoll's mind. They were largely intangible, tantalisingly skimpy and in a kaleidoscopic disorder. And there was a girl. Pretty. Young.

"There's a girl," he muttered, now rubbing and massaging his forehead in frustration.

"I don't know," Pete told him. "I think I've exhausted what I know."

The man was looking back at the photograph of himself. "Can you show me what you've seen on the Web?" he asked.

"If you think that's a good idea. If you think it'll help."

Pete placed his laptop on the desk, called up the Web and typed in Marcel Bartoll at SNEL. He watched closely as the LinkedIn pages for Marcel appeared on the screen and the man before him started reading about himself. "This is a very strange experience," Pete thought to himself. "Watching someone rediscover themselves."

"It's like coming out of a dream," Marcel observed.

Pete began to feel more comfortable – as if a crisis point had been passed. Marcel Bartoll had not collapsed into a mental quagmire or physically attacked him in some sort of fit of frustration. Confident he could leave the man alone for a short while, Pete said he needed to make some telephone calls and moved to a different office where he phoned SNEL in England. Eventually he got through to Steve Oldbury who he knew of from what he had read on the company's website. The man was heading the organisation in the aftermath of the Gulf of Guinea disaster.

"You don't know me, Mr Oldbury," Pete started by introducing himself. "I work in the Democratic Republic of the Congo for an international NGO. You need to prepare yourself for a shock, Mr Oldbury, though I believe this will be extraordinary good news."

"I'm intrigued," Steve Oldbury replied.

"I have in my office here in the Congo a man who has without doubt totally lost his memory. Through various checks including looking at sites on the internet, there is absolutely no doubt he is Marcel Bartoll, your missing CEO."

"Good God!" exclaimed Steve.

"Physically he's OK but mentally he's in a mess," Pete told him.

"Are you sure it's Marcel?" asked Steve. The news was just unbelievable.

"There's no doubt," Pete assured him. "And though he hasn't a clue who he is, there's evidence he's had a pretty good clout to the head and my guess is that's why his memory's gone. But there are indications he's starting to recall things. I'm no expert on this – far from it – but I reckon it's a short-term loss."

"I'm astounded, Mr Anderson," said Steve. "I don't know what to say. How did he get there?"

"One of my truck drivers picked him up," Pete told him. "But how he got to this part of Africa I've no idea. There are lots of questions at the moment but no answers. But the big question is, Mr Oldbury, what do we do next?"

Chapter 45

Sum Taeyoung approached the meetings in the mining village with a mix of anticipation and trepidation. He had high expectations of doing business with a certain Chinese dealer who had expressed interest in buying the cobalt being recovered from Black Bart's Bay. But he approached the meeting with ISIS with far less certainty. It had taken torturous amounts of time and mountains of frustrations to eventually secure agreement to meet their senior representatives at the mining village. He was driven there by members of his SDBI team. Their journey started badly. Not far from where he was picked up from his hotel, Sum Taeyoung was surprised when their way was blocked by Wandoran soldiers who advised them not to drive out of town on the main road because of some local disturbances. When asked what sort of disturbances, they were told a small riot was being put down. Sum Taeyoung was very troubled to hear of civil unrest. He asked for more information. The most senior soldier of the group was called to provide answers. Apparently, some local citizens had taken to the streets and were demanding an end to army rule and the formation of a democratic parliament. A few hundred people were involved but were being dispersed by water cannon and rubber bullets.

"We have the matter under control," the army man reassured him. "It's virtually all over."

Sum Taeyoung made a mental note to raise questions with Moussa Ehouzou and Major Moustapha Abass about the incident. He would need their assurances that any public insurgence was being properly and thoroughly stamped on.

During the drive from Porto Wandora, the South Korean took the opportunity to question his men about the missing SDBI 4x4 and its occupants, an unresolved mystery but subsequently overtaken by the ISIS attack. Certainly it was now no longer a matter of great concern to Sum Taeyoung. He had far more important issues occupying his mind. Nevertheless it was a mystery and one he hoped would eventually be answered. As it was, the SDBI men had nothing to tell him of any substance. Their knowledge was all based on rumours and conjecture.

As they approached the mining village, Sum Taeyoung was deep in thought as to how to tackle the forthcoming meeting. The enticement that had eventually encouraged the ISIS people to agree to meet was the prospect of some sort of business arrangement which would be to their advantage. When the first 105mm shell from a L118 Light Gun exploded on the edge of the village, a couple of hundred yards from Taeyoung's vehicle, the South Korean jumped in shock. A second shell, like the first, exploded just short of its target – the main administrative block of the mining operation. Also like the first it fell into the soft sandy ground with a dull but loud thud and sent a large amount of sandy soil into the air. Otherwise it, like the first, was harmless. However, the impact of the two explosions sent men scurrying in all directions, mostly towards the motley collection of armed trucks in which they had arrived. The third shell was more damaging. It blew a large section of the administrative block to pieces.

Sum Taeyoung was apoplectic with rage. Under most circumstances and even when encountering the most stressful of pressures, the South Korean prided himself on his self-control. But this unaccountable attack on the mining village – just as he was about to open delicate negotiations with ISIS, was such a shock and interruption to his plans. But what really blew his self-control was the news when he tried to contact Moussa Ehouzou that his Minister was away – out of the country – would be gone for a month – that sent him into a frenzied temper. How could he have gone away without telling him? It would seal the fate of Moussa Ehouzou.

"Who's attacking the mining village?" he demanded of the poor person at the other end of the telephone line who had had the misfortune to answer the call.

"We know nothing of such an attack," the man from the Ministry of Armed Forces replied in a slightly quivering voice. He had instantly recognised Sum Taeyoung's voice and immediately wondered what he had done to upset the Gods. How come he had been so unlucky to answer this call?

"Someone must know," Taeyoung bellowed down the phone. His car had done a rapid U-turn and driven away from the village with the sounds of more bursting shells now accompanied by heavy machine gun fire. "Put me through to the army barracks."

As he waited for the call to be answered a light tank drove by some hundred yards away, heading towards the village. It kicked up significant clouds of sand in its wake but not enough to conceal from Taeyoung the flag flying from its radio aerial. It was blue and clearly not the flag of Wandora. Taeyoung recognised the armoured vehicle to be a PT-76 ex-Soviet amphibious light tank of which he knew the Wandoran army had six. He made it his business to know about such things.

Army headquarters at the barracks received the venomous call from the South Korean but could shed no light on the attack on the mining village.

"I've just witnessed what I am sure is a Wandoran tank flying a United Nations flag heading into the area of fighting. I need an explanation! What's happening?"

The most senior ranking officer who could be summoned to the phone seemed totally perplexed by the news of the attack. He promised to make enquiries and call back.

Alarmed and totally mystified by the scene unfolding before him, Taeyoung sent two of his SDBI men out to see what was happening. He was, he told them, especially baffled by the blue flag he had seen on the passing tank. Twenty minutes later they were back. The attack was over. The ISIS fighters had surrendered and several had been killed. The attackers appeared to have a number of small tanks and light field guns and had simply outgunned the ISIS insurgents.

"Did you see any more blue flags?" Taeyoung asked them. All his men had. It seemed all the attacking vehicles were flying them.

"And were the men with them wearing blue helmets?" he asked.

His men looked at each other in bewilderment. They were not sure what their leader was talking about.

"The attacking force. Did the men have blue helmets?" he asked again, more forcibly and with his temper just in control.

The negative answer puzzled Taeyoung even further. Blue flags normally meant a United Nations force. But UN forces wore blue helmets. Apparently these attackers had not. So who the hell were they?

As Sum Taeyoung drove back to Porto Wandora, mystified by what he had seen and angry beyond words at Moussa Ehouzou, Major Adrian Rego surveyed the scene of destruction before him and the line of bedraggled and defeated ISIS men.

"Mission accomplished," he reported down the phone of his command jeep.

In Porto Wandora, Kevin Forsythe congratulated his new ally and replaced the phone in its cradle. "Now for phase two of this mad plan," he thought.

Chapter 46

Steve Oldbury assembled the SNEL team together in their Marchwood offices and broke the news about Marcel. Their reaction was much as his own, a mix of elation and delight, confusion and perplexity. The team had so many questions he could not answer including what would happen next. He basically had no idea but one task had to be fulfilled as a matter of urgency and only he could do it – breaking the news to Charlotte McDonnell. Lotty had not come into the office today. Some days she did. Some days she did not. Since the explosion and the disappearance of the mini-sub, Lotty's life had lost all sense of meaningfulness and direction. On the days when she did turn up for work her mind was elsewhere and her contribution to the life of the company was questionable. But nobody had the heart to tell her to go home. On this day she had not turned up at Marchwood so Steve drove to the apartment she and Marcel had developed as their home. With a large degree of apprehension he pressed the intercom button at the entrance door.

"Hello," came Lotty's voice.

"It's Steve," he answered.

"Gosh," she responded, obviously surprised by this unusual visit. "Come on up." The door catch clicked and Steve entered the apartment block and headed for Lotty's. He still thought of it as Marcel's home and he realised he had not been here since Lotty and Marcel had teamed up. So it was not unexpected that Lotty should be surprised to find Steve visiting her in the apartment. Dressed in a jumper and jeans, she welcomed Steve with a quick hug and offered him a drink. She looked frail and tired, black eyes suggesting lack of sleep.

"No thanks," he responded. "Let's just sit down and let me break some news to you that you may have difficulty dealing with. It's good news. But be prepared to be shocked."

"Goodness," said Lotty and sat down on the couch in readiness. Steve sat alongside her.

"It's Marcel," said Steve. "He's alive."

Lotty gasped. The colour drained from her face and Steve thought she was going to faint. He put his arm round her in support.

"He's been found in Africa," he continued. "But he seems to have lost his memory. He doesn't know who he is."

Lotty was sobbing now, almost uncontrollably. Her whole body was shaking. Steve went to the nearby kitchen and poured a glass of water which he took to her and placed gently at her lips. She sipped at it which seemed to help calm her.

"Is he alright?" the words came between the sobs. "Apart from his memory problem. Is he OK?"

"I believe so," Steve told her. Then slowly, as Lotty regained her self-control and the sobbing ended, he told her everything he knew. She listened without interruption and only when Steve had concluded the whole story did she say anything.

"Has he forgotten me?" she asked tentatively.

"As I understand it he's forgotten everything," Steve told her.

"We must go," Lotty told him emphatically.

"Where?" asked Steve.

"To him. To where Marcel is. We must help him recover his memory. If he sees me surely he'll remember?"

"We can't be certain Lotty," Steve cautioned. "You have to prepare yourself for a difficult time."

"I can make him better," she said. She knew she could.

Steve thought about it and rapidly concluded she was probably right. Anyway, nothing would stop Lotty flying out to wherever Marcel was and he, Steve, had a responsibility to accompany her. It would be a tough journey but she was right. They had to go.

"How quickly do you want to go?" he asked.

"Now," she told him. "Right now."

"I need to make some calls," Steve told her.

"From here?" she asked.

"No," he told her. "I'll do them from the office. The numbers I need are there. Anyway, if we're flying off somewhere it will be easier to organise from the office than here. I'll keep you posted as to what's happening. You prepare yourself for a sudden departure."

Back at the office, he phoned Pete Anderson and updated him as to what was happening. He and Lotty would be flying out to meet Marcel.

"Just hold on," the Australian told him. "No point coming to the Congo if we're not here. And at the moment it looks like we're heading for Wandora." And he went on to tell Steve about the conversation with Kevin Forsythe.

"Not easy sometimes to know what he's on about," Pete confessed. "Talks in riddles – Shakespearian most of them. All a bit beyond an Ozzie bushman! But he's asked if I would take Marcel to Porto Wandora. Said something like though Wandora's a tiny country things are happening that will 'test how far that little candle can throw its beams.' I think he was off into Shakespeare country again but clearly something significant's going on there. So we plan to head there."

On that basis, Steve started to make arrangements for he and Lotty to head to Wandora to meet Pete there.

Chapter 47

Gene Bond could not make out what the smell was. No doubting it was there, filling the night air with a strange aroma that he ultimately concluded originated from the old coastal tramp cargo ship they currently stood alongside. Goodness knows what mix of cargos it had carried in recent times that created such a smell now mixed with a good helping of diesel fuel fumes and miscellaneous dockside aromas. He had no idea what she was carrying now in her forward holds that occupied at least two thirds the length of the ship. The rest was taken by the aft-located wheelhouse and entrance to the crew's quarters located on a lower deck and now largely taken over by those paying for the privilege of being transported from the harbour in Benin to Porto Wandora, a distance of less than 100 km. The journey would take about an hour and a half by road. It would take appreciably longer as this old tramp followed the coastline and chugged its way through the night.

Joe had stopped only for fuel as he drove them more or less the whole length of Benin to the coast and the harbour at Porto Novo. On the way he heard news that the mining village of Wandora had been taken over by an ISIS squad but that they in turn were now surrendering to what appeared to be a United Nations force. Joe was puzzled. Normally he would have been automatically forewarned such an action was going to happen. Worried by the apparent break in his line of information he phoned his Nairobi HQ but was told the UN knew nothing of any such action by their forces in Wandora. Nothing had been planned by the UN. Nothing had been implemented. There was no UN force in Wandora. It was, it was suggested, Joe's own intelligence that was wrong. Perplexed, Joe had no alternative but to put the matter to one side. He would try later to find out more.

Having reached Porto Novo, they were all now standing by the car and close to the black and daunting side of the ship that would be their home for the next few hours. She looked dark and unwelcoming with only her navigation lights and one small light at the bow and another at the stern. Joe had been instructed by Kevin Forsythe to simply drive to the harbour and wait. And that is what he, Nakki, Pete and Bond were doing on what was a dry but dark night with thick clouds rolling fast across the sky driven by winds which, Joe pondered, might make the sea a little lively. Even in the protection of the harbour there was sufficient of a sea swell to cause the old cargo ship to strain against her mooring ropes which creaked and groaned under the stress. Meanwhile they waited. What for they did not know. And the longer they waited the more likely they were to become conspicuous to the authorities – in whatever guise that might be. So there was a nervous tension between them.

The amount of activity around the harbour at this time of night was minimal. Time ticked on slowly and Nakki and Pete eventually retired back into the 4x4.

When another vehicle approached and drove towards where they were standing, anticipation and nervousness rose rapidly. Hopefully, at last, something was going to happen. Hopefully it would be positive. The vehicle stopped nearby and they watched as four people got out and one – the driver – unloaded bags. Once his task was complete he drove off, leaving the group – two men and a woman, a short distance away from where Joe and company stood now with Pete and Nakki who had left the comfort of the 4x4 to join them. One of the men walked towards them.

"Good evening," he said in a very refined English accent. "Which one of you is Joe Wright?"

"I am," Joe replied, responding to the other's extended hand which he shook.

"I apologise if what I'm about to say sounds over melodramatic. As will ultimately become apparent to you, there's considerable sensitivity concerning my two fellow travellers for whom I am their official spokesperson – at least for the time being. Until you're told otherwise, you are not to speak to them – unless they first speak to you. Is that quite clear? Can I have your assurances on that and that of your friends?"

Joe looked at the others who had been listening intently to the brief exchange. The three men nodded in agreement. Nakki had no idea what was going on and clearly posed no threat to the stranger and his companions.

"Very good," he responded and walked off to the gangplank and onto the ship. The two groups of people stood apart from each other and waited. Ten minutes later the man was back and ushered everyone onto the ship. They encountered nobody between the harbour and the room into which they were eventually ushered. During the short walk, Gene Bond had, probably like the rest of his group he thought, tried to see who the mysterious fellow passengers were – who they were instructed not to speak to. It was easy to see one was a man and the other a woman, perhaps a young woman. But with their coat collars pulled up and their heads always bent low, it was hard to see anything more.

The man who had made himself known to Joe took charge. The room was not very large, had a table at one end, some seating against its walls and a selection of loose chairs. An assembly of bottles clanked against each other to the movement of the ship as they stood in their container on a large tray which also included some paper bags containing an assortment of refreshments.

As they all took off their coats Gene could see the man and woman fellow travellers more clearly. The man, probably in his mid-30s, was strikingly well-dressed in a western-style sports jacket and open-necked shirt. He was obviously of African origin as was the young girl who accompanied him. Nakki, Gene noticed, was seemingly hypnotised by the other young girl's presence.

The man who had taken charge of everything went to the one door of the room, looked out from it as if to reassure himself nobody was nearby, then shut it firmly. He had every appearance of being a European and from his accent was as English as could be.

"I'm sorry for the cloak and dagger stuff on the harbour," the temporary orchestrator of events apologised. "But you will quickly understand why. Our mutual friend, Kevin Forsythe, can be blamed for it all!" It was only much later that Gene Bond realised that he never did get to know this man's name, who he was or who he worked for.

"Sir. Ma'am," he continued, addressing the man who stood by the young girl. "May I introduce to you Joe Wright of the US government and based in Nairobi; Gene Bond from England, internationally respected expert on sustainability; Pete Turner, an English geologist; and Nakki who these good people rescued from the north of Wandora – a story on its own."

And turning to the others he said; "May I please introduce you to the Oba of Wandora and his daughter – the Crown Prince, Christopher Kpotsra and Princess Sylvia."

He paused while this bombshell of information was digested.

"Needless to say, their identify needs to be kept a close secret. Lives depend upon it – including yours. I am not sure how secure this room is. I doubt it is. So it will be prudent if any conversation from now on is of a general nature, mentions no titles or anything remotely political. When we arrive at Porto Wandora we will be taken immediately to see Kevin Forsythe at which time a more comprehensive explanation will be provided."

With the introductions completed, the crown prince shook hands with everyone while his daughter made friends with Nakki who seemed to be in awe of what was happening and overwhelmingly delighted to find someone she could talk to in her own language. The two young girls huddled together and the talking between them did not stop for the whole sea journey. The crown prince seemed especially interested in Gene Bond.

"What brings you to this corner of Africa, Mr Bond?" he asked.

Gene Bond was still in shock about whose company he was in – and why? He remembered hearing the royal family had flown the country in the aftermath of the bomb that killed the president. And now here they were – or at least a key member of it – on their way back to Wandora. He could not wait to hear more from Kevin who was obviously a key player in whatever was going on.

"Sir, it's his fault," Bond responded, placing an arm round the shoulder of the young geologist. "He brought me here because of the rare mineral cobalt."

"Ah yes, cobalt," the crown prince replied. "I hear there maybe cobalt offshore Wandora?"

"Yes sir," said Bond, surprised at how well the crown prince was informed. "There's supposedly an expedition going to search for it but it's been delayed because of the tragedy that recently happened with another offshore Wandora diving expedition."

"I heard about it," the prince nodded in solemn memory of the event. "Tragic."

"Kevin Forsythe and I also travelled to the DRC to see the artisan mines where young children are used as cheap labour in the extraction of cobalt. It's another tragedy but on a massive scale. I'm ashamed our civilisation seems to condone what's happening there."

"Tell me more, Mr Bond." The crown prince pressed Gene Bond for more information. Their journey to

Porto Wandora was virtually taken up by the two men in energetic conversation and agreeing that such use of children had no place in the modern world.

"There is much to be done, Mr Bond. Much. And it will not be easy. But things have to change."

"Amen to that," agreed Bond and they undertook to discuss and explore the matter further once they were with Kevin Forsythe.

Chapter 48

As if a French farce was coming to its crescendo finale, so in the Palm Trees Hotel, Porto Wandora and the nearby apartment of Kevin Forsythe, all the key players assembled. In his suite of rooms on the hotel's top floor, recently returned from his aborted trip to the northern mine to meet ISIS, South Korean chaos entrepreneur Sum Taeyoung still seethed at the absence of Moussa Ehouzou. The man had let him down badly. Now he would pay for that. On the journey back to Porto Wandora various messages were sent to spark action that would hopefully placate his frustrations. Once back at the hotel, he summoned Major Moustapha Abass to seek more information about who had attacked the mining village and why. But Abass genuinely seemed to know nothing. Taeyoung was appalled. The feeling that control was slipping through his fingers was growing all the time. He was very disturbed by it. Control was the crux of most things. Ehouzou had badly let him down and reneged on his duties.

Things moved fast in response to Taeyoung's calls from his car. It was early evening in Switzerland and Moussa Ehouzou glorified in the calm coolness and gloriously fresh air as he walked from the conference in the Montreux Music & Convention Centre to his nearby hotel. His mind ruminated over optional prospects for the evening. The primary objective of this trip was for him to indulge himself and he was working hard at it. This evening – perhaps a shower first. Then a massage. Depending on who applied the massage, maybe that could develop into a sexual romp. The evening would conclude, he thought, with dinner in the garden restaurant overlooking the lake. A splendid prospect.

He could have exited the Centre via its front door and walked down the town's streets. Instead he elected to relax and savour the stunning environment of the shoreline pathway separated from the gently lapping waters of Lake Geneva by the resplendently full and immaculately maintained flowerbeds. Across the blue lake the distant mountains with their white-topped peaks provided a dramatic backdrop to complete a picture of utter tranquillity. He shared the pathway with young loving couples, business people, the elderly many of whom sat on the wooden benches and just watched the world go gently by. As in any such scene in any part of the world, a few individuals disturb the slow pace. It was no different here with the occasional skateboarder weaving through the slower pedestrian traffic.

Ehouzou saw the young girl – tall, lean, leggy and wearing the shortest of shorts and with a sports top with hood covering her head – just before she seemingly momentarily lost balance and crashed into him.

"Pardon Monsieur," she muttered as she regained control and went on her way. He was left with a fleeting image of a delightfully shapely young lady, blonde hair escaping from inside the hood, an attractive face such as

303

he saw of it – and a pin prick in his left arm he did not even know was there.

Ricinus communis is a highly potent toxin. Ricin when purified is so lethal a few grains no bigger than table salt can kill a human. It became infamous when the Bulgarian dissident writer, Georgi Markov, was assassinated in 1978 in London by ricin fired into him from an umbrella. Ricin also killed Ehouzou. He had not progressed much further towards his hotel when he collapsed. He was dead before his body hit the pathway alongside Lake Geneva. Paramedics declared he had died from a heart attack. It was only later that a post-mortem would reveal how Sum Taeyoung had disposed of a liability.

Back at the Palm Trees Hotel, Porto Wandora, also recently arrived was Gary Marchant, keen to link up with Ken Burlington's expedition in the harbour so he could report back to Sum Taeyoung and hopefully ensure Vanessa did not suffer more. He knew the South Korean occupied the top floor of the hotel and hoped to meet up with him. He should by now be confident his wishes were being met. That should release Vanessa. Gary hoped for a positive meeting with the South Korean but before that could happen he was to have the biggest shock of his life.

Bond, Pete, Joe and Nakki had also recently arrived at the hotel, the royal element of their party from Benin having gone straight to Kevin Forsythe's apartment to which they too would soon be summoned.

Just arrived from the Congo were Pete Anderson and a still highly bewildered Marcel Bartoll. The Australian was anxious to meet up with Kevin as it was he who suggested their journey here. But the phone number he had been given seemed to be constantly engaged. He had, however, made contact with Steve Oldbury, also now encamped in the hotel with Lotty McDonnell. They made arrangements to meet in Steve's room. It was, Steve Oldbury thought, going to be an extraordinary meeting. Would Marcel remember Lotty?

Kevin Forsythe meanwhile was increasingly feeling schizophrenic – like his world was becoming a fantasy and a delusion. His natural inclination was to yearn for peace, solitude, comfort – a 'dully sluggardized life in shapeless idleness' – a carefree retirement in comfort. Yet here he was, centrally orchestrating the lives of goodness knows how many people – including royalty. It was lunacy!

The prince, his daughter, the man who had accompanied them from Benin and Major Adrian Rego were in Kevin's apartment. The Englishman was trying to update Wandora's senior member of the royal family.

"The most comforting development is news that the armed forces are keen to support any move that ousts the current controlling regime. That is so, is it not, Major?"

The young military man nodded in agreement.

"And there is growing civil unrest against the current rulers. We have recently had rioting on the streets. It has not been extensive but our intelligence tells us it is indicative of widespread disillusionment. We also have many indications that the return of the royal family would be popularly welcomed."

"What about the ISIS matter?" the Prince asked.

"We believe, sir, it is now dealt with, at least for the time being. The insurgents who took over the mine are now in the hands of the army," Kevin told him.

"Can we expect reprisals from ISIS?" the Prince asked.

"We hope not, sir," Kevin tried to reassure him. "We were worried about that – that Wandoran action against the ISIS raiding party might invoke a bigger attack. So we tried to disguise our actions."

"How?" asked the Prince.

"It's highly illegal, sir. I'm sure you would not have condoned it or authorised it. I take full responsibility though the Major here was responsible for implementing my idea. But when our forces attacked ISIS we flew the blue flag of the UN on all our vehicles. We know from interrogating ISIS fighters afterwards they think they were overwhelmed by a UN force. That is what we hoped for. Our rationale was that whereas ISIS might have taken retaliatory action against Wandora for what happened at the mine, if they thought it was a UN force that had defeated them they might hold off and think twice about attacking us."

"A risky strategy?" the Prince suggested.

"We considered the risks and concluded it was a sensible approach. Communications around this part of Africa are so confused at the moment that something like the action we took and how we did it will only accentuate that. Our prime objective was to stop ISIS spreading into the rest of Wandora. If they had taken over the port, for instance, it would have been a catastrophe."

"Do you agree with this?" the Prince asked Major Rego.

"Without doubt, sir," the young military man answered with firm assurance. "And to reiterate what Mr Forsythe said, the armed forces are standing by to support any move you make, sir, to replace the current disastrous governing regime."

"I need to know about that in detail," the Prince told them. "And while you do that perhaps we could call in all the others you suggested I should meet."

Back at the hotel, Pete Anderson received the call inviting him and Marcel to a meeting at Kevin Forsythe's. He phoned Steve Oldbury to find he too had received a similar invitation. Between them they decided to meet up with Marcel and Lotty prior to heading to Kevin's. They would meet in Pete's room.

"I think I need a drink before we do this," Marcel told his Australian companion who was never one to refuse such an opportunity. They headed for the hotel's bar via the reception foyer through which they passed just as Sum Taeyoung, dressed flamboyantly in his colourful flowing robes, strode purposefully on his way out of the building. Marcel and Pete had to stop as he swept by. The encounter meant nothing to them. But it did to the South Korean whose photographic memory always held him in good stead. So it did on this occasion but Sum Taeyoung did not hesitate in his stride or show any facial response to seeing alive a man he thought he had been responsible for killing some time ago. How had the man escaped the sinking of his mini submarine? Sum would need to make urgent enquiries – and seek to get his money back from Janka Koldun. The Eastern European had made some sort of catastrophic mistake.

Or, heaven forbid, had the contract not been explicit enough? Taeyoung could not remember. Had the contract specified a sinking or a killing? Did one assume the other? He would have to check. Could the failure still impact somehow on the prospect of mining cobalt offshore Wandora – assuming the stuff was there?

Pete and Marcel walked into the hotel bar. As they did so a man sitting on a high stool at the bar looked casually up towards them as he had done when anyone walked in. Pete had never seen anyone lose their colour so quickly and dramatically. But it was hardly surprising. Gary Marchant felt the blood drain from him and his legs go weak as he watched a dead man walking towards him. The young English barman who had just served him a drink thought his customer was going to pass out.

"You OK, sir?" he asked. "You look as if you've just seen a ghost."

"I have," Gary Marchant spluttered in response.

Chapter 49

Major Moustapha Abass was completely out of his depth. His guiding mentor, the man who had got him into this mess, was still missing. Rumours were flying that the man was dead. News from Switzerland was confused but it increasingly appeared that Moussa Ehouzou had had a heart attack and died. Moustapha wondered cynically if, assuming the news to be true, over-indulgence had been the cause of his demise. Whatever the reason, he now felt very much on his own and vulnerable. All the demands of Sum Taeyoung were now directed at him – and quite simply he did not know what to do.

Summoned to meet in what used to be the President's main office in the São João Baptista de Wandora, Sum Taeyoung's barrage of testing questions left Moustapha in no doubt his fears about his various lack of ability were well justified.

"Have you determined who attacked the mining village yet? Was it a UN force or not and if it was why was it using Wandoran military hardware?" the South Korean snapped at him.

"The matter is still being investigated," Moustapha responded.

"Which means you don't know," barked Taeyoung.

The major looked back at him blankly but said nothing.

"And these rumours the royal family are returning. What do you know about that?"

"I've also heard rumours," Moustapha agreed.

"Which means you don't know about that either," Taeyoung was running out of patience. "And if there is any substance in the rumour, how much will the military support the family's return?"

Moustapha shrugged his shoulders. "It's difficult to tell."

Taeyoung was starting to pace up and down the room, hands clenched behind his back.

"And the uprising on the streets. Has it been put down?"

"I believe it has been contained," the major responded.

"What the fuck does that mean?" Taeyoung snapped back. "Has it been put down or not?"

"There's no rioting at the moment," Moustapha told him and watched the South Korean pace up and down, fearful of what he might say next.

"We need more soldiers on the streets of Porto Wandora," Taeyoung eventually said. "And more tanks. Wherever the rioting flashpoints have been to date we need high military visibility. You understand?"

"Yes, sir," Moustapha responded. "Our forces are well stretched at the moment because many of them are still involved in the tsunami clean-up and rebuild."

That seemed to mean nothing to Taeyoung. "The control of Porto Wandora is paramount," he told

Moustapha. "Bring the forces back so you can do what I order. Understand?"

"Yes, sir," Moustapha agreed timidly. The negative impact that would have on the post tsunami rescue programme would be significant but there seemed to be no point in arguing with the South Korean – especially when arguing might mean life itself coming under threat – again.

"And anything you hear about the royal family or their plans you will communicate to me immediately."

"Yes, sir."

"And do you know anything about the survival of the man who was supposedly killed when the scientific submarine sank off our shores? I either saw a ghost in the Palm Trees Hotel or the man somehow survived."

"I know nothing about that, I regret," Moustapha apologised. He again watched as the South Korean paced silently up and down, clearly in a greatly agitated mood.

"Seems to me you know nothing about anything," Sum Taeyoung told him bluntly. Moustapha waited while the South Korean paced more before he eventually said: "The people detained during the last riots, how many were there and are they held under arrest? Is it planned they go on trial?"

"I'm afraid I don't know," Moustapha reluctantly admitted.

The South Korean stopped his pacing and stood immediately before the military man. "You are close to being a total waste of time, aren't you?" The question was rhetorical. Moustapha flinched but said nothing. "You will find out by tomorrow how many people were detained and under what legality. Whatever is in place you will cancel. However many people there are will be recharged with treason and brought to the court which will hold a special trial on Independence Day. That will give the royals something to think about though I have more surprises for them."

The South Korean stared at the man who stood right in front of him. He could see fear in the man's eyes. That was good.

"You understand?"

"Yes, sir."

"And you understand the penalty of failure?"

"Quite clearly," replied Major Moustapha Abass in a voice that failed to conceal a quiver.

Chapter 50

BBC Central African Correspondent

Fears of a civil war in the small African state of Wandora appear to be evaporating as rumours persist that the royal family is soon to make a return to power. Skirmishes between different factions of the Wandoran army were not the precursor to an out and out civil war many predicted though civil unrest is still happening in the country's capital, Porto Wandora. The royal family fled the country after the assassination of the president but are rumoured to be back.

Mystery still surrounds the defeat of an ISIS group that took over a mining village in the north of the country. Reports that a UN force had overwhelmed them have been strenuously denied by the UN from their Nairobi African HQ though locals still report the invaders have surrendered to what was thought to be the UN.

Chapter 51

"My God!" exclaimed Marcel to Pete Anderson as they entered the bar of the Palm Trees Hotel. "That's the bastard who tried to steal my company. What the hell's he doing here?"

Pete was completely taken aback. This was the first time Marcel had shown the slightest glimmer of remembering anything from his past. Now, suddenly, it was as if the memory loss had never happened.

"I thought you were dead," said a white faced and badly shaken Gary as his former business partner moved towards him.

"I guess you'd prefer it that way," Marcel suggested, bitterly. "It would resolve some problems for you."

Gary was at a loss as to what to say. Still deeply shocked, he could not get over who he was talking to.

"But what happened? Everyone said you'd been killed."

"I don't know," Marcel told him. "I can't remember a thing. Strangely though, I knew you as soon as I saw you. The man who stole my company. Not to be forgotten – obviously."

"That's in the past Marcel," muttered Gary. "But I can't get over you're here."

"Well, clearly I am," Marcel replied in a voice that did not conceal the anger he was feeling. "And what you did may well be in the past. I may have forgotten a lot, Gary, but I haven't forgotten you and what you did. You're nothing more than a thief and a crook. I set you up in business and you robbed me – went into competition against me. You're a bloody traitor."

Gary was at a loss as to how to respond. He was shocked to the core. Marcel being alive created huge complications. He could not get his mind round them all. He was stunned by Marcel's resurrection. A barrage of thoughts rushed through his mind not the least were all the problems about sea bed mining for cobalt killing off the sea anemone Marcel was hunting for. It was not a discussion he wished to have – and certainly not with Marcel and certainly not now.

"It was business," he eventually told Marcel. It was a poor response but the best he could think of.

"Fuck off Gary. It was daylight robbery. A con." Marcel told him. "If I'd had my way we'd have been in court by now. Maybe one day. Don't think you've got away with what you did. I'll get my own back – sometime. Just don't cross my path again."

And with that, Marcel turned away and he and the man he was with headed for a corner of the bar as far away from Gary as was possible.

"Who the hell is that?" Pete asked.

"A former business partner who did the dirty on me big time," Marcel told him.

"And you remember that?" Pete was amazed at the transformation with Marcel who up to now could not remember a thing. This man Gary was totally recognisable to Marcel as was whatever had happened

315

between them. Deeply puzzled, Pete used his phone to access the Web and looked up memory loss. The entry he elected to read told him "Post-traumatic amnesia is a state of confusion or memory loss that occurs immediately following a traumatic brain injury. The injured person is disorientated and unable to remember events that occur after the injury and may be unable to remember who they are and their name."

Pete passed this onto Marcel who nodded. "Seems to fit," he agreed. Pete was conscious that Marcel could not stop looking across to where Gary was and was relieved when the man finished his drink and departed. It was as if a tension had left Marcel.

The meeting with Lotty was extraordinary. As they headed to meet her in Pete's room, Pete was conscious that Marcel was still seething from the meeting with Gary. But he hoped what he had witnessed with Marcel's memory recovery would happen when they saw Lotty. Any doubts were quickly dispelled.

The young girl was in tears as she stood at the door, Pete beckoning her in. Marcel has been standing by the window looking vacantly out to the sea view but his mind elsewhere. He turned as Pete opened the door to welcome the pitiful sight of a very pale Lotty, tears streaming down her face.

"Foutu enfer! Lotty!" Marcel moved quickly across the room to wrap his arms round Lotty who seemed to melt in the moment. Pete stood and watched, transfixed by the passionate meeting between the two and astounded that Marcel was again showing clear signs of memory recall.

"I'll see you in the bar," he said to the embracing pair and made a diplomatic retreat from his own room to leave them to their so unexpected reunion. How much and how quickly would Marcel remember their previous time together? It was an extraordinary situation but one which needed the two to be left alone. Pete headed back to the bar.

Chapter 52

Kevin Forsythe could not have been a better host for such a meeting. All his diplomatic career experience came to the fore as he took great delight in reintroducing the prince and his daughter to Gene Bond, Joe, Pete Turner and Nakki, the latter overjoyed to be with the princess again. Major Adrian Rego was also meeting the prince for the first time though Kevin had already talked extensively to the prince about him. The prince was also meeting for the first time, the Australian Pete Anderson, Marcel Bartoll and Lotty, shaking hands while the visitors who, not being sure what protocol to observe, nervously bowed their heads in a gesture of deference to the young royal. Gene Bond noted with interest that the man who had initially introduced them to the prince in Porto Novo was also present but seemed detached from the meeting, said nothing of consequence to anyone, and left before the meeting ended. Though he was to encounter him again, Bond realised later he never did find out who he was.

The prince listened intently as he heard for the first time from Pete Anderson about the Great Green Wall idea being advanced for the DRC. He pressed the Australian for as much detail as he could give but noted the response reflected Pete's cynicism and concerns about corruption and ISIS.

Marcel updated him as best he could about the two explorative projects – his own hunt for the sea anemone though he could still recall nothing from the moment the expedition's boat had left Porto Wandora, and Gary's search for cobalt on the sea bed in Wandoran territorial waters.

"I do worry, sir. From what I've been told about the explosion that ended our hunt for the sea anemone, it may have killed it off. It was, apparently, a substantial explosion and I fear for the damage it may have caused. The expedition hunting for cobalt is in its very early days and as far as I know hasn't yet started exploratory drilling. Just to remind you, sir, as others have reminded me recently, minerals extraction from the sea bed is quite a contentious environmental issue at a time when there's growing global concern about the overall impact of the human footprint on our oceans."

Kevin intervened. "Just to further update you, sir, there's quite a substantial amount of cobalt on the coast at Black Bart's Bay. It came ashore during the tsunami and its existence was part of the evidence that supported the expedition now about to look for the mineral offshore. I believe Sum Taeyoung is about to start to recover it from the bay."

The prince listened intently to what they all had to say. "I'm learning so much from you guys," he told them. "And Gene has already told me what he witnessed in the cobalt mines in the Congo. It's quite an inhuman situation."

After a break for refreshments, the prince told them of his plans.

"Obvious though it may be, I cannot stress highly enough the sensitivity of what I will tell you. And from the start I want to thank our host Kevin for the role he's played to date in helping me be here. I see this man as someone I can trust and a man with considerable experience."

"As you may or may not know, Wandora Independence Day will soon be with us. Normally it is a day which passes without much recognition. It was established to celebrate our independence post our colonial days. That significant happening is now distant history and this year we still have the aftermath of the tsunami impacting on many of our citizens. Celebrating is hardly the most diplomatic or sensitive thing to do at the moment when so many of our people are suffering."

"However, this Independence Day is going to be different. On that day I will make a very public announcement that the royal family has returned from exile. I will immediately abolish the existing Administrative Committee and announce Wandora from now on is a constitutional monarchy with me as its non-political head and members voted into a new parliament through a democratic process. We will hold elections as soon as is practical."

"Mr Sum Taeyoung will be deported. We could stand him on trial for at least drugs and gun running through our country. We have enough evidence to make that stick. He would end up in gaol. But I do not want him on our soil any more. He is a cancer at the centre of many of our problems. So he will be deported."

"Taeyoung's right hand man, now Major Moustapha Abass since Moussa Ehouzou died in mysterious circumstances in Switzerland, will be arrested and tried for treason. Major Adrian Rego here will take over control of all Wandora's military with immediate effect. We believe we have the military on our side in this matter, is that not so, Major?"

Major Rego nodded in agreement.

"A new administrative structure will be launched. It will be headed by Kevin. Mr Forsythe has stressed to me that he should have retired an age ago. That may be so but I have persuaded him to take on the challenge, reporting to me. We both hope we can bed all of this down quite quickly and that Mr Forsythe will be able to finally enjoy his much desired retirement – but not quite yet!"

"We will quickly pass a new law about mineral extraction in Wandora and its territorial waters. We cannot afford to take the mining process into nationalisation. We have neither the money nor the expertise. But we cannot have Taeyoung or anyone like him pocketing the profits. They have to be taken into the national exchequer. But we can nationalise the selling process. So we will buy all minerals extracted in Wandora then sell them on to the appropriate markets. In this way we can ensure a percentage is taken into the national coffers. I have decided on this route instead of introducing a tax regime."

The prince turned to Kevin.

"And I would like to rush this law through so we can apply it to the cobalt being recovered by our South Korean friend from Black Bart's Bay. That will come as a nasty shock to him!"

"I'm very taken by what Mr Anderson has told us about plans for a Great Green Wall in the DRC and adjacent territories. I need to know more about this. If this is a way of eradicating the use of children in the minerals extraction process, Wandora will do all it can to support the idea. We are a poor country with little resources and many problems of our own. But if we can help that initiative we will."

"So, gentlemen – and ladies," the prince nodded in the direction of his daughter and Nakki who had now been joined in a sort of feminine cluster by Lotty, "all I have told you I'll announce on Independence Day. With the help of the Major here we will stage a military parade so that the world can see that the return of the royal family is supported by the military. I hope the parade will raise spirits, excite a new national pride and open a new chapter in the history of our country."

Chapter 53

Wandora Independence Day dawned with the promise of sunshine unbroken to sunset. A sizeable workforce was so early on site in the wide open square of the Place de l'Indépendance they disturbed the resident red monkeys from their slumbers just as the local birdlife launched into their chorus to greet the new day. As the sun rose over the horizon there was already a bustle of activity as finishing touches were made to the temporary grandstand and other necessities of the grand parade taking place later in the day. This included a security sweep of the whole area, the open space of the Place de l'Indépendance and its surrounding buildings – or at least as good a security check as could be managed with the limited resources available.

A sense of anticipated excitement had grown ever since the announcement of celebrations to mark the young prince's homecoming. A motley array of banners appeared across Porto Wandora in support of the royal return. It was clearly a popular development and a welcomed move away from the despised, depressing military control.

Much had happened in the short time since the meeting in Kevin Forsythe's apartment. Under the authority of the prince, Major Adrian Rego assembled an elite group of senior ranking officers representing key elements of Wandora's fighting forces. In a rushed but nevertheless stately event, these officers attended a ceremony in the São João Baptista de Wandora to swear allegiance personally to the prince who spoke to each one individually, to the royal family and to the nation of Wandora.

By now the prince's return had fuelled increased patriotic fervour on the streets of the capital and elsewhere throughout the country. It was obvious to everyone this was a popular development.

But not quite to everyone! Sum Taeyoung and Major Moustapha Abass found their own plans being overtaken by events. The new wave of patriotism was palpable wherever anyone went and despite his best effort, Major Abass found he had been outmanoeuvred by Major Adrian Rego and the armed forces were largely, but not totally, aligning themselves behind the prince. A small faction of military people, seeing the rapid wind of change spreading across the country, sought to asset strip Wandora as best they could by grabbing anything of value and seeking to escape the country. Taeyoung had other ideas.

"The parade the prince has organised for Independence Day is an opportunity to stop this nonsense," he told Moustapha Abass. "The prince and his supporters will all be present at the same time and place. It's a God-sent opportunity. In a single strike you can wipe them all out and we can regain control."

"Me?" Moustapha did not miss the emphasis on his potential role.

"Who else?" the South Korean asked. "You are mostly responsible for the mess we're in. It's up to you to sort it."

"But what do you expect me to do?" Moustapha was almost pleading.

Sum Taeyoung frowned and lent towards the military man. "It's your problem, you incompetent little man! You sort it!"

Moustapha looked back at him in fear and confusion. There was a heartless coldness in the eyes of the man in front of him – a steeliness – a lack of anything resembling humanity.

"I don't care how you do it," Taeyoung added. "Just do it. You might die in the process. But remember – you most certainly will die if you don't try. At least the option of trying gives you a chance to live. The alternative doesn't – of that you can be assured. You have my personal guarantee."

On the coast of Wandora, diners and drinkers at the Pirates Rest and those simply enjoying the delights of Black Bart's Bay suddenly had their peace and serenity shattered by the arrival of a convoy. The miscellany of vehicles included earth-moving dump trucks, excavation equipment, a variety of SDBI-badged 4x4s and some heavily armed trucks. They trundled down the beach towards the rock and rubble surrounded sand dune. It was now known there was not only cobalt at the back of the dune, hidden from the rest of the beach, but also under the sand of what looked like a near six metre high dune but in reality was a very substantial pile of rocks and rubble, including cobalt, all of which had been thrown up by the tsunami then covered by a thick layer of sand.

Threatened by his changing circumstances, Sum Taeyoung was wasting no time in recovering whatever valuable minerals he could and transporting them to a waiting ship in nearby Porto Wandora. It was something he had planned to do for some time but rushed into action as part of stripping Wandora of any assets he could quickly get his hands on, just in case his time in the country was ending.

In fact, the South Korean had established a temporary new base on the ship, vacating the comparatively palatial facilities of the Palm Trees Hotel – a precautionary measure to aid a safe evacuation. If Abass was successful in doing what he had been tasked to do, Taeyoung would quickly re-establish his more desired base in Wandora. If he failed, the ship provided a route of escape and a means of capturing some of the value Wandora's land amassed cobalt provided.

So when a heavily armed assignment of commandoes raided the Palm Trees Hotel to execute a court warrant for the arrest of Sum Taeyoung, the man was long gone. Much of his personal belongings remained as if the occupier of the room had every intention of returning. But not one element of his business interests had been left behind. There were no files, no mobile phone or computer, iPad, note books – nothing.

Meantime Major Moustapha Abass gathered around him elements of the military keen to rebel against the prince to protect their own individual, corrupt activities. With an operational base of sorts established in the now dilapidated buildings of a long since bankrupt vineyard north of Porto Wandora, the motley gathering of mixed senior ranks from various elements of the military plotted to reverse the fortunes of the prince's popular return. There was no dissention to the idea Independence Day would create the best opportunity to take action. The big question was – what action?

Back in Porto Wandora, at the request of the prince, Kevin Forsythe's Independence Day was destined to be closely attached to the programme of the royals, especially the public element involving the parade and the speech by the prince. Everyone else who had assembled at the initial meeting with the prince received an invitation to watch the proceedings from an area of the grandstand reserved for VIP guests. There were three exceptions. Major Adrian Rego tasked himself to be key orchestrator of the celebrations. As such, he allocated himself no specific duties but tried to ensure all aspects of the day, led by the military element of the parade, were properly delivered. He did allocate himself one specific task – leading the parade.

Joseph Wesley Wright II also declined the royal invitation, preferring to remain free to roam around the city whilst the celebrations took place, keeping eyes open for anything that could help lead him to the source of the armaments and drugs being trafficked into Africa via this country. Just one other from the meeting in Kevin Forsythe's apartment was missing from the group assembling in the grandstand. He was to play a pivotal role in the events soon to unravel.

The grand procession was scheduled for 12 noon and would follow the speech by the prince. Since the announcement of the event, the idea had grown in popularity and, despite the impoverished and disaster-struck state of the nation, local community organisations asked to take part. The prince was delighted. This would no longer just be a military event but more like a celebration by the people. Once the parade was over, the VIP party would move to a special reception in the São João Baptista de Wandora.

By late morning of Wandora Independence Day, Joe Wright was standing in the shade of a cluster of trees on the edge of the square some 100 yards from the grandstand, watching as crowds poured in to enjoy being part of the procession or to simply spectate. Many carried the national flag. Others had banners with slogans of support for the prince. A wide variety of colourful costumes were on show. There was a noisy, relaxed carnival feeling in the air but one also of excited anticipation as to what the prince would say.

By half past eleven the royal party arrived together with Kevin Forsythe and the others who had all last been together in the Englishman's apartment. With just ten minutes to go before the Prince spoke, Joe felt his mobile phone vibrate. Reluctant to take a call, he looked at its screen and was more than a little surprised to see the code words and numbers reserved for CIA operators. It was only used within the organisation and rarely in Africa. In fact, Joe had never had such a coded prefix to a call during his whole career to date in Africa. He was certainly not expecting any such call now. Puzzled and reluctant to answer the phone with the prince so close to speaking, he nevertheless felt duty-bound to answer it. He immediately recognised the refined English accent of the man who had been accompanying the prince.

"Joe. There's no time for explanations. You must evacuate the prince and the royal party from the grandstand now. There's to be an assassination attempt and an explosion as soon as the parade starts. Taeyoung's also using this as a diversionary cover to move cobalt from Black Bart's Bay to the port. I'll tell Adrian Rego. Can you get Forsythe or Bond to evacuate the royals? Now!"

"Jesus," muttered Joe. "How the hell do you know?"

"I've had Moustapha Abass bugged since this morning."

"Holy shit!" exclaimed Joe, taken utterly by surprise. "Who the hell are you?"

"Enough of an ally of yours to show you the code you responded to," said the mysterious man. "There's no time for explanations. Just do it." And the call ended.

For a split second Joe stared incredulously at his phone. It was the CIA code that validated the call. Without that he might not have taken the call so seriously. With the code he had no option but to act. Looking towards the grandstand, he decided his fastest bet was to phone Kevin. He tried but the phone was dead. Switched off. Instead, he dialled Bond's mobile. As he did so he looked around, taking stock of what was going on. To his left, some two hundred yards away, the procession was assembling, virtually ready to move – military at the front, a colourful and noisy array of civilians in its wake. They were waiting for the moment after the prince's speech to move forward across the square and parade in front of the grandstand. As far as he knew, Rego was in the lead vehicle, an ex-Russian PT76 light tank of which the Wandoran army had six, recently used against the ISIS in the north.

"Hi Joe," Gene Bond's cheery voice responded to his call.

"Gene. No time for explanations. Just listen then do as I say – immediately. You've got to get the royals and your lot off the grandstand – now. There's about to be ..."

His words were cut off as a massive explosion erupted less than 500 yards to his right. A large cloud of black smoke spiralled upwards. He could hear screaming mixed with the sound of the blast as it echoed around the city. Large numbers of people were running away from the seat of the explosion. Others were running towards it to help. Joe saw Major Adrian Rego leap from the lead tank and run towards the developing chaos, smoke and general carnage. Shortly a new sound came to him, the unmistakable noise of a tracked vehicle moving on a concrete surface. A second tank was moving past the still stationary first tank Major Rego had vacated, its turret turning to its left and the gun menacingly swinging round to line up on the grandstand. Its intentions were blindingly obvious.

Gene Bond, like everyone in the grandstand, ducked down automatically as the bomb exploded but with the words from the interrupted call from Joe still dominating his thinking, he headed towards the prince. The explosion had caused bedlam. Everywhere around him people were trying to move – to get anywhere away from the explosion and any subsequent danger. Only half a dozen people separated him from the royals but in the chaos it needed fast action.

"Kevin," Bond screamed at the Englishman a dozen people away. "Get the royals out of here. Someone's going to try and assassinate him."

Kevin, like everyone else, was still shocked and confused by the explosion. Like many others around him, at the moment of the blast he had involuntarily bent double, head close to knees, as if to shelter from any blast. Momentarily he did not comprehend what was happening. He was aware Gene Bond was shouting but not necessarily that it was at him or why.

"Kevin! Get the royals out of here."

Bond's second shout spurred Kevin into action. He virtually grabbed the prince's arm in as tight a grip as he could and hauled him towards him.

"No time to explain," he told the young royal. "Got to get you off the grandstand."

By now others from the VIP party were responding to Bond's call. Pete Turner grabbed Nakki and the princess, while Pete Anderson pushed at the prince while Kevin pulled. The young prince was trying to protest and resist. He was minutes from making his important speech and though he had heard Bond shout he had not gathered why. Marcel held Lotty's hand tightly as he brought up the rear of the retreating party.

The first shell from the tank of Moustapha Abass burst short of its target, hitting the lower front part of the grandstand still thick with spectators. Death and destruction was instant and widespread. The whole grandstand structure shook violently on the impact. Body parts, wood and metal pieces flew into the air, cascading down on those trying to escape. A terrified

Gene Bond became aware of a new deadly noise adding to the bedlam as Abass turned his tank's machine gun onto the collapsing grandstand. He virtually tumbled down the steps at the rear of the structure, pulling a still protesting prince with him. The rest of the party followed as best they could, scrambling through tightly packed bodies as other spectators fought to get down the steps at the rear of the grandstand.

Abass told his driver to keep his tank moving forward towards the grandstand. In his seriously restricted line of vision, he saw his first shell fall short of its target and in anger turned to sweeping everywhere with the machine gun. It was a bloody massacre with bodies flying in all directions making it impossible for Abass to see where the prince and his guests were. With his shell loader telling him another round was available to fire, Abass brought his tank to a stop and carefully aimed the second explosion to hit where the royal party had been minutes before. The resulting slaughter was considerable but the target it had been meant for was gone.

It was only minutes since Joe Wright had phoned Bond. With some relief he saw the prince failing in his attempts to resist being manhandled off the grandstand but in horror saw the Abass tank fire off its two shells and machine gun the spectators. The whole area now seemed like a war zone with chaos to his right where the bomb had exploded and now a bloody scene in front where the grandstand was collapsing under shell and machine gun fire. Instinct and training launched the American into action. A stationary tank is easier to attack than one on the move. Grabbing two scaffolding poles from a small pile left by those who had built the grandstand, Joe ran up to the tank from its rear, out of view of those inside it, heaved and rammed the steel into its wheels. As he did so, the tank lurched forward, Abass wanting to close in on his target. With a screeching grinding noise, the steel poles buckled and became caught in the tank's tracks. It stopped.

Joe, intent on climbing onto the tank and somehow attacking the crew inside it, heard someone shouting. He turned to see Major Rego running back from the bomb area, a grenade launcher in his hands. Having reached the scene of the bomb explosion and realised straight away there was nothing he could do to help that was not already being done by others, his thoughts turned instantly to the need to protect the prince. He spotted the grenade launcher left presumably by someone now involved with rescue activity – and instinctively grabbed it.

Joe could not hear what the major was shouting but the message was clear enough – Major Rego was lifting the grenade launcher to his shoulder. So Joe turned and ran as fast as he could. As he did so he heard the grenade launcher fire. He threw himself to the ground as the tank took the first hit. The grenade hit the tank's gun turret, just as Rego had hoped it would. With any luck it would create a shock wave inside the vehicle. Almost immediately the hatch on top of the turret was thrown back and Moustapha Abass appeared, his back to Joe, one hand heaving himself out of the tank, the other holding a sub-machine gun.

Joe, some 50 meters from the tank, drew his Glok 19, aimed, fired and started running closer to his target. He knew he was on the limit of his gun's range but it was worth a shot. He missed. Abass, presumably having heard Joe's gun go off, turned, saw Joe who was now stopping to take a second shot, and started to lift his sub-machine gun to fire at Joe. But the American got his second shot in first. Now well within the range of his pistol, this time he hit his target in the head. He saw Abass drop his weapon and disappear from view back down the hatch. By now Adrian Rego had arrived at Joe's side.

"Was that Abass?" he asked breathlessly after his run across the open square.

"Yes"

"Dead?"

"I hope so. The tank seems to have gone quiet."

"Thank God," the major looked towards the remains of the grandstand and the slaughter there. "Is the prince alright?"

"I've no idea," Joe replied and rang Bond on his mobile. "They're all OK," he reported to Adrian Rego.

Rego looked around him at the chaos. Rescue squads and medics were scrambling round the remains of the grandstand. "Not much I can contribute here," Rego told him. "I'm going after this guy Taeyoung. See if I can intercept the cobalt he's trying to take out of the country."

And with that the young major ran to his tank and set off with three others in his wake. Joe decided to climb onto the Abass tank and see if anyone inside had survived. Sum Taeyoung had been right. Whichever of the two options he offered Major Moustapha Abass would lead to his death. Joe's shot had ensured that.

Chapter 54

They met in one of the many side rooms of the São João Baptista de Wandora. The Oba of Wandora, Crown Prince Christopher Kpotsra, wore a plain, unpretentious, light suit tailored for him on his last visit to New York. His open-necked shirt enhanced the unceremonious, western look. He was in a relaxed mood amongst friends and though this was a meeting of considerable consequence to the future of his country, he was conducting it in a very informal manner. He was conscious that everyone present was still to one degree or another in shock after the horrendous events of Independence Day. The casualty count from the initial explosion then the attack on the grandstand totalled 54 people dead and more than 100 injured.

"My friends, firstly I want to thank you all for the actions you took that day. I owe my life to the intelligence that forewarned us what was to happen and the rapid response that followed. Images remain vivid and my heart bleeds for those whose lives were devastated by the evil actions perpetrated that day."

Gene Bond reflected on being counted as a friend by this royal man who he had last seen as he physically dragged him off the wrecked grandstand when it was under machine gun fire. Never in his wildest dreams could he have foreseen circumstances in which, with no consideration to appropriate decorum, he would so roughly haul a royal personage like an oversized sack of potatoes. Once they were at ground level, with panicking people scrambling down the stairs behind them and chaos reigning in every direction, they had managed to link up with Kevin Forsythe and gather their group together.

The nearest point of sanctuary was the São João Baptista de Wandora and once within the walls of the old fortress they were able to take stock of the bumps and grazes they had all accumulated during the chaotic evacuation. Nobody was in any way badly hurt and a few plasters and bandages were applied where necessary. The prince and Kevin were soon immersed in meeting various people and telephoning others leaving Bond, the two Pete's, Turner and Anderson, Princess Sylvia and Nakki, Marcel and Lotty, all in various stages of shock, talking about what had happened and of their own escapes.

It was two days later that they all gathered together again at the bequest of the prince. They sat around a large, very modern, reinforced glass-topped boardroom table in a room which contrasted the brushed and oiled oak wooden floor with the original arrow slit windows cut through the thick stonework of the modified ancient castle.

"Major Rego," the prince turned to the only uniformed person present. "So we all know, what happened to you?"

"I was in the tank at the head of the parade when the bomb went off in the Place de l'Indépendance. I ran to see what help I could offer but by the time I got there those unscathed by the explosion were helping those who had been injured. Medics were also arriving. I don't know why I looked back at the parade but I did and saw Major Abass's tank passing mine and lining its gun up on the grandstand. I could also see Joe Wright heading towards the tank with some scaffolding sections in his hand."

"What caused you to do that, Joe?" asked the prince, interrupting Major Rego.

Joe told him about the strange phone call he had had. "How the man has a CIA code I've no idea. Incredibly, he told me he had been bugging Moustapha Abass all day. Does anyone know who this guy is?"

Blank faces provided no answer. "He was introduced to me by the British Foreign Office," said the prince. "He made all the arrangements for the princess and me to travel to Wandora and to meet up with Joe and Mr Bond. He travelled with us but I never found out who he was. He never offered his name and somehow it never seemed right to ask him."

Major Rego continued his account, recalling how Joe shot Major Abass and how he had checked the major was dead. "We took my tank and three others and headed off to the port to intercept the convoy coming from Black Bart's Bay. We took them so much by surprise there was not much of a fight before those in the armed trucks fled. I have the rest of the convoy vehicles under guard and those who didn't run are under arrest – or dead."

"Have there been any signs of the South Korean, Sum Taeyoung?"

"No, sir. But the ship that was waiting to take on

board the cobalt from the trucks has set sail and is out of our territorial waters."

The prince reflected on that before saying "so we are rid of the South Korean terrorist?"

"It appears so," said Major Rego.

"If I may say so," interjected Gene Bond. "I'd be careful about making such an assumption. I have crossed swords with this man many times and he is very persistent and extremely devious. And he has an interest in the expedition that's searching for cobalt in the sea bed offshore Wandora."

"But for the time being we've put a stop to drugs and weapons smuggling through Wandora into Africa," said Joe. "That certainly ticks one of my boxes and should make life here a bit easier."

"All I am saying, Joe," Bond responded, "is that Taeyoung is determined, ruthless and powerful. While he thinks he has a chance of gaining profit out of Wandora I would not assume for a moment that he has gone away for good."

The prince looked down at his notes for some time before speaking again.

"What's happening to the expedition to find cobalt off our coastline? Mr Bartoll. What can you tell us?"

Marcel looked up in surprise. Somehow he had not expected to be asked to say anything.

"Early drilling has now started," he reported. "But, your highness, it is very early days. It will be some time before it's known if there's cobalt in the sea bed off Wandora."

"Is Sum Taeyoung not funding that expedition?" asked the prince.

Nobody seemed to want to reply. Eventually Gene Bond did. "I guess the truth is nobody here knows for sure but we think he is. Which is why I suggest you may not have yet got rid of Sum Taeyoung for ever. He will, somehow, hang around to protect his interests."

The prince reflected on that response. He turned again to Marcel. "And what about the sea anemone? Is that project dead?"

"We don't know," Marcel responded. "We don't know if the explosion terminally damaged the species. We are negotiating with the expedition insurers but because the origins of the explosion have still to be determined they're reluctant to pay up. Without that funding I don't know whether another expedition is possible."

"What happens," asked the prince to nobody in particular, "if cobalt is discovered and the sea anemone lives on?"

"You'll end up," Gene Bond answered, "in the contentious debate about mineral extraction from the sea bed. It's a very uneasy debate. It will be especially sensitive and difficult for Wandora."

"Why?" asked the prince.

"Because my guess is you need the potential value of the cobalt to reinvigorate your poor economy yet there may be a potential of damaging the sea anemone if mining happens nearby.

"A quandary," observed the prince.

"Quite so," agreed Bond.

The prince paused again. "What's happening to cobalt on the world market?"

"It continues to surge," Bond told him. "And forecasters say that's likely to be maintained for some years as the automobile industry turns to electric power."

"It seems to me," the prince told the meeting, "we confront many imponderables. The way ahead for my country is not going to be easy. There is so much to do and so little resource by which to do it. However, with the help of Kevin, I am confident we will quickly establish an efficient constitutional monarchy with a democratically elected parliament."

"Those involved with the atrocities of Independence Day will stand trial immediately." He nodded towards Major Rego who acknowledged this was within his responsibility. "And the same applies to members of the armed forces who rebelled against the state."

"Whilst Kevin Forsythe leads the reforming of our administrative structure, I would like to contract with Mr Gene Bond to continue to provide advice and guidance on all matters to do with the creation of a sustainable economy that is harmonious to our environment."

Gene Bond raised a hand in acknowledgement.

"I am very interested," the prince continued, "in what Mr Anderson told us about developments in the DRC. The proposed Great Green Wall project is ambitious. I share Mr Bond's abhorrence about the use of young children in the artisan mines and that the developed world is reliant upon them for the cobalt essential to their sophisticated societies. That has to stop. We all have responsibilities in regard to this and I will do whatever we can to alleviate this child slave labour. The modern world should hang its head in shame."

"The new contact with the CIA in Africa will be of great value to us and I hope, Mr Wright, we can maintain our new friendship. Illegal drug and weapon running, the threat of ISIS spreading to this part of Africa – these are all threats to our stability and forward prospects best tackled in partnerships."

Joe Wright nodded in agreement.

"I will continue to maintain a personal interest in the prospect of the Gulf of Guinea Sea Anemone providing value to the pharmaceutical market. Wandora will support any further expeditions needed to progress that."

"Thank you," said Marcel.

"To you all – and to our absent and still unidentified friend with powers to bug senior military people in my country, I again say, thank you. Kevin, is there anything I have not covered that I told you I wanted to deal with here?"

"No, sir," Kevin replied, turning to Gene Bond, "the prince mentioning our absent friend reminds me that he asked me to give you something. And from the inside pocket of his jacket he pulled a small envelope and passed it to Bond who looked at it quizzically. Bemused, Bond opened it and took out a small piece of paper. On it were the handwritten words "Georgi reminds you he still has a stock of Caucasus brandy in need of consumption!"

Fact and Fiction

- The quotation about children
- Shakespearean quotes
- Everything about cobalt. I am especially grateful to Professor Peter Slater who advised me on this and allowed me to write him into the book
- Lack of eco-life in the Gulf of Guinea
- Experiments on venom from the sea anemone, the plant-like cousin of the jellyfish
- The largest tsunami in history when the eastern flank of the island of Cape Verde blew off
- There may be 5,000 new varieties of fish yet to be found
- We currently discover about 150 new species of fish every year!
- The Centre for Strategic Elements and Critical Materials, University of Birmingham, UK
- Welsh pirates Bartholomew Roberts and Howell Davis
- ISIS movement in Africa and other terrorist organisations
- The artisan mines of the DRC and the child labour
- University of Birmingham
- Everything about batteries
- The Gulf of Guinea Interregional Network
- The Critical Maritime Routes Programme

- Bromley Murton
- Richard (Rick) Steiner of Oasis Earth
- UN HQ in Nairobi and all about it
- Attack and loss of life of US soldiers in Niger
- University of Plymouth report
- The size of Africa
- The café in Methodist Central Hall
- Local food and drink ('borrowed' from Togo and Benin)
- Concrete block swept from Japan to America
- The 2013 bomb blast in Nairobi
- Type 92/QSZ-92 pistol
- The Burnees
- Post Gaddafi armaments
- Type 56 assault rifle
- Grand Hotel du Niger
- Cap Banga restaurant
- Ex-Soviet Navy Whisky Class P2 submarine – was for sale
- Voodoo – from web research
- Sir Nick Stern's Perfect Storm
- Culinaire Bazaar
- Colombian Pacific coast submarine manufacturing – from web research
- The Committee on Cooperation, International Relations and Conflict Resolution
- World Bank report on auto industry use of cobalt – from web
- Bloomberg report – ditto
- US Major General (quote), US special operations in Africa – from web
- Great Green Wall
- Dr Kartik Sunagar of the Centre for Ecological Sciences – from web

- Quote from University of Exeter and Greenpeace
- Economic report on auto industry move to electric cars – from web
- Bloomberg report
- Tanguieta in Benin
- Flying Bird Tea Shop and all to do with it
- The size of Africa
- King Leopold as land owner
- The Spinnaker Tower
- PRN Newswire
- Montreux Music and Convention Centre
- Ricinus communis – a highly potent toxin.
- Georgi Markov's assassination in 1978 in London by ricin fired into him from an umbrella.
- Post-traumatic amnesia – from web
- Glok 19

FICTION

- Everything to do with Wandora
- The Gulf of Guinea Trench
- The specific tsunami referenced in the story
- Everything about, and everyone within, SNEL
- The European Secret Service, its communications centre and people
- Everything to do with SDBI
- BBC Central African reports
- Idea of a second Great Green Wall

 Matador

For exclusive discounts on Matador titles,
sign up to our occasional newsletter at
troubador.co.uk/bookshop